I0535744

Red Tape

Kathy Kulig

RED TAPE

Red Tape Copyright © 2014 by Kathy Kulig

All rights reserved. This is a work of fiction.
Names, characters, places and events portrayed in this
book are either the product of the author's imagination
or are used fictitiously. Any similarity to real persons,
living, or dead, places, businesses, events or locales is
purely coincidental.

No part of this book may be reproduced or used
in whole or in any part or by any means existing without
written permission from the author. For information contact: kathy@kathykulig.com.

Edited by Joyce Lamb
Cover design by Wicked Smart Designs

Published by Burnt Stilettos Press
ISBN: 978-0-990343912

Dedication

To my husband, Joe. Always…Thank you for understanding the life of a writer, for the many sacrifices and fabulous dinners. And thanks for the original idea—"Bondage in the White House."

Chapter 1

Jason Merritt swung his racket hard, but missed another easy shot off the back wall. The racquetball bounced past him. *Fuck*. Two points down, with an audience, and he was losing to a man twenty years older.

"Have you talked to Zoe yet?" his opponent asked.

"Not yet, and when she finds out I recommended her, she better not have a loaded gun." Jason's gut clenched as he considered that conversation. He'd tried calling her two nights ago, right after she started her new job, but had gotten her voice mail. His opponent hit a driving serve. Jason swung again and missed. "Fuck."

"If I didn't know you better, I'd say you were letting me win." The older man glanced sideways at Jason.

"Sorry, Mr. President."

President Douglas Bryson laughed. "Not to worry. When do you plan to call her?"

Three Secret Service agents peered through the Plexiglas partition like frozen automatons. They couldn't hear their conversation, and no one else was in the swanky health club. Once a week, the president reserved the entire club for his private use. The silence descended into a surreal Stephen King novel.

"I haven't talked to her since our last mission more than six months ago. I thought I'd let her get settled into her new position first."

The president nodded. "Make it soon. We need her brought up to speed."

He failed miserably in his attempt to smile. On the other side of the partition, the Secret Service guards held their robot expressions.

The president patted Jason's shoulder. "We already had her in mind. Zoe's the perfect type. Blond, attractive, physically fit, top-level clearance and trained for undercover work. We used you as a reference since you worked with her at Langley. Tell her that."

Jason nodded. "Yes, sir."

"Your past relationship won't interfere with this project." It was a statement, not a question.

"No, sir, Mr. President. We've worked on missions together before. She was trained for intelligence gathering, not this."

"I'm aware of your other missions. It's a role like any other undercover work," President Bryson added, locking eyes with Jason. "Get her briefed. Celia was one fuck-up too many. This operation needs Zoe."

If Bryson knew everything about their last mission, would he have selected her? Or was the organization that desperate?

The president checked his watch. "One o'clock and I have an early meeting. Our games may have to be postponed until after the peace talks. You have a busy day, too."

"I'll get on it." He couldn't afford another screw-up.

* * *

Zoe Summers retied her scarf for the third time, then checked in the hand mirror she kept in her desk to make sure it covered the scar. She had another hour of work to do and desperately needed coffee. As late as it was, there might be a few White House staff left. She hated when people stared at her neck, hated it even more when she had to make up some lie instead of explaining that a mission went horribly wrong. Pity she didn't need. What she needed was to forget and end the nightmares.

She dug an armful of manila folders out of the old, metal file cabinet and tossed them onto her desk. The last batch before she'd head home. This was an honor, not Langley's way to avoid outright firing her. Secret documents, archiving, filing. This was *not* the drudgery that would crush the living soul out of her body and damn her to file-clerk hell.

She leaned back in the desk chair, gazing around at the

dusty, basement office surrounded by a dozen filing cabinets. There were always rumors and conspiracy theories by people who had too much time on their hands. She'd escaped one lead-lined dungeon for another, but White House or not, suspicious activity or not, this felt like a demotion. She should have been out in the field, interacting with terrorists, transporting sensitive documents, carrying a gun, not moving papers.

Rubbing her temples, Zoe glanced at the clock on her desk. Ten p.m. Coffee. The door to the hall was open a crack to ensure the guard would check in on her during his rounds. It was best he get to know her since she planned on working a lot of late nights. Maybe if she exceeded expectations and did a really good filing job, they'd move her on to bigger projects.

Even for a basement, she was surprised by the amount of after-hours activity. A group of people came downstairs, entered one of the rooms, then left after an hour or two. It had happened the night before, too. She was never able to see who they were, but couldn't help feeling paranoid after what the Big D had told her. He'd heard rumors and suspected something was terribly wrong at the White House but gave no specifics. The lack of security cameras on her level seemed odd when there were plenty on the upper levels.

Taking her cell phone out, she listened to Jason's message again. The message was three days old. After several playbacks, she still hadn't decided whether to call him back.

She yanked open the drawer of her desk to lock the files away while she went upstairs. The drawer slipped off its track and jammed.

Crap. Banging it with the heel of her hand, she pulled the drawer free and placed it on the floor. She checked inside for papers that had fallen behind. Lying on the floor inside the desk was an employee ID badge with two keys attached and another key ring with a set of five keys.

Turning the badge over in her hand, she examined a red piece of tape dangling off one of the keys like a one-inch flag.

Nothing was written on it. The photo on the badge was of a young blond woman in her late twenties with a pretty smile. The woman could've been Zoe's sister if she had one. *Celia Aldridge, Researcher.*

Had the previous worker lost the badge and keys or had they been left behind? She turned the badge over and studied it closely. A six-digit number was scribbled in faded marker. Zoe pursed her lips and rolled her eyes. People who couldn't remember PINs or key codes sometimes wrote them in inappropriate places. Even intelligence agents, men mostly, were known to use 36-24-36 as a pass code.

Did this woman get promoted? Transferred? Did she quit or get fired? Normally when an employee left, security destroyed the ID badge. Who was she, and why had she left? Maybe she worked in another department and Zoe could return the badge. Sitting at her computer, she typed in Celia Aldridge's name to do a search, her finger hovering over the ENTER key. She wasn't at Langley. Anything she typed in on the White House computer could be traced by the IT guys. Frank Phillips in security had warned her about unofficial use of the computers. She could be violating a confidentiality rule. She deleted her entry.

"Zoe, you still here?"

Zoe cried out, palming the woman's badge and slipping it into her blouse. As she rose, she tugged on her scarf. "God, Melissa, I didn't hear you come down."

Melissa Tadeshi, assistant to the press secretary, stood in her doorway. "I was going to leave this under your door. It's tomorrow's schedule." Melissa held up an interoffice envelope. "You're leaving now, aren't you?"

"I had a little more work to do. I was going for coffee." Zoe took the envelope, dropped it on her desk and gestured Melissa inside. "I thought you left hours ago. Is Julia still here?"

Melissa rolled her eyes. "Long gone. What work? We finished our training today. Want to go for a drink?"

"No, thanks. I'm trying to make a dent and make this office

livable. I guess housekeeping doesn't clean this room. It doesn't look like it's been dusted since the Kennedy administration." Considering the late hour, Melissa still looked gorgeous and professional, like an Asian Victoria's Secret model in her early thirties. Although Zoe thought Melissa pushed her professional attire to the limit for the White House. She'd wear heels a bit too high, skirts a little too short and blouses cut way too low, but no one seemed to mind. Her long, black hair was fastened neatly with a simple clip, and even her makeup looked fresh. Other than making sure her scarf covered her scar, Zoe hadn't checked her appearance in six hours. She hated to think what she looked like. "Besides delivering tomorrow's schedule, why are you here late?"

"We finished up a few meetings over an hour ago. I was doing some prep work. The president's meeting with a number of foreign reps, so expect another crazy early morning."

Zoe inched toward the door, expecting Melissa to follow.

Melissa looked inside the office and noticed the drawer on the floor. "Do you need help with that?"

Zoe hesitated for a second. "No, just cleaning out the desk."

"How's everything going?"

"Good. It's not hard work. I'm surprised they just didn't hire a college intern for this. My old boss said someone at the White House recommended me for the position. Did you know about that?"

Melissa glanced at the stack of files on Zoe's desk. "Probably because you had top-secret clearance working in the CIA."

"Any clerk can get a security clearance." Zoe didn't mean to sound so cynical.

"Security threats are always a concern. You of all people should know that," Melissa said, very serious now.

The hairs went up on the back of Zoe's neck. "You're right."

"Don't ever let your guard down."

"Don't get me wrong, I'm grateful to be here. But when I was hired, I expected it was for something more exciting than filing."

Melissa smiled, back to her pleasant mood. "Give it time. Trust me, working here is never dull. The White House wouldn't have hired you unless they had a reason and needed your expertise. They need people they can trust above all."

"I can be trusted," Zoe said, more to herself than Melissa. She stuffed the folders back into the file cabinet, got the drawer back on its track, and then closed and locked it.

Melissa gave a small laugh. "Go home, girl. It's late."

Home. Where silence and four walls only reminded her how long it'd been since she was on a mission? If she hung around, she could do an unsupervised tour. She held up her dust-smudged hands. "I need to wash up first."

Melissa groaned. "Hurry it up. The guards get twitchy when we stay too late."

"I won't be long." Zoe locked her office, but Melissa hadn't moved to leave. "By the way, do you know who worked in here before me?" Zoe watched Melissa's expression.

Melissa's mouth quirked slightly, a nervous gesture the average person wouldn't notice. "I don't know. She must've left before I got here."

"She?"

Melissa huffed. "She...he...whatever. I don't know. This office has been empty for a while."

"Does anyone else work down here? Meeting rooms?"

Melissa frowned and narrowed her eyes. "It's a basement. Nothing more than storage rooms, space for electrical, boiler, and mechanical equipment. Why?"

"Just asking." Zoe wasn't going to mention the late-night visitors until she gathered more information. She didn't want to sound like a paranoid idiot.

The atmosphere chilled between them. "Look, I'm sorry," Zoe said. "It's too quiet down here. See you at lunch tomor-

row?"

Melissa smiled. "Sure." She checked her phone, punched a few keys with her thumbs, then headed for the stairs. "See you tomorrow."

Zoe used the restroom and scrubbed her hands. When she strode out of the ladies' room, she stopped in the hallway and contemplated the door at the end of the hall, holding Celia's badge in her hand. The door had a key-swipe lock and keypad. Could it be this easy?

* * *

"Anything you need me to do before the presentation?" Jason asked Julia. He wanted out of there, wanted to get to Zoe and tell her to resign before she learned anything about the program. At Langley, they may have parted on a sour note, but she would trust him this time. By not trusting her partner, she'd compromised their last mission and much worse. If he told her to leave, she would. Once she was briefed about Red Tape, it'd be too late.

"No, we're ready." Julia's nails clicked on the computer keyboard with enough force he expected to hear them snap. He shifted in the stiff Victorian chair in front of her desk. Waiting was torture. His cell buzzed at the exact moment Julia's buzzed. The target had just left the hotel. *Fuck.* Julia glanced at him with an anxious look. He hated when a mission was starting off on the wrong foot. Already, this one was behind schedule, and everyone was on edge. Not good.

Julia swore. "Where the hell is Melissa?" The petite woman got up and paced the carpeted room. The razor-cut ends of her red hair brushed the collar of her crisp business suit.

"I'm sure she'll be here shortly." That wasn't happening. The text he got said Zoe hadn't left yet but would soon. *Come on, Zoe. Just this once, leave something half-finished.* Melissa couldn't drag her out of there unless she hogtied her.

His schedule as one of the first lady's Secret Service agents was hectic, and he suspected it was about to get insane. Julia gave an impatient huff and checked her watch again for the hundredth time. "If she doesn't come up soon…"

"She will." Jason stood and walked to the window, watching for the black cars that would arrive at the back entrance. If he had been in charge, it would never be going down like this.

"After this presentation, we'll schedule Zoe's training." Julia sighed. "We're pressed for time."

"Zoe's a professional. I won't have a problem training her."

Julia's smile wasn't a friendly one. Her green eyes flashed rage and worry. "What makes you think you'll be training her?" Her tone had a slight edge of condescension.

He stuck his hands in his pockets to keep from clenching them. "For this program to work, wouldn't she feel most comfortable with someone she knows well?" He took a breath, attempting to keep the conversation from breaking down into a shouting match.

She smiled again, and this time, Julia placed a gentle hand on his arm. "You mean someone she knew intimately, Jason. Training doesn't work that way."

"How then?" Before he finished the sentence, reality slammed into him. "Who'll be training her?" Heat rose in his face, and he took a step closer to her. The idea of Zoe thrown into the most dangerous part of the mission, unprepared, grabbed him by the throat.

"Now is not the time." She checked her watch, standing a little straighter, which didn't help her height but made a point. "You know what's involved." She walked over to her desk and leaned on it.

He didn't answer.

Three sharp raps on the door and Melissa barged into the office, giving both Jason and Julia a grim look. "Sorry I'm late. She's still here but should be on her way out." Melissa crossed her arms over her chest. The tight business suit she wore and low-cut blouse pressed the curves of her breasts higher. No

wonder the first lady chose her for this particular position.

Julia groaned, hands clasped together and held under her chin. "We need to make this count, people. There's no room for errors."

"Zoe's been working during the setup and practices this week. She wasn't a problem then," Melissa offered.

"No, I don't want the chance of her running into our guest." Julia's voice rose to a level bordering on hysteria.

Jason checked his watch, then looked at Julia, who tapped her tiny, pointy shoe while glaring at Melissa. Four men in business suits walked into the office, the first lady's private security guards.

"The first lady is on her way down," one of the men announced. "And the target will be here in ten."

"We're out of time," Julia said to Jason. "Get her out of there."

Chapter 2

Did she dare? Zoe hadn't even tried her own badge and code on the door at the end of the hall yet. She padded to the men's room door to make sure no one was around, then knocked. "Hello? Housekeeping." No answer. She entered, and it was much larger than the ladies' room with two more showers and a condom dispenser. Zoe frowned at that. *Are you kidding me? In the basement of the White House?*

She left the men's room, and tiptoed down the hall, trying each door she passed. All locked. Not surprising, but her curiosity was focused on the door at the end. Why would a room for storage or mechanical equipment need a keypad access?

She swiped Celia's badge and punched in the PIN, but the light remained red. She tried again, slower, and still got red. Then she tried the PIN in reverse.

The light turned green. She turned the doorknob, walked inside a small vestibule and was blocked by another door, locked, of course. Like Alice in Wonderland, the mystery begins with doors and keys. She flipped on the light in this small antechamber. The key on Celia's badge with the piece of tape opened the next door.

Illuminated only by the light from the vestibule, this room appeared spacious. A few objects or furniture stood in shadows. The scent of leather and disinfectant mingled in the warm air. She felt along the wall for a light switch then decided against it. Using the backlight from her cell phone, she crept around the room, examining each object. One large chair stood in the center. It was elaborately carved with straps attached to the arms and legs.

Zoe stiffened and took a step back. An interrogation room. Not a meeting room. Her mind flashed to Turkey. They'd tied her down when the deal went bad. Her hand reached for her neck, and her body shook, remembering the pain when the knife

blade broke her skin. Sweat soaked through her underwear.

She shoved the memories out of her head. The White House was the last place she expected to find an interrogation room. In one corner was a bed with pulleys and more straps. On the other side of the room was a table with several small objects she suspected were torture devices, instruments for pain and truth serum drugs. Her stomach rolled, and the taste of bile rose onto the back of her tongue. At the far wall in the shadows was a tall, wooden cross. That looked familiar, but she couldn't place it. What kind of torture did they do in the White House?

As she moved around the room, she thought she heard voices in the walls. She shook her head. It wasn't real, only memories. The voices continued.

She dropped her phone and covered her ears with her hands. *Go away, you're not real.*

"Zoe. What the hell are you doing in here?" Jason's voice. She *was* hearing things.

Zoe spun around and saw a figure silhouetted in the doorway. "Jason?"

"Yes, you have to get out of here. They're coming." He picked up her phone and handed it to her. It started buzzing, and her thoughts sharpened.

Jaw clenched, she marched up to him and clamped her hand around his throat. The weight of her body continued the momentum until she slammed him against the wall. Her knee pressed into his groin, and her nails dug into his neck. "What the hell happened to you? You dump me after Turkey, then left Langley without a word. Or were you looking for an excuse?"

He winced from the pain in his throat or groin, she wasn't sure. "I didn't dump you at all. I was reassigned and sent out of the country while you were visiting your dad. I couldn't contact you."

"Six months ago," she argued, not releasing her grip. "You could've left a message that you were heading out. When did you get back?" Why didn't he just say the fuck-up in Turkey was her

15

fault? Maybe then they could move on.

"Couple weeks." He groaned. "I work here. Secret Service."

She fought the urge to rush into his arms. Every muscle in her body ached for him. God, she missed him. As reality quickly registered, her body chilled on the inside. Their last job hadn't accommodated relationships and emotions. Why would it be different now? She grabbed her phone and turned her back on him. "If you didn't trust me as your partner, you should've told me. Instead, you disappear."

"I can't explain it now. They're coming. We have to go now."

"Who's coming? What's going on? Is there a security problem?" She blinked several times and adjusted her scarf, but it wasn't necessary. Jason was the only person who didn't gape at the ugly scar.

He grabbed her arm, turned her to face him. "I'll give you details later."

Her body stiffened. "Are they bringing someone down for interrogation?"

"What?"

"Isn't this an interrogation room?"

"Interrogation room?" He chuckled. "It's a bit more complicated." Again, the voices emanated from behind the walls. He looked toward the sounds and held up a hand to be quiet. At least she wasn't crazy. He'd heard them, too. Then silence.

Footsteps approached down the hall. "Shit, too late," he said as he closed the inside door. The room swallowed them in utter blackness. Zoe held up her cell phone for light. Jason flicked on a penlight.

"Which way?"

"In here," he ordered. He grabbed her arm and shoved her into a small storage closet, then closed the door. Her cell buzzed. "Phone off."

Zoe glanced at her phone and let out a sigh as she turned it off. "Thank God."

"What?" Jason asked.

"It's Damien." Zoe let out a breath. She hated when her brother was late, even when he was beating the crap out of her in the Words With Friends game.

Jason's expression softened. "Iran?"

She nodded, her eyes adjusting to the dim lighting.

"Turn it off. Now."

"Okay. What's happening?" As much as she wanted to be angry at him, her stomach fluttered with excitement and her sex throbbed. He always managed to turn her on, especially when they were in danger. He smelled so good, too. A new shampoo, body wash? Whatever it was, it made her remember so many scorching-hot nights, breathless from hours of fucking. She wanted him again, wanted him now.

He took the phone, made sure it was off and stuffed it in his pocket. His penlight was still on. "Now listen to me. We cannot leave this closet or make a sound until it's over, under any circumstances. Do you understand?" His frown grew fierce and his eyes wild.

"Yes."

He cupped her chin with his hand. His mouth was close to hers as he whispered, "I'm sorry, Zoe. I should've called, should've explained." He squeezed his eyes closed then looked at her again. "Please, trust me."

"Trust you? But I don't know what the hell is going on."

"Zoe, please."

She knew that tone, knew him well enough not to argue. Trust wasn't always easy for her.

"No sound." He turned off the penlight.

She leaned against the wall, listening. A rush of adrenaline surged through her. The sound of her heartbeat pounded in her ears. *Like old times on a mission together.* The doorknob to the room rattled. Then the door squeaked open, and a sharp click of the light switch sent a shudder of excitement through her. The sound of people entered the room. Zoe tried to estimate the number. At least three, maybe more. Women and men by the voices and heeled shoes. She gasped but only a whisper. He placed a hand over her mouth, and she nodded. She held her breath.

"Anything you need before the room is sealed?" a male's voice asked.

"No, we're good. Seal it." Was that the first lady? Slowly, Zoe's eyes adjusted to the darkness, and a sliver of light appeared beneath the door. Another sliver of light cut through the doorframe where the old wood had warped. Angling her head just so, she squinted through the crack, trying to get a fix on the outside room. As they moved around, four people came into view, two men and two women.

Good God, one woman wore leather fetish wear—a corset, thigh-high boots and stockings. And the other with blond hair wore a black scholar robe. Beneath the robe she wore five-inch heels. Their faces were covered with elaborately decorated Mardi Gras masks. Two men were also present. One young guy with a muscular build was dressed in a black T-shirt, tight pants and wore a leather face mask. Between the robes and the guy all in black, the scene had a Gothic, macabre feel. What kind of rendezvous was this?

The older man wore business clothes. He was the only one without a mask. When he turned, Zoe thought he looked familiar. He was a small man, middle-aged and not very attractive. By his smile, he appeared to be enjoying the encounter. Zoe studied the furnishings now that the room was lit. *Shit*. This wasn't an interrogation room. It was a kinky-sex dungeon. Under normal circumstances she'd have been laughing. This wasn't funny. This was the White House.

The blonde had to be the first lady. The voice, the mannerisms. *Oh my God.* Shock and panic ripped into Zoe. She didn't want to be here to see this. Zoe tugged Jason's arm to take a look. He tapped her hand once, their signal for "no." Then he paused and did a series of two taps. She took that to mean, yes,

yes, he knew. So quickly they fell back into their old patterns where they could communicate without speaking during a mission. Why couldn't they talk about their love life? Why had he left months ago without a word?

The woman with dark hair must be Melissa. She had the same build and hair. The first lady was into kinky sex? Who knew? Did the president know? No wonder Jason had looked terrified.

Oh God, oh God. Jason must've heard her ragged breathing. If this hadn't been the White House, or if this had been a torture scene, she could've handled it, but she hadn't been prepared to observe a scandal at this level. He squeezed her shoulders and rubbed them gently. She took a slow breath in and let it out easy. What the hell?

Quiet. She must be quiet. Peering through the crack, Zoe watched the woman with the long, dark hair strut up to the older man and whisper something to him. Yes, it was Melissa. She'd shown Zoe those boots the other day when she noticed the box by her desk. Melissa had called them her party boots. Zoe hadn't thought anything of it.

"Let's get started," the first lady announced as she untied the robe, revealing her outfit. Her breasts thrust high over a red corset, thigh-high stockings and spike heels. Matching satin gloves came to her elbows. She strode to the table, picked up a crop and smacked it in her hand, then came around to stand beside Melissa. Both women kept their bodies angled in a particular way so their backs always faced the one wall with an intricate mural of American national parks.

"I'm Mistress D," Melissa said to the man as she stroked his back, speaking in a soothing tone. "Remove your clothes, please. Place them on the chair, then present yourself to me. When I ask you to present yourself, I want you to stand with your legs slightly apart, hands behind your back, right hand over your left and eyes looking down at the floor. Understand?"

"Yes, Mistress." He lowered his head and began to undress.

Shit. If only she could figure out who the man was.

"Mistress R is here to observe only," Melissa said, referring to the first lady. "If she feels the scene is getting out of hand, she'll signal by smacking her crop or stopping the scene."

The first lady stepped to an area out of Zoe's view.

Jason placed a hand on Zoe's shoulder to pull her back. She responded with a one-finger tap to his hand.

The man was standing as Melissa had requested. She made a few adjustments. "Very good. This is how I want you to stand when I ask you to present yourself. It's a small task and a way for me to break up our time together. I can also see how well you're handling my session."

Melissa picked up a leather flogger, smacking the knotted thongs on the nearby table. The man jerked, but he didn't look up. Naked, he stood sideways, fully aroused. His cock jutted straight out. Melissa approached the man and brushed the thongs across the tip of his cock.

"Kneel," she ordered, pointing to the bench. He complied. She hit him on the back and buttocks gently with the flogger in caressing strokes, a warm-up. Then harder and harder. Zoe cringed with each strike, her fingers digging into the doorframe.

The encounter was like watching a burning building in slow motion, mesmerizing and scary. Zoe knew people got into this bondage stuff. It didn't do much for her, although her body heated up with each strike. His moans were of pleasure mixed with pain. He was enjoying this. After a time, Melissa stopped, bent down. "Are you okay?"

"Yes, Mistress," he answered with enthusiasm. There was an accent, Middle Eastern, Zoe thought. She knew six languages fluently as well as basic words in a few others.

"Do you like this?" Melissa asked the man.

"Yes, Mistress."

"Good. We'll see how well you obey."

"Yes, Mistress." He rocked on his hands and knees and shifted side to side.

"Relax. Stop fidgeting. You'll enjoy this more."

He took a deep breath and stopped moving, except for his toes and fingers.

"You know the rules and have your safe word."

"Yes, Mistress."

Melissa then picked up a cane from the table. She touched his buttocks with it, not hitting, just touching as if teasing. She did that several times. After the fourth or fifth time, she smacked him hard, and he swore in Arabic. The moans and strikes were loud. Zoe wanted to cover her ears. She cringed and squeezed her eyes closed.

When she opened her eyes again, the man followed Melissa over to the wooden cross shaped like a giant letter X. "Present yourself to me," Melissa ordered.

The man stood in front of the structure, arms at his sides, head bowed. Melissa walked around him and studied his position. "No, this is not correct," she scolded. "Right hand over the left." He made the correction.

When Melissa was satisfied, she directed him to lean against the cross, facedown. She strapped him down in a spread-eagle fashion.

The implications of what was going on in this room were beyond imagining. If the public found out about this, what would happen to this administration? The peace talks? This was more damaging than a stained blue dress. This was a nightmare.

Jason touched her shoulder. His fingers slowly skimmed down to her upper arm, where he grasped her and tugged her closer. Outside, the bondage ordeal continued. Red marks crisscrossed the man's back and buttocks. She'd seen enough. Jason's other hand slipped to her waist. He leaned into her. Warmth, hardness, and the scent of male. She shouldn't be so turned on. The hairs on her arms stood up. Her breasts felt heavy, and her nipples grew tight. What was Jason thinking? After all this time, he wanted to get busy with her in a closet? Really?

She pulled away and tapped a "no" on his arm.

He tapped "yes" on her hand and slowly turned her around, pulling her against his body. God, he felt good. So many nights she'd imagined Jason in her arms like this. She had to control her breathing to keep from making any noise. The real torment was being trapped inside the closet. Sex with Jason had always been the hottest when they were on a mission. Why couldn't they have sex and a relationship like normal people?

They didn't know how to do day-to-day. Everything they once had came tumbling back. She wanted him again, wanted to give in with complete and utter abandon. Her body was on fire, throbbing, needing him now at the wrong place, the wrong—

Craaack!

In the next room, a flogger or cane smacked what sounded like bare, taut skin in quick repetition. The man cried out.

"Do you want me to stop?"

"No, Mistress, more, please." Another sharp crack sent shivers up Zoe's spine. How could he stand the pain, let alone enjoy it?

Jason's warm, moist mouth pressed on her ear, her neck, and she sucked in a little breath. His tongue drew a line to the hollow of her throat.

Yes, she ached to say, yes. Jason's touch was torture, sweet, sweet torture. She gave in a little, pressing her sex against his hard shaft bulging beneath his pants. She did want him but not here, not now.

On his arm, she tapped "no."

He hesitated long enough for her to wish she had said "yes." After all these months, they'd barely had enough time to say hello and already they couldn't keep their hands off each other. Nothing had changed. He rested his forehead against hers, and she heard his intake of breath and a long sigh. Outside, Melissa shouted orders, and the man groaned. Jason pressed his lips to Zoe's ear and barely mouthed, "I want you."

Then why did you leave me?

Outside their closet, in the dungeon, voices and the smack-

ing got louder. Inside, Jason pulled her against his chest and stroked her hair. She breathed in his scent, and time slipped away to the many heated nights he'd held her close. He knew how to draw out every exquisite sensation with his touch. Before she got too worked up, she backed away, slowly because she didn't want to knock into anything in the tiny closet. The sex party going on was so loud, Zoe doubted they would have heard anything.

His hands slid around her waist, holding her captive. "Sorry. Missed you." His words tore through her, ripping her heart in half. If he wanted to continue where they left off, she couldn't.

She leaned toward his ear. "Missed me? You'll have to do better than that."

His mouth came down on hers, and she sensed his hunger, felt her own heating up her body. His tongue slid across hers, drawing the passion from deep in her core. Her hands reached up along his hard chest, moved up and around his head, where she tangled her fingers in his hair. She resisted the urge to spread her legs. To encourage him would only make their situation more difficult.

Clinging to him, she gave in this time and melted deeper into the kiss. She couldn't fight him here. His hand reached under her skirt and slipped inside her pantyhose. Her sex was so wet, he easily parted her folds and thrust a finger inside her channel. With a silent gasp, Zoe broke away from the kiss and lifted up on her toes. He steadied her against his body. Matching his thrusts to the rhythm of groans and strikes outside the closet, she rode his hand closer to orgasm.

On impulse, she reached for his cock. The hard ridge bulged against his pants, and she pressed the heel of her palm along his length until she heard his intake of breath. The roughness of his hand rubbed her clit. Heat and throbbing intensified, coiling deep, bringing her to the edge of release. *Yes!* She wanted to scream and tell him not to stop, but it was sweet torture having to remain silent. Almost there.

23

"Did you enjoy yourself?" Zoe heard the first lady say. She pulled her hand away from Jason's cock at the same time he slipped out of her pantyhose. Her body continued to throb, her vagina clenching at empty space and aching. When she peeked out through the crack in the door, the first lady had already slipped on her robe.

"Very much," the male guest answered. "I must say this type of American hospitality was unexpected."

"Our pleasure." She handed him his clothing, and the man finished dressing. "Secret Service will escort you to your car."

"Thank you."

The group left. The man in black was the last to leave, switching the lights off and closing the door. Again, Jason and Zoe were surrounded in blackness.

"Now what?" Zoe whispered.

"We wait a few minutes."

The walls of the closet closed in. "You want to tell me now or later?"

"About what went on out there, or about us in here?"

"Either, both." She leaned against the door and crossed her arms. "You leave Langley without a word months ago, and then you end up here, like me. Funny coincidence. You act like nothing ever happened."

"Not a coincidence. You were handpicked for a project, like I was."

"What project?"

He hesitated. "You'll be briefed soon, but I suggest you don't take this job."

She groaned. "Why would I be briefed about someone's sexual activities?"

He cleared his throat and took a breath. "Zoe." His voice softened. "You should leave before you learn any more."

"Learn about what?" She laughed. "I don't know anything except the first lady might be a sex addict. Oh God. Does the president know?"

He groaned. "Zoe, quit your job, resign. Go back to Langley."

She shoved at his chest. "I can't go back. I think the Big D arranged this job to avoid firing me."

"Firing you?"

She nodded, although he couldn't see her. "Turkey was my fault. He probably doesn't want a repeat."

"It was my fault, too." He swore.

Silence rose between them. "Is that why you left? You didn't want to be my partner anymore and they wouldn't reassign you?" Now that he was stuck with her again, he wanted her to leave. Her throat tightened.

"No. That's not why I left. It was a mission ordered by the White House. I can't tell you more yet."

She laughed. "Whatever it is, it looks pretty entertaining."

"Trust me, you don't want to be involved with this."

"Well, I'm not quitting. Can I have my phone back?" She heard him moving around, then the phone was pressed into her hand. "Thank you." She checked Damien's message. He'd made a play. "Forty-three points? The bastard." She'd check the game later. She had three E tiles among her seven and didn't know what word she could make with that. Sometimes the small, insignificant words had better scores. It was all in the placement. At least Damien was back at the base instead of on a mission somewhere in Iran or Afghanistan, where much of the fighting was.

"How's Damien?" His words had softened a bit.

"Conditions aren't great over there. Deteriorating, from what I hear. Damien's been out on a number of missions. I'm worried. And the peace talks aren't helping. He should be coming home on leave in a couple months." She couldn't wait. At least she could count on him.

"That's good."

Three hard thuds hit the closet door. Zoe launched herself into Jason's arms. It sounded like Goliath outside pounding with a club. "Jason? We're all done here," a man's voice said. He

25

chuckled. "Need a hand in there?"

"Funny, smart ass. No, I'll lock up."

She swallowed and pressed her hand to her breast, feeling her heart slamming against her chest. She never heard the guy come in or turn on the light. Light streamed in beneath the door and through the crack. "Who was that?"

"Don't worry about it. We can go now." He opened the closet door. The man had gone, and the door to the room was closed. When they stepped into the room, Jason gave her a long look.

"How did he know we were in the closet?"

"He's Secret Service." He grimaced, as if that explained it all.

She strode over to the table and examined the implements of fetish toys and bondage equipment. Floggers, dildos, vibrators, cuffs, canes, gel lubricant, clamps, rope and a few things Zoe couldn't identify.

"What you saw obviously can't be taken out of this room."

"I'm not sure what I saw. Why don't you explain it to me?"

"Not tonight. You'll get a full explanation if you stay, but I recommend you don't." The man was a master at hiding his emotions. She wasn't sure if he hated the idea of working with her again or if there was something about the job she should be concerned about.

She stuck her hands on her hips and glared at him. "And do what? Get a job as a detective in the suburbs? You need to give me more than just telling me to quit my job. If you don't want to work with me again, just say it."

He rubbed his face and looked around the room. "It's not that, Zoe. It was a mistake. They shouldn't have hired you."

She raised her arms up in the air and dropped them by her sides. "Why? Julia and Melissa seem to think an ex-CIA agent is perfectly qualified for filing or whatever they want me to do. All I want is a chance to do something that matters, something important."

He smiled sympathetically and stroked her cheek with gentle fingers. "I wouldn't tell you to leave unless there was good reason." He was dead serious. The pained look in his eyes twisted at her heart.

"Maybe. But I don't walk away from anything unless I have a good reason." The silence stretched between them. Sadness and regret crept into her soul.

"I know." He took her in his arms and hugged her close. Months of anger, bitterness, and pain dissolved. At least some of it. She stepped back and gave him an up-and-down look. Damn, he looked better than she remembered.

She forced a smile. "The suit's a good look for you." They never dressed so formal while gathering intel overseas. His trim dark hair had a more professional look, less military than the last time she'd seen him. The suit couldn't hide the well-toned bodybuilding frame. Even at five-ten, Zoe felt short and small next to his six feet, four inches.

His mouth quirked in a slight grin. With the mix of emotions running through her head, she didn't want to address their relationship right now. The churning in her stomach she attributed to the Chinese food she had for dinner. "I need to go home and walk Dexter."

"Dexter?" He frowned.

"My black Lab. He's still a puppy. My neighbor lets him out and feeds him when I'm home late."

"He's probably eaten your couch by now." His eyes glittered when he smiled this time. "You bought a house, a dog, really settled down. Not the Zoe I remember."

She shrugged. "I guess I'm all grown up." The teasing look in his eyes changed to sadness. She was sure he knew she was failing miserably in her attempt to live a nine-to-five life.

"I'll walk you to your car." He put an arm around her shoulders.

The door to the room opened, and a man dressed in black walked in. He glanced at Zoe and gave a small nod. He could be the one who wore the black leather face mask. "You're wanted upstairs, Jason."

Jason murmured a few words to himself. He didn't sound pleased. "Great. How'd it go?"

The man shrugged. "Okay, I guess. We're about to find out." He narrowed his eyes at her. "Why is she here?"

"Long story. It's not a concern."

"She shouldn't be in here until she's briefed." The man continued to stare at her, and Zoe knew he was considering whether there had been a breach in security. Not knowing what was going on, she kept her mouth shut and let Jason talk his way out. If there was a way out.

"Julia instructed me to explain the program to Zoe," Jason said. "I haven't gotten to all the details yet."

The man nodded, seeming to accept that explanation. "You'll have to save the rest of your tour for another time. Julia wants us in her office now."

"I'll be right there," Jason said as the guard walked out, leaving the door open. Jason turned to Zoe. "Can you wait for me? I'd like to walk you to your car. It's late."

She laughed. "I can take care of myself."

He frowned. "I know that, but it's a hike to the parking lot."

She knew what he was thinking. "Turkey was different," she snapped. "Stop trying to protect me. I could take down a linebacker with a .357 pointed at my back."

He held up his hand. "Okay. Sorry. See you tomorrow." He pulled out his phone and punched in a quick text.

"You're supposed to tell me what was going on down here."

"Not now."

"Why?"

"Plausible deniability. I'm hoping you'll quit."

"Don't count on it. Should I be worried?"

"Very."

Chapter 3

By the time Zoe left the White House, it was almost one a.m. She yawned as she speed-walked to her car. Why bother leaving when she had to be back to work at seven? Her car was a couple of blocks away. The night was chilly and the streets quiet. Unusual for Washington. Checking her phone, she saw that Damien had played the word D U N E. He was beating her by fifty-nine points. She still had a chance to catch up. She'd planned a few options, but all she could play was one word with two of the E's she had. By using an X and D already on the board, she added the word E X P L O D E and clicked PLAY.

Moments later, she received a text from him.

How's the job? Talk to Dad lately?

He ended the e-mail with an ASCII art of an owl. She stopped walking and took a few breaths.

The owl was Damien's sign meaning he was heading out on a mission. Asking if she'd talked to Dad was his way to say, "Let Dad know." Who knows when she'd hear from him again, and she knew how bad the situation was over there. Since the new Iranian president had taken power, corruption and violence in Iran and other countries had escalated, creating monumental challenges for Iran's citizens. Oh God, the word she just played. What an idiot.

A few moments later, her phone buzzed with another text. Damien again.

Rough day? Can't sleep?

He thought she was home in bed, considering it was one in the morning.

Not really. New job.

K. Get some sleep, sis. LU

LU2.

She slipped the phone back into her purse and continued walking. Footsteps followed behind her, matching her pace at first then speeding up, moving closer. Slowly, she slipped the strap of her purse over her head so it lay across her body. Her hands tightened into fists. A man, by the heaviness of the steps. She planned her attack, depending on which side he approached. Two strikes—forearm and fist, then knee.

Out of the corner of her eye, she noticed his approach from her left. She took a breath and raised her left arm.

"Anyone ever tell you not to text—ooph—"

Zoe spun around and struck his solar plexus with her elbow. A rush of air expelled from his lungs. As she continued around, she was about to smash his nose with the heel of her hand, but something in his voice sounded familiar. She eased up on the momentum of the punch, hitting his mouth instead. He went down, and she climbed on top, her knee pressed on his chest.

She sucked in air as if she'd run a mile, adrenaline pumping in her ears. She blinked, staring at one of the people who interviewed her for the White House job, Frank Phillips, the security adviser. "Jesus, Frank, you scared the daylights out of me."

"Scared you? Christ, Zoe. I was about to say it's not safe to text at this hour walking alone. I stand corrected, er, not exactly standing. Can you let me up?"

"Sure. Sorry, I hit you. Are you okay?" He was ex-military, built solid like a carved pile of cinder blocks.

He rubbed his jaw. "Better than my pride. How's your hand?"

"Okay." She continued walking toward her car, and he paced alongside. "Merritt call you?"

"What if he did?" Frank turned and looked behind them and around each car, shrub or tree they passed. Were all ex-military this paranoid?

"I told him I don't need protection." She picked up her pace, and he matched her steps.

"I see that. But the orders come directly from the first lady. The special tactics team involved with the current project re-

quires personal protection."

She stopped and stared at him. "What special tactics team? Protection from what? No one placed me on any team. I'm filing papers in the basement." She marched toward the parking lot before he had a chance to answer. Her keys were out, and she pressed the key fob. It unlocked the car with a chirp and flash of headlights.

Every ounce of her body was exhausted. She didn't have the energy to get more out of Frank. She doubted he'd tell her much anyway.

"A lot has been going on with the peace treaty," he said. "Security risk is high. Go home and get some rest."

"Thanks for walking me to my car," she said.

"Anytime. Maybe I should have you walk me to mine."

She laughed and considered that a compliment as she got in the car and started it. He gave a wave and watched her leave.

When she got home, Dexter, sleepy-eyed and tail wagging, met her as she walked through the door. After Zoe petted and hugged him, he charged for the back door. Zoe let him out to pee. Mrs. Snyder had left a note on the kitchen counter saying Dexter had been fed and walked at six p.m. When she let him back inside, he went straight to his food dish.

Zoe petted him. "How does one so little eat so much?" She added an extra scoop of food to his dish and checked his water, then glanced around the room and sniffed. She was on the lookout for any doggy presents. She didn't smell anything unsavory. What she did find was white paper everywhere. It took her a minute to realize he'd unrolled the toilet paper from the guest bath and decorated the entire first floor. "Nice job, Dexter."

How could she be angry at him? He was one of the few things in her life she could depend on always wanting her, trusting her, needing her. At this hour, she was too exhausted to scold him. The little guy had been bored all day. She'd have to get him a few more toys and keep the bathroom door closed. At least he hadn't eaten the couch.

At noon the next day, Zoe sat in the employee cafeteria, sipped her fourth cup of strong coffee and waited for the caffeine to kick in. She poked at a Caesar salad.

Normally, the White House was a busy place, but today the employees looked especially haggard and worried. Most of them didn't stop to sit and eat lunch. They ate on the run. A few Secret Service agents in dark suits, sunglasses and coiled ear pieces marched in, grabbed food, then sat down at a table against the far wall. All of them adjusted their chairs so that their backs weren't facing the door. *Typical.*

Zoe smiled at the image the men brought to mind—the movie *Matrix* and all the controllers in dark suits hunting down Mr. Anderson.

The remaining tables were mostly empty. She kept watch for Melissa or Jason. There were a lot of unanswered questions, and it was time someone filled her in. National news highlighted the foreign diplomats in town, meeting with the president, UN officials and advisers involved with the controversial peace agreement. From the looks on everyone's faces, the talks weren't going well. All heads in the room turned toward the television screens up on the walls when CNN announced the escalating violence in the small country of Chad, giving the latest numbers of casualties. Surrounding countries were descending into chaos and soon would be caught up in the momentum. The increased fighting in Africa only added to the continued war and brutality in the Middle East.

"Hi." Melissa plopped down at her table with a tuna sandwich and coffee, out of breath. "I have exactly ninety seconds for lunch. I heard you and Jason Merritt from Secret Service used to work together."

Zoe studied Melissa, waiting for her to mention the sex dungeon and mystery man from the evening before. The woman gave no indication of anything out of the ordinary. She could've been an intelligence agent. "Where did you hear that?" Zoe asked.

"Jason. I thought he was going to give you an orientation."

"Haven't heard from him today." Zoe shrugged, glancing around at the rush of people coming and leaving. "Is this what happens every time we have diplomats visiting?"

"Pretty much." Melissa took a bite of tuna sandwich. "Worse this time. Stressful situation overseas," she said under her breath.

"So I hear." Zoe nodded toward the television. She lost her appetite for the rest of her salad. "The media says we're heading into two wars on two continents. What a military nightmare. The world is like a patchwork quilt splitting apart at its seams."

"This peace treaty has to pass." Melissa glanced around the room as if making sure they weren't overheard. She promptly changed the subject. "Jason didn't call you?"

"No, was he supposed to?"

Melissa's eyes narrowed with that bit of information. "What time did you end up leaving last night?"

"About one. I got started on another file, then Jason stopped in and wouldn't let me leave until then." The time she left could be checked. She didn't have to give details.

Melissa put her coffee cup down and stopped chewing. Her face went pale. "Why so late?" There was an edge to her voice.

"There must've been a meeting or security issue late last night."

"Oh? What makes you think it was a meeting?" Melissa was convincing in her act.

Zoe shrugged. She came up with a lie. "I don't know. Jason had to lock me in until it was over. And I heard a number of people come down the stairs. I know the Situation Room is down there."

"Not in your section," Melissa argued. "How long did you two work together at Langley?"

Zoe kept her tone even. "Three years."

"He's a good guy." Her friend forced a smile and averted her gaze. "You look exhausted. Try to get home early tonight."

"I plan on it." Clearly, Melissa had no intention of telling Zoe about the sex dungeon and the wild parties.

"Hey, Zoe. Hey, Melissa. Love the scarf, Zoe." Alana MacKenna practically bounced over to their table. "Need a little icing to perk up your day?" Alana was a White House researcher who worked with Melissa and had more energy than Zoe and Melissa put together. Maybe she got more than three hours of sleep last night.

"Alana, you've been warned about this. Zoe hasn't been briefed yet," Melissa said, checking her watch. "Crap. Gotta go. We have to go out for drinks some time. I know where all the hot guys hang out."

"I'll take you up on that." Zoe wasn't sure about the hot guys. Seeing Jason had stirred up more than old wounds and mixed emotions. Their heated encounter last night was still fresh on her mind and filled her with a deep ache and longing. She was over him, or wanted to be over him. Whatever they once had was a brief affair. Messing around like a couple of teenagers in the closet was not the beginning of a relationship. It was opportunity and hormones, nothing more. Initiating another affair was a bad idea. He'd only disappear again. Did she want to go through that pain all over again?

Melissa frowned at Alana. "Best you keep your distance until it's all over." Her warning didn't dull the sparkle in Alana's green eyes. She retied her long, red hair into a neat twist and clipped it. "I know, but Zoe should see this anyway. She'll be part of the program soon enough. Icing is what makes our job worthwhile." She grabbed Zoe's salad, didn't ask if she was finished, and dumped it in the trash. "Hurry. You have to see this."

Melissa walked in the other direction, shaking her head in disapproval.

"Pull your phone out," Alana said softly as they walked toward the Oval Office. "Act like we're waiting for a meeting or

something. I'll tell you where to stand."

Zoe pulled out her phone and pretended to text someone. "Why are we doing this?"

"Icing," Alana said again. She stopped, and they stood along a wall, several steps from the main entrance to the Oval Office. Alana ducked her head and checked her phone but had her gaze focused on the doors. Several staff members and Secret Service were around, so they were inconspicuous as far as Zoe could tell.

Be a ghost, don't make eye contact, blend into the background was Zoe's gut instinct. For what, she didn't know yet. "What are we waiting for?" she whispered.

"See those three foreign guys standing at the door?"

Zoe nodded.

"They're security for the Iraqi dignitaries who are speaking with the president right now."

"About what?" Zoe asked.

Alana sighed. "Inside the Oval Office right now is the cake."

"Cake?" Zoe didn't get it.

Alana's eyes widened with delight. "Yes, cake. Proof that we were successful at our job. Watch their expressions when they come out the main entrance. They'll come out in a couple minutes."

"Their expressions. That's the icing?" Zoe was confused.

"Exactly."

"Does this have to do with the peace talks?"

"It'll all be explained to you."

Shouts came from inside the room. And the doors burst open. Two Iraqi delegates charged out, faces red and teeth flashing as they snarled. The Iraqi president shouted orders to his guards in Arabic. Zoe studied his face, and he wasn't the man she saw in the sex dungeon the night before. So why was he so angry? The group stood at the door, shouting, while the Secret Service tried to usher them out of the White House. A Secret

Service guard closed the door to the Oval Office.

Zoe glanced at Alana who had a slight smile that was barely noticeable to anyone around. The woman had backed into the shadows of the crowd, a ghost, blending into the background. But why?

"Icing?" Zoe asked.

"Icing." She nodded. "The cherry will be the announcement this afternoon at the press conference. The Iraqis just signed the peace agreement."

Zoe skimmed and copied documents in her office until well past the dinner hour. She was stalling until she could do more exploring. Jason hadn't explained what had been going on beyond the walls of the sex dungeon, when they both heard the voices coming from another room.

Tonight she would find that room—and hopefully some clues as to what was going on there so late at night while the first lady had been getting her rocks off next door in the sex dungeon. Remembering her director's warnings about keeping her eyes open, she was determined to uncover any security risk if there was one. She felt a bit uneasy with her plans, but until she knew who to trust, this had to be done.

The files in her hands were old journals from numerous first ladies or their secretaries. They documented dates, times and names of well-known political figures, foreign diplomats, ambassadors, princes, presidents. These women had met with the high-ranking officials for tea or cocktails, dinners or lunches in various rooms in the White House. Acting as hostesses prior to important meetings with the president?

There was so much Zoe didn't know about entertaining foreign dignitaries. These guests had the power to start or stop a war, murder or save thousands with a nod, or invade another country with the push of a button. How did you serve coffee and dessert to these people with a smile? She locked the files away and shut down her computer.

She hadn't heard from or seen Jason all day. Should she be surprised? She ground her teeth. The man was true to his old ways. Torment her with sweet, hot sexual attention, then vanish. At ten thirty she put her work away and left her office, since it was unlikely anyone would come downstairs this late at night.

If she figured out who belonged to the voices behind the walls, the rest might make sense. Armed with keys and the ID badge she'd found, she stopped in front of the door adjacent to the sex dungeon. Silence engulfed her. If there were spare offices at this level, she doubted they were being used.

A habit from her old job in counterintelligence was to be hyperaware of her surroundings. One trick she'd learned: If she wanted to hide a secret, put it on the ceiling and to the left. Most people rarely look up and instinctually look to their right first or turn right when entering an unfamiliar place.

If trying to hide a secret message, write it on the ceiling to the left.

Zoe didn't see anything besides a cracked plaster ceiling, but high above the thick Colonial trim around the door, she did notice an odd drawing. It was approximately eight or ten inches across, a symbol consisting of three interlocking triangles that created a nine-pointed star. A double eagle and a crown were etched in the center of the star. Beneath the eagle was the phrase *Deus Meumque Jus*. Latin for "God and my right." It was a Masonic symbol.

Did the Masons have anything to do with choosing the bald eagle as the American symbol? Her father and grandfather were both Freemasons. They had told her brother but never her. Zoe found out by accident after her grandfather died and she'd helped her grandmother go through his personal items. Zoe discovered the lodge manual and her grandfather's Mason ring. When she confronted her dad, he shrugged it off as being a guy thing. Just like her job as an intelligence agent wasn't as important, or as dangerous, as Damien's job. He'd never used those words precisely, but it was clearly implied.

With the set of keys found inside her desk, she tried them one at a time until she found one that fit the lock in the old doorknob. The lock turned, and she entered the dark room.

Chapter 4

Jason's phone buzzed in his pocket. *Meet me in the parking lot in ten.* The text message was from Melissa. Now what?

Outside, the night was clear, but with all the security lights in the parking lot, only a few stars were visible. When Jason reached the employee parking lot, Melissa was pacing back and forth, checking her phone and frantically working her thumbs on the keypad.

"What's up?" he asked. Just because it was eleven p.m. didn't mean White House staff went home like most nine-to-five workers. At least the people in her vicinity were long gone. Still, only a few cars remained, including Zoe's ten-year-old hybrid. "She's still here."

"No kidding. And you haven't told her about the FLC." She glared at him while she finished her text. The air was brisk for an October day and smelled fresh like snow. He liked the snow, since he never saw much of it while growing up in Texas. A breeze blew her long, dark hair about her face. She didn't seem to notice. "Julia doesn't want her down there during a presentation until she's formally a member. We don't want a Celia repeat. Tell her."

Jason groaned and rubbed his forehead with the tips of his fingers. He was dreading it and now he hated himself for bringing Zoe into this. He still cared for her, but hadn't realized how much until now. "She's not right for the FLC. Not this part. I thought she'd be helping me with surveillance."

"Are you crazy? It's too late for that."

"It's true she can role play a drug or arms dealer, but she doesn't know the dominance and submissive lifestyle."

"We needed someone to replace Celia with top-level clearance," Melissa said.

The mention of Celia's name left a sizable hole in his chest. Everyone took Celia's tragedy hard. Celia had never been right for the FLC. "Isn't there someone else we can bring in?"

She shook her head. "It's taken months to plan this. You know what will happen if we fail."

"You don't understand. I almost lost her on a mission. I won't let that happen. I'm not setting her up for something dangerous."

Melissa placed her hand on Jason's arm. "I do understand. Zoe's well trained and won't do anything stupid. Secret Service and you will make sure she's safe. But it has to be Zoe."

He swore under his breath then nodded. "All right, all right."

Melissa frowned. "I knew we could depend on you."

***

The air in the room was cool and smelled damp and slightly moldy, but there was also an odor of incense. Zoe found a light switch and flipped it on. Light flickered from a small, antique chandelier and gave a dim, surreal glow.

The room appeared to be staged like an old office of a hundred years ago. A heavy antique desk stood in the center of the small room with a brocade wingback chair that faced the door. Heavy red brocade drapes covered some of the walls, while others held a few faded canvas pictures. Some were drawings of iconic Washington structures—the Capitol, the Lincoln Memorial and the Washington Monument. Other canvases showed strange symbols. One she recognized. A ruler and compass with a G in the center. The same symbol on rings worn by both her father and grandfather.

Was this room a meeting or meditation room for Masonic study or rituals? Above the door faded painted words—*In Hoc Signo Vinces*—caught her attention. She'd have to check to see what that meant.

Arranged on the desk were a skull—it looked like a real human skull—a candle and a metal bowl holding a powder of some sort. It reminded her of voodoo, but she knew a little about the Masons, and although their rituals appeared strange and mysterious to some, they were benign. She sniffed the powder. It had a strong, unpleasant odor. Not the woody oil scent she detected when she first entered. Maybe wood polish?

This room creeped her out. Did the president use this room? Past presidents had been Masons. She'd read where the main structures in Washington had been designed by Masons, their cornerstones set in formal ceremonies. What was going on down here? First, a sex dungeon and now a Mason room. What next?

A draft of stale air swirled into the room, and the drapes moved. Behind them, she discovered an opening about two and a half feet wide. A passageway. The air here was cold and the tunnel completely dark. She thought about running back to her office for a penlight but remembered her cell. It gave off enough illumination to light her way.

She walked for several yards and tried not to think of rats or bats or other creepy things that might live in dark spaces. Maybe this was an old escape route in the event the White House was taken over? It hadn't been that long ago that the country had been in the midst of the Civil War. The White House could've been seized back then.

Far ahead, she thought she saw another door. Then she heard the noise. A scratching or shuffling sound. *Oh God. There are rats.* She froze and looked down at her feet. *Please, no rats.*

Then a hand clamped around her mouth. She raised her elbow, about to jam it with enough force to crack ribs, when she heard Jason's voice.

"Shhh. Don't scream and don't kill me." He chuckled softly as he turned her in his arms and pressed her against the wall with his body.

"Bastard. You scared the crap out of me."

"Sorry. I couldn't yell down the tunnel. Voices carry. What the hell are you doing?"

"Gathering intel. Um, exploring," she said. Neither sounded like a good excuse. "I was trying to figure out where those voices came from last night."

"You can't go wandering around in the White House," he said. Her back was against the wall, and he was facing her, his thigh planted between her legs. God, she was getting turned on.

"I work down here. I'm authorized," she argued. "Is this an escape tunnel? Has it always been here?" In the light of her cell, his gaze was intense. She couldn't tell if he was angry or not. Heat radiated through her in so many naughty ways.

He took a breath. "This isn't your grandmother's house where you can go off exploring every nook and cranny."

"I know." She leaned her head back, tilting it in a defiant pose, and gave him a smirk. "So where does it go?"

A grin twitched at his mouth, and he licked his lips. He had to do that. Her sex tingled as fond memories recalled what that mouth was capable of. "Another part of the basement." His vague answer pissed her off.

"Guess I'll have to find out for myself." She tried pushing past him, but he caught her arm, slammed her against his body and pressed her into the wall. His thigh rubbed on her pussy. Instantly aroused and wet between the legs, she felt his cock harden.

His mouth came down on hers in a rough kiss. Tongues plunged into each other's mouths, desperately drawing her deeper and deeper, as if all the air had been sucked out of the tunnel and she was gasping for the last few breaths of it.

His arms wrapped around her and pulled her in tighter. His cock pressed into her belly. Large hands moved around her front and kneaded her breasts, then he groaned and yanked her blouse from the waist of her skirt, lifting it high and shoving the bra clear.

His mouth clamped down on one nipple. Groaning, she tried arching her back to meet his mouth, but the confined space wouldn't allow it. Zoe had an image of two people trying to fuck inside a coffin.

"God, Zoe. What are you doing to me?" He pulled up her skirt and reached for the top of her pantyhose. She heard the rip of material as he shoved his hand down and found her clit. "Damn, you're soaked. I want to taste you."

His fingers worked her sensitive flesh until she was on the edge of climaxing. "Jason," she moaned and gripped his shoulders, moving with the rhythm of his hand. "Yes."

Then his finger plunged into her channel. And she cried out. "Shhh," he said as his mouth captured hers and silenced her moans.

The heel of his hand rubbed and stimulated her nub until it was raw and throbbing.

"Oh God, like that." Her head rested on his shoulder as her body coiled on the edge of the most intense orgasm she'd had in a long time.

Then he froze.

No, don't stop now.

"Damn, now? They're early," he said, pulling his hand out of her ruined pantyhose.

She heard it, too. "Someone's coming." She said it in barely a whisper.

"Stay here." He left her in the darkness. She straightened her clothes, then checked that her phone was on vibrate. She slipped it inside her skirt pocket to douse the light.

A moment later, Jason returned. "We can't go back, but I know another way."

This was going to be hard to explain to security later. Jason led Zoe down the narrow passage in the pitch dark. She was amazing, beautiful and irresistible. He couldn't resist her back then, why should it be different now? For months he'd tried telling himself they were better off apart, she'd be safer not having him as a partner, but the truth was, he wasn't sure if anyplace was safe. Right now, he needed to concentrate on the matter at hand. The FLC mission and the unauthorized use of this passage. Secret Service had rules to follow, and he was about to break a couple. His gut tightened. He'd have to explain his appearance on the security cameras pointed at this location.

"My purse and car keys are in my office," Zoe said. "Will I have a chance to go back and get them?"

He had to smile. She was worrying about that now? "Not tonight. I'll drive you home."

She groaned. "Crap."

"What?"

"My keys to my house are with my car keys."

"Stay at my place tonight. I'll drive you in early."

"Can't. Dexter's at home."

He felt a fist punch his shoulder. "Ow." Good aim in the dark. "What was that for?"

"You planned this," she snapped.

"How could I have planned this? You're the one who went snooping. I was doing my job, checking…out the rooms." He didn't want to say his job had been to either check that she'd gone or make her leave. "We'll figure out something."

"You came down to make sure I left so I wasn't down here like last night. Right? Was there another sex rendezvous or secret meeting planned?"

"This passage splits into two around this point." Jason felt along the walls. "We don't want to make the wrong turn. It's a maze down here."

"What else could it be?" She sounded worried. She should be, and that ripped a hole in his chest.

"Just like when we worked at Langley, the details will come when it's appropriate for you to know. I can't tell you more for your own protection and the program's."

"So there is some program. I suspected that." She sighed. "I know, I know, details as needed. But we're not at Langley, and this is different. Something doesn't sit right with me. I'm worried that the president is in danger. What if there's a security breach? Remember the Russian double agent?" That agent had worked in their office at Langley for two years before he was discovered. He had a wife and two kids, and his family had had no idea.

Jason stopped and took her into his arms. "Zoe, I can't tell you right now. The president isn't in danger. I promise you that. The world is in a very dangerous state right now, more than you know. What's going on down here is vital for keeping the world from self-destructing."

"In other words, stay out of it." She rested her head on his shoulder, and he held her tighter.

"For now. I'll explain it later." How could they have brought her into this? *Damn it.*

"Anything I can do to help?" she asked.

"Right now we need to be quiet. We'll be hitting a set of stairs soon for the first floor."

"Where does this come out?"

He groaned. "You really don't want to know."

Zoe walked on tiptoes in her business heels up the old wooden stairs behind Jason. The steps creaked. How someone couldn't hear them coming a mile away, she had no idea.

At the top of the stairs, Jason pulled out his iPhone and turned it on to illuminate the passage. A keypad and key swipe were on the wall next to a panel. No door.

He swiped his card and punched in a six-digit code then eased the panel open a crack. "Thank God, no one's in here. Hurry."

Disoriented, Zoe followed him into the dark room. She looked around. "What is this place?"

"The president's private study."

"Oh crap. Maybe we should've waited downstairs until that meeting was over."

"Not a good idea." He took her hand. "This way before security comes." There was an odd catch to his voice. Could he be involved in a plot against the president? She didn't believe that Jason was capable of being a double agent or working with a criminal group.

"Are there other secret panels like this in the White House?"

He didn't answer.

"Oh, come on. Is there one in the Oval Office?"

He gripped her hand so tight it hurt. "You know nothing of these tunnels and passageways. Do you understand?"

"Yes, and you're hurting me."

He swore under his breath as he loosened his grip. "Sorry. There's a lot going on."

He'd never been this nervous before as an agent, and they'd worked together on a variety of missions. On one, they did a two-man carry of documents containing underwater-weapon specifications. While they stopped for gas at a Stuckey's in Kansas, three armed men pulled in and surrounded him while she was in the bathroom. They were after the documents. Jason had no idea how their cover had been blown, but he managed to wound two of them and subdue the third by the time she'd made it back to the parking lot. Kansas state police arrested the men. After proving their identities, Jason and Zoe had given statements and left.

"Let's go. I'll take you home." He unlocked the door and opened it, then took a step back. Three armed guards stood blocking the doorway with stern expressions.

"Hi, guys," Jason said calmly. "Didn't mean to alarm you. I suspect we'd set off the motion sensors. Ms. Summers wasn't aware of the foreign diplomats coming in this evening for a private meeting. When I saw the group coming down the hall a few moments ago, I didn't want to compromise the delicate negotiations by our presence, so I pulled her into the closest office."

The one in the center frowned then gave a slight smirk. "Private meeting, huh? Foreign diplomats? I haven't been notified of any meetings or special guests this evening, sir."

"The president doesn't want these meetings publicized."

The guard made a grunt. "Right." Obviously, he wasn't

buying it. They were screwed. "Well, Mr. Secret Service." He picked up Jason's ID badge and glanced at it, then glanced at Zoe's. "Mr. Merritt and Ms. Summers, next time you decide to have a *private* meeting, do it someplace other than the president's study."

"Will do," Jason said in his humblest of tones.

The guard made a slight tilt of his head. "Get out of here."

Chapter 5

Melissa Tadeshi knocked on the press secretary's door and held her breath, waiting for her boss to answer. She was used to working these late hours.

"Come in." Julia had a weary, apologetic tone to her no-nonsense voice. Normally, Julia's eyes shone a hazel green that flared when she was ripping into someone. Secret Service agents or White House guards gave her a wide berth when passing her in the hall. Melissa had seen the woman poking a guard in the chest with her finger and yelling while the guard nodded like a scolded child. But Julia's face had no fight in it tonight.

The woman didn't approve of Melissa's position, barely approved of the FLC, but if the president needed this, she'd go along with it.

"Is he here?" Melissa asked as she strutted into the room. She wore a long London Fog raincoat over her outfit.

"Just arrived." Julia peered down at her shoes and scrunched her nose. Melissa had on medium-heeled business pumps. "Are those the heels you're wearing?"

Melissa rolled her eyes and gave a snort. "Of course not. I know how to dress the part." She opened her large leather shoulder bag and pulled out a pair of lace-up, knee-high boots. The heels on those babies were six-inch, including the platform. "I'll put these on just before I go in."

"They'll do. What are you wearing?"

She unbuttoned her coat, then tossed it on a chair in front of Julia's desk.

"Wow," Julia said as she leaned back in her chair. "Where the hell do you shop?"

"At a little fetish shop in Georgetown." Melissa wore a black leather corset with studded spikes across the breasts. A leather thong barely covered her sex. She held up a decorative mask. "I have two of these."

"Good. You'll both need them. I'll have all three cameras going. Are you nervous?"

Melissa leaned on one foot, hands on her hips. "I was a professional Domme for six years. I can handle clients."

"Have you ever had one you couldn't handle?"

Melissa hesitated for a minute. She'd tried lying on her application for the White House job. She should've known better. The application had asked if there was anything in her past that might be viewed by the public as lewd or immoral. She left out her BDSM history and career. She'd always been discreet. During her interview, that was the first thing they asked about. They had dates, times and places.

Then she was offered a position. She'd suspected they did a lousy job on the security check. They hadn't. Shortly after she started at the White House, she was propositioned for her Domme experience.

"I did have one bad incident. My partner is a switch. He plays both the dominant and submissive sides of a scene. Usually, he's present, sometimes to assist, sometimes to protect me with a new client. We each have our own apartments, and we rent a third that we use as our dungeon. This particular time he was away. He's a race car driver and travels frequently. I had a new client who was anxious."

"But your partner wasn't available. Why didn't you reschedule?"

"The money was good, and this guy came with a recommendation."

"So you were a prostitute?" Julia asked, but her comment held no judgment.

Melissa got that a lot, and it annoyed the hell out of her. "No, I was not a prostitute. I never had sex with my clients. I helped clients realize their fantasies in a safe environment. A highly intensified and dramatized fantasy, but that was my purpose and expertise."

"What went wrong?"

"The client wasn't a submissive. He was a ballbuster. He wasn't into exploring his fantasies. He was into a royal mindfuck at my expense, and I almost got raped in the process. Fortunately, I had a knife handy. Threatened to cut off a few of his favorite body parts if I ever saw him again. If not me, then my partner would."

"If things get out of hand in these situations, don't make threats of any kind. Do you understand?"

"Yes, ma'am." The realization of her next scene and what she had to do sent a shiver through her. Her hands were shaking. Her hands never shook before meeting a client.

"If they do get out of hand, raise your pinkie finger, and either the first lady or the Secret Service guard present will step in."

"I understand." Melissa ran through the scenario she had planned and hoped it would satisfy her sub.

Julia stood and took the handful of papers she had on her desk. "We can't mess this up. So far, it's all working well. But we'll need to bring Zoe into the FLC sooner than expected."

"Why?"

"Talks with representatives from Iran, Somalia, Afghanistan and others aren't going well. The war continues to spread out on several fronts. The UN advisers have suggested a small reception at the White House as a sign of goodwill. Many of the delegates will be entering the country early. The schedule for our program will have to move up."

"I'll talk to Jason. We'll start her training," Melissa assured her. "By the way, who is our target this evening? Usually, you tell me who he is and some background."

"I can't say."

"Don't you think I should know?" Why was this one different? A list of possible reasons raced through her head, all of them bad. A few of these targets had known connections to terrorist groups.

"You know his preferences and his limits. It's best that you don't know more."

Melissa nodded. She opened her mouth to ask if she was in any danger then changed her mind. Of course she was in danger, they all were. Everything about the project exposed them to unforeseen hazards.

"Do you have a question?" Julia asked as her phone rang.

Melissa shook her head.

Julia picked up the phone. "Yes? We'll be down." She hung up and stood. "They're ready."

"Good." Melissa put her coat back on and stuffed her boots and masks back in her bag. "I want to get this over with."

Melissa followed a guard and Julia down the stairs to the lower levels of the White House. She passed Zoe's office and was relieved to see the door closed. The text she'd gotten from Jason several moments ago—*Z out*—was all she needed to know. This encounter was too important to fuck up. At the end of the hallway, three more guards stood in front of the Red Tape entrance.

"Is he ready?" Julia asked the guard standing at the door. All three men were well above six feet tall and built like bouncers.

He nodded. Melissa's stomach turned sour. Never in all the years as a Domme had she felt nauseated before meeting a client. He *was* just a client. Dropping her bag on the floor, she kicked off her shoes and slid on the knee-high boots.

"I need to make a quick stop," Melissa said, pointing to the ladies' room. Her mouth went dry, and her tongue felt two sizes too big.

Julia made a face. "You have sixty seconds."

Without a word, Melissa dashed into the bathroom and turned on the faucet, splashing cold water on her face. She willed the contents of her stomach to remain where they were. *Please, please, get a grip, Goddamn it.* She leaned against the sink and took three deep, slow breaths. She could do this.

After drying her face and hands, she touched up her makeup from a bag in her coat pocket, slipped on a pair of long, black gloves and donned the mask. The Mardi Gras mask, made of black satin and decorated with feathers, sequins and glitter, covered half her face. She had another one to match for her partner in crime.

She removed her trench coat and hung it on a hook by the showers, ran her hands down the front of her corset to her hips as a way to center herself. Swinging the door open, she strutted down the corridor toward the waiting group. Julia looked about ready to burst a vein in her forehead. "Ready now?" she said without holding back her annoyance.

Melissa had to give the three guards credit for their professionalism and training. They didn't flinch or blink an eye when she came out in her Domme outfit. "By the time I'm through with him, he'll be a whimpering mass of flesh. And you'll get him to do whatever you want."

"All well and good. Just stick to the program." Julia slid her ID card through the key lock, punched in the code and the door clicked open. The guard held the door as Julia stepped aside and Melissa walked through alone.

The guard closed the door again. With a loud ripping sound, Julia pulled out a length of red duct tape and stretched it across the door, attaching it on a diagonal to the thick oak trim. Then she cut another length and did the same in the opposite diagonal, creating a giant X, as if marking the area with crime-scene tape, except this was red tape, not yellow.

"No one leaves or enters until the first lady opens this door or Secret Service from inside cuts the tape," she told all the guards.

"Understood," the one closest to her stated, standing a bit taller and taking his position in front of the X.

Julia walked down the corridor toward the stairs. She'd wait in her office like she usually did on these nights. This would be another late and tense night.

RED TAPE

Chapter 6

Jason couldn't believe they'd almost had sex in the White House. What was he thinking? When it came to sex, they always went a little crazy. Working together was going to be a challenge, especially when her training began. He kept his eyes on the road, even though the streets of Washington were pretty deserted at this hour.

"If you stay with me tonight, we can get the key from your neighbor in the morning to take care of Dexter."

"No, you live too far," Zoe said, digging through her purse. "Let's go to my place."

"Without keys, can you break into your house at this hour without setting off all sorts of alarms and waking your neighbors?"

She gave him a sideways glance. "I used to be CIA, remember?"

He turned the car and headed in the other direction.

"Maybe the robes, the masks, the bondage have to do with some bizarre ritual, or it's all just kinky sex," Zoe said, as she stared out the passenger side window. "Does it have to do with the Masons?"

"The Masons?" Jason chuckled. Where did he start?

She pulled out her cell phone and punched away on the keypad.

"Who are you calling so late?" he asked.

"No one. I'm looking up something. I knew that other room had to do with the Masons. My grandfather was a Freemason, but I never knew it until after he died and I found his ring and lodge manual. I've seen those strange symbols on the walls in that room."

"What did you find?" His chest swelled. Even though she was way off track, he admired how she took clues and managed to look at situations from all angles.

"It's a Chamber of Reflection. A meditation room for Masons," she said, still staring at her phone.

He was trying hard not to think about how hot and sexy she was just a few moments ago. She looked so good and felt so amazing. Now that they'd started, he'd never get enough of her. Would they be making a mistake by getting involved again?

"What else did you find?"

"A Chamber of Reflection is for serious meditations. A room to reflect upon present or future plans or decisions. Quite appropriate for the president of the United States, especially for those who were Masons. Fourteen of them were, you know."

"I knew George Washington and Franklin Roosevelt were. I didn't realize there were fourteen."

"Now that Latin phrase on the wall makes sense. I found the translation of *In Hoc Signo Vinces*. It means, 'By this sign thou shalt conquer.'" She looked at Jason. "Were those men coming downstairs Masons heading to this room for a meeting or to the dungeon room for sex?"

Jason looked straight ahead. "This is your street here, isn't it?"

"Yes, park in back."

He found a free parking space for visitors. "What time do you want me to pick you up?"

Zoe groaned. "It's almost one. It's too far of a drive for you. Stay here, and you can explain what's going on."

* * *

Wearing her decorative mask and Domme outfit, Melissa slowly stalked into the Red Tape Room, pleased to see her target's eyes widen. The first lady introduced her to the delegate. Melissa held her stance—tall, chin up—and locked her gaze with his.

"My pleasure, Mistress," President Kasim Rutu from Somalia said as he smiled and nodded in a polite gesture. Although he requested to be her submissive for the scene, his intense brown eyes held an element of power, and his stocky shoulders didn't cower in the slightest. He would be pushed and submit only as far as he derived pleasure from it. The handsome man had short, dark hair and looked to be in his mid-forties.

Retrieving the other mask from her bag, she walked over to First Lady Faith Bryson and handed it to her. The next thing she did was select music from the iPhone seated in a docking station. Seductive music with an exotic beat filled the room, something that might have been played at an upscale strip club. There was a reason for the music. Like there was a reason for everything.

The first lady put on her mask, a signal to the audiovisual room to begin recording, and backed off to the side of the room. Melissa instructed him to stand, eyes down, hands behind his back, legs slightly parted in a parade rest stance. Her first test to see how receptive he would be to her commands. He obeyed without hesitation. She relaxed a little. Usually, when it came to sex, Melissa had men in the palm of her hand. But she was always ready for the unexpected with these men.

"Good." Melissa strutted straight over to the table that held floggers, canes, clamps, vibrators, dildos, ball gags, an electrical wand and a few other items. She didn't expect to need most of them. One item they would never have in one of these sessions was a hood. It was very important that the subject's face be clearly seen at all times. Even a blindfold was permitted only briefly.

Ignoring him, another test for her subs, also put her in a position of authority. Considering this man's high level of authority, she knew that was quite a feat. Talk about a power exchange. Glancing down at her hands, she noticed they still shook. She tightened them into fists while she scanned the items on the table, planning her scene.

During their time together, she would not think of this man as a leader of a nation with connections to terrorists, one who was resisting the current peace negotiations, making him a major threat to global security. He was her submissive, like any other client. Her only role was to satisfy his needs. She selected a leather collar from the table and walked back to her sub.

"Take off your clothes and put this collar on," Melissa ordered in a firm but casual voice. "You may put your clothes on the bed."

He hesitated for only a fraction of a second then began to unbutton his shirt. His eyes met hers for an instant, testing her authority.

"Eyes down," she ordered. "I didn't give you permission to look at me." With her heels, he was about her height of five-foot-ten, and his dark hair framed his wide face, giving him an innocent appearance. "When I give you an order, I expect a 'Yes, Mistress' in return. If you don't understand something, you may ask."

"Yes, Mistress." He lowered his gaze and moved faster with his undressing. Melissa noticed he had a hard-on. Good sign, thank God.

Walking back to the table, she examined the various tools of torture. She already had a plan, but wanted to give him time to think and worry a bit. So she picked up different ones and tested them. She smacked a cane across the table, testing its flexibility, then placed it back on the table. Then she selected a flogger, smoothed the cool leather through her hand. The smell of new leather could get her turned on. Stretching the thongs out in her other hand, she took a few practice swings. The leather cut through the air with a whoosh followed by an exploding crack. This was her meditation, her way to calm her nerves, get her worked up, even aroused. Surprisingly, she was getting turned on by this. Besides being a Domme, Melissa was a sadist. She enjoyed inflicting pain. Normally, she gave pain or humiliation only to those who desired it. She was careful and respected limits.

In this situation, the subject desired pain and humiliation, but he had no idea the true pain would begin after the scene, after he left. Whether her part in this manipulation scheme was honorable depended upon which side of the political arena one sat.

Holding her hands out above the table, Melissa smiled to herself. Her hands no longer shook. Behind her, the rustle of clothing and sound of a buckle being hooked caught her attention. She picked up a cane and spun around. Faith was helping him put on the collar. His eyes locked on the cane and widened. He quickly lowered his gaze then folded his hands over his semierect penis and bowed his head.

A cruel master of a country was now in a subservient pose to her. Wow, what a rush. This would be a piece of cake. She hoped.

Behind the floor-to-ceiling wall hangings was the hidden video equipment. The canvases were translucent enough to record the events in the room.

Melissa strolled over to the man. He didn't look up.

"Do you like the feel of the collar?" she asked.

"Yes," he said.

"Yes, what?" she asked with a warning tone. He was pushing her, wanting to get punished.

He hesitated for a moment. "Yes, Mistress?"

"Did you forget so quickly?" She swatted him on his ass, and he jumped.

"Sorry, Mistress." He wasn't sorry. He liked pain. Good, she liked giving it.

"I will call you Romeo tonight. And if you trust me, I can take you to places of pleasure and pain you've never experienced before. But the pain is only to intensify the pleasure, never to harm and never to go beyond what you can handle." He nodded. Not using his real name helped to keep him in the fantasy. "I'll give you a safe word to let me know when we've gone too far. Jupiter is your safe word. Repeat it to me, Romeo."

"My safe word is Jupiter, Mistress."

"Good. If you need me to slow down or ask me a question because you're unsure of something, you'll say yellow. Under-

stand?"

He nodded.

"What is your caution word?" she demanded.

"Yellow, Mistress. May I ask a question?"

"Yes, Romeo."

"How long do I have with you?"

She hooked her fingers under his chin and raised his head. "Our time together will be over when I say it's over. Or when you call your safe word."

He nodded, eyes wide.

"I don't want you to come too soon, because then our session would be over too soon. So I have something I'd like you to wear." She released his chin and walked over to the table and picked up the device. Test number one. This would tell her how much he was willing to trust her.

As she approached him with the device in her hand, she watched for his response. He stared at it and cringed.

"Ever wear one of these before?" She held up a contraption called the Gates of Hell for him to see. He knew what it was by his expression. Behind him, the first lady had a slight smile.

He shook his head. "No, Mistress. It looks painful."

"Not as painful as you may think. But you will have to concentrate on keeping yourself from getting too hard, or it will become painful."

A series of five metal rings were evenly spaced and held together by a strip of leather. "Hands at your side."

He complied. She took his cock in hand and slid the rings down his semi-hard shaft. The first ring pressed at the base, and the top ring encircled the crown of his cock. "Doesn't that look hot," Faith said with a seductive tone. "Turn him toward me so I can get a good look."

Melissa placed her hands on her sub's shoulders and guided him slowly around. Now Faith could see, and those who were watching could, too. "He does look hot, doesn't he?"

Romeo's cock twitched and swelled against the rings.

"Don't get too excited. If it does become painful, let me know. I won't promise to remove it, but I want to know." Melissa walked him toward a piece of furniture, a spanking bench. "Kneel for me."

He did. She stretched his arms out on the armrests while stroking his shoulders and back. "Comfortable?"

"Yes, Mistress." She picked up a bottle of scented oil from the table, poured a few drops into her hand and rubbed her hands together.

"When Faith had you to tea, you said you wanted to experience the feel of a flogger on your skin."

"Yes, Mistress." His body vibrated on the bench, and he gripped the armrest.

"How about a cane?"

He didn't answer for a long time.

"Romeo, when I ask you a question, I expect an answer."

"I don't know about the cane, Mistress. But if it pleases you." He lowered his head and voice, which told her a lot about how he felt about the cane. Part of being a good Domme was being able to read body language.

"We'll use the cane as punishment."

"Yes, Mistress. I'll try to please you so I won't need to be punished."

She massaged the oil into his shoulders. He trembled beneath her touch. Slowly, she moved down to his back, buttocks and thighs. He sighed, and she could feel the muscles relaxing, his breathing slow. When she used the flogger on him, she'd have less of a chance of breaking the skin.

Melissa put the oil down, then stood in front of her sub. "You like the boots, don't you?"

"Yes, Mistress." She noticed him moving his ass when he answered.

"What would you like to do to these boots?"

"Mistress, I would like to lick them or kiss them if it would please you."

She waved over the first lady. "And what about my assistant's shoes? Aren't they pretty? Would you like to lick her toes, too?"

Faith wore a pair of red five-inch platform peek-toed heels.

"Yes, Mistress." He breathed heavy now and groaned.

"Is your cock getting too hard?"

"I'm trying to be good, Mistress."

She put her hand under his chin. "The cane will be punishment. Licking boots and toes will be a reward, later. For now, you must look straight ahead at that mural of Niagara Falls."

"Yes, Mistress."

She chose a flogger with knotted thongs. This would be especially painful and guaranteed a response and marks. Quite a few bruises. She needed a number of marks to show. She worked across his shoulders, watching him flinch with each strike but not making a sound. As the skin became rosy, she moved down to his buttocks and then his thighs. He cried out when she struck his ass and thighs. She stopped and stroked his back, gently running her nails over his skin until he shivered.

"How are you doing, Romeo? Is it too hard?"

"Not yet. I like it. I like pleasing you, Mistress."

"Good answer." She increased the intensity, and Romeo whimpered and moaned with each strike.

She continued to strike him over and over, not hitting the same place twice but working up into a fevered rhythm. Red marks rose on his skin, but she was careful not to break the skin. He was a bit of a masochist. If she kept the rhythm up, he might drift into subspace. In this altered state, a submissive reached a level of extreme comfort and acceptance, physically and emotionally. If she wasn't careful, she could go beyond his limits, even harm him, while in this state. That would please her audience.

"Hmmm. Ahhh," he moaned and slumped on the bench but kept his head up. His eyes looked a bit glazed. He was getting close.

She stopped for a moment, checking him and admiring the network of red lines across his back, buttocks and thighs. "Want me to stop?" she asked.

He hesitated.

"I asked you a question. I expect an answer."

"If I say yes, will you punish me?"

"I will punish you for not answering or lying to me. Have you had enough?" she asked, raising her voice.

"Yes, Mistress."

"I don't think so. I think we're just getting started." She picked up a paddle and held it against his ass. "Do you think you could handle a few whacks?"

He breathed rapidly again. "Oh yes." She whacked him hard, but not too hard, on one buttock. She didn't want to finish him off too soon. He cried out and sounded angry.

Then she smacked the other side. He mumbled something under his breath but kept looking at the mural.

"Did you say something?"

"No, Mistress." The purpose wasn't to hurt him as much as she could. Well, in a way it was. She wanted to push him to surrender to her. Right now, he was enjoying the pain and showing off his ability to withstand it. That was defiance, not what she was going for. She wanted an exchange of power, respect.

"Get up. Over to the cross." She stood alongside him, making sure he was steady on his feet. If he was going into subspace, he might stagger like a drunk. He was a little wobbly but okay. She purposely walked him around, displaying him in clear view for their hidden audience. Faith gave her a slight nod of approval.

When she brought him up to the St. Andrew's Cross positioned in the center of the room, he immediately leaned, face-forward, without instruction, arms wrapped around the juncture and legs stretched out, resting against the thick wooden planks.

Melissa didn't even need to strap his wrists and legs to the cross with leather restraints. He was quite a willing participant.

This time, she took two floggers, one in each hand, and rapidly struck him in a Florentine fashion like a pinwheel.

After several minutes, Romeo moaned, pleaded for more, then begged her to stop, but didn't call out the safe word. He slumped against the cross, knees buckling. Moaning and mumbling to himself, he was gone, far into subspace. Melissa felt she couldn't and shouldn't go any further. She glanced back at Faith.

The first lady drew a slow slashing motion across her neck, making an inconspicuous "cut" motion. The signal that the session was done.

"Okay, Romeo. I'm going to get you down now." The first lady pushed a chair over while Melissa helped him step away from the cross. The two women guided their sub into the chair. He stumbled and swayed, barely able to hold himself up. "Here, let me get this off." Melissa slid the Gates of Hell off his cock. Romeo sucked in a breath as if in pain for a moment. Then she took off the collar.

"Did I come?" he asked.

Melissa giggled. She saw no sign that he had and found it interesting that he was so far into subspace that he didn't know himself. "Yes, you were wonderful. Here, have some water, and we'll help you get dressed. Someone will take you back to your hotel."

Unlike Alana, who liked to see their victim's reaction, Melissa didn't want to be anywhere around Rutu when he heard the news.

Chapter 7

Zoe's old townhouse in Georgetown felt more like home than his own place. She lived on a quiet street, had nice neighbors she actually knew and had a backyard. The only thing missing was the picket fence and a man mowing the lawn.

"Mrs. Snyder won't complain about you waking her up this late?" Jason yawned as she rang Mrs. Snyder's doorbell. A mixture of exhaustion and guilt weighed him down. As much as he wanted to tell her about how she got the job and what she was in for, it was late and they were both exhausted.

"How long have you been up?" she asked him.

He checked his watch. "About thirty hours. Even my hair is exhausted." He yawned again. Damn, he still wanted her bad.

Zoe knocked on the door. "Mrs. Snyder? Beth? It's Zoe."

The door swung open, and an attractive woman in her seventies blinked up at the two of them. She eyed Jason suspiciously. "Is everything all right?"

"Yes, this is my coworker, Jason. I'm so sorry to wake you, but we got involved in a late project, and my keys are at the White House. Can I have my spare?"

"Are you sure you're okay?" She studied Jason again.

"Yes." Zoe laughed a little. "Jason's an old friend."

"Oh." Mrs. Snyder smiled and nodded as if she got the inside joke. "I've got it right here. I let Dexter out around six and gave him his food." She retrieved the key on a table by the door and handed it to her.

"Thank you," Zoe said. "Sorry to wake you."

"Enjoy your evening," the woman said with a smirk as she closed the door.

"My way of breaking in," Zoe said.

"Nice neighbor. Guess I'll be going." The lack of sleep was quickly catching up to him.

"No, you're staying here. You're not driving across town at

this hour. I don't want to hear about you falling asleep and getting into an accident."

"Hmmm. You want me to stay? I think I'm getting my second wind." He grinned as she unlocked the door.

She play-punched him in the arm. The moment she opened the door, Dexter was there to greet her and Jason. He jumped up on her, offering licks to her hands and face, then looked at Jason cautiously for a few seconds then, deciding he was a friend, leaped onto him as well.

"Dexter, down," Zoe ordered. The pooch half-listened. "Push him down if he keeps jumping, I haven't been home much to work with him."

"Down, Dexter," Jason said with a firm tone, and the dog sat instantly and looked up at him, anticipating the next order.

Zoe rolled her eyes. "Terrific. My dog takes orders from a stranger. He'll make a great watchdog."

Jason laughed. "He'll be fine. He's still a puppy. Once he has a hundred pounds behind him, no stranger will come into his domain without facing consequences."

Jason followed her inside with Dexter at his heels. Zoe flicked on a Tiffany lamp on an end table, placing the room in a soft glow. The place was spotless, with simple traditional furnishings, hardwood floors, and lots of stained woodwork.

"Can I get you something to drink?" She opened the back door and let the dog out.

"I'm good." He examined the fireplace in the living room. "Does it work?"

"Yes, wood-burning."

"Great." He took a breath. This was probably a bad time for spilling guts. "I guess I owe you an explanation."

"For tonight?"

He shrugged. "That and for why I left Langley without telling you."

She sat on the sofa and put her feet up on her coffee table. For a neat freak, that was an odd thing to do. "At first I thought you went on a mission that ran into some complications, then I heard you left or were reassigned. Later, Big D said you left but gave no details. Typical. I figured you lost interest."

He sat next to her on the sofa and took her hand. "That wasn't quite right. I did get reassigned. But I should've contacted you. I wanted to. I got involved in a complicated project and was sent overseas right away."

"It's late. Let's talk about this another time." She got up and let Dexter inside. He got a drink of water from his bowl, then curled up on his doggy pillow in the living room.

"Okay. We'll talk about it later." Jason patted her thigh.

She got up and walked into the other room, her bedroom, he assumed, and closed the door.

Crap. That was that. He deserved it. What did he expect? That she'd forgive him and jump right in the sack? At least the sofa felt comfortable. He took off his shirt, pulled a throw blanket from the back of the sofa, and stretched out. Dexter hopped onto the couch and curled around his legs. He considered pushing him off, but the dog looked at him with soulful brown eyes. "Okay, I don't know the rules, so just this once." The dog gave a loud sigh.

Zoe dug through her dresser drawer, looking for her sexy lingerie, the black lace shift with red ribbons running through it. The cups barely covered her breasts and made her look two cup sizes larger, thanks to a little padding and underwire. She left her scarf on the dresser. Jason was the one person who understood and either didn't see the scar, or ignored it. She loved him for that.

Was she a fool getting involved with him again? Feeling his body and his response in the hidden passageway was more than she could resist. There always had been amazing heat between them, and for what was going on in that secret passage, she knew he wanted her as much as she wanted him.

Details could come later. They were adults. They could en-

joy each other's company if they wanted. If a relationship was meant to be, they could work it out.

She knew he cared, had really cared for her once. They'd worked on a few dangerous missions. You learn a lot about a person during a crisis, even someone who was trained to deal with crisis situations.

The first one had been in Israel. They'd been gathering intel on arms dealers. One of the dealers left his grandmother sitting in a chair near a flower vendor as a lookout. Zoe was to take photos of the people coming and going from the building, not approach. The building was under renovation and empty except for construction workers. But when a contractor's truck blocked her view, she decided to go inside. When the grandmother noticed Zoe enter a building, she alerted her grandson. Jason almost blew his cover, and the mission, to rescue her before the men got to her.

He shouldn't have returned to the scene. He'd had the intel he needed even without her photos. The information was too important and the risk too great, but he risked his life anyway.

The incident in Turkey had been even worse. That nightmare she'd rather forget. Months later, he'd left Langley without a word. All this time, he was working Secret Service.

Had another woman stepped in? Or another mission? Or had he lost interest? If that was the case, she would walk away. Either way, she'd survive and put it behind her. Right now, she wanted him. Every cell in her body was hot for him. She didn't care what he did or who he'd been with. Her pussy was soaked, her nipples hard and sensitive. In those secret passages, he'd worked her up, and now she needed a release.

Leaving her bedroom, she walked into the living room where Jason lay on the sofa, asleep, snoring softly. Months ago, that hard body had made love to her in the most exotic places. Dexter was also asleep at his feet. He wasn't supposed to be on the couch, but she didn't want to disturb Jason. Her body reacted to Jason's nearness, but she didn't have the heart to wake him. *Fuck.*

She drew the throw blanket over his chest, turned out the lights, went back into her room and went to bed.

The next morning she woke to the smell of bacon and coffee. Rolling over, she glanced at her clock. 8:55 a.m. They'd gotten to bed after three. She climbed out of bed and made a quick stop in her bathroom. As she suspected, makeup had left dark smudges under her eyes, and her hair looked and felt like a bale of hay stomped on by a horse.

After running a comb through her hair and quickly brushing her teeth, she wrapped herself in a silk robe and headed for the kitchen. "Something smells good."

He stood at the stove, barefoot, shirtless and wearing only his trousers. Dexter sat on the floor munching on something. She assumed a slice of bacon. Jason knew how to win him over.

"Morning," he said over his shoulder as he continued cooking the eggs.

Her insides thrummed, ached for him all over again. She marched straight for the coffeepot and poured two mugs.

"I can't remember the last time you cooked breakfast for me."

"It was at my condo. It's been awhile." He brought the plates of food to her dining table in the next room.

They sat down and began to eat. She sipped her coffee. "I assume you still live in the same condo in Chevy Chase?"

He shook his head. "I have a place in McLean Gardens now."

Of course, McLean Gardens was pretty close to the White House, so maybe that was where he moved to be closer.

The silence grew awkward between them. Then he reached across the table and touched the sleeve of her robe. He rubbed the peach silk between his fingers. "This is pretty. Were you wearing this last night?"

She nodded. "You crashed. I didn't want to wake you."

He gave her a crooked grin. "You should've."

"The eggs are good. Thanks." She munched on the buttered toast. "We can shower quick, then go get my things. Are you working today?"

"No, I'm off."

"Odd that we're working together again." She hadn't thought about it much, considering all that had happened. But now that she did think of it, wasn't it a bizarre coincidence?

"I suppose," he said. "Are we showering together?"

"Maybe." She leaned back in her chair and waited for his response. He didn't say a word. "One good thing about not working at Langley anymore, we can tell each other where we're going and talk about our jobs."

"To a degree. I'm not authorized to chat about certain aspects of my job."

Zoe stood up and got more coffee and more cream. She huffed. "I know that." She topped off his mug with more coffee, splashing a little onto the table. She resisted the urge to clean it up. He used to tease her about her compulsive cleaning.

After a minute she couldn't stand the drips of coffee and grabbed napkins and soaked up the spill.

She was sure he noticed, but he didn't mention it. Dexter stood by the back door, his signal to be let out. Zoe opened the door for him.

"Did I ruin your plans last night?" Jason asked.

"My research project in the basement?" She sat back down and sipped at her coffee, unable to finish the rest of her breakfast.

Her robe slid off one shoulder. He reached over and slid a finger beneath the lacy strap of her chemise. "Not what I meant. Did you have plans to make love?"

"Perhaps. It was awfully late."

"We can manage now." He smiled, and his gaze turned dark and sultry. The look was intoxicating, and her stomach gave a flutter. "I have a lot to make up to you."

She felt all hot and horny inside. Yes, she wanted him, and

she probably could have him right there, but then what? He'd walk away again? "Promises, promises." She smiled, but it was a bittersweet smile. She stood up and carried the dishes into the kitchen. Starting over brought up the uncertainty and fear of what would happen later.

He followed. "It was damn hard leaving you," he said. "I was afraid that if I didn't, you'd be killed or tortured, or we both would."

"You don't think I was a good agent?" She glared at him, arms crossed, wrapping the robe tightly around her.

"You're an excellent agent. Maybe a little too fearless at times, but smart, and you have nerves of steel."

"I think we worked well together. We had a couple of bad missions." She touched his hand.

"Don't you want this?" The pain in his voice ripped a hole inside her.

"I want you so damn much." Her words choked in her throat. She forced a laugh to keep from crying. "Hell, we can't seem to keep our hands off each other."

"Should we try?" He stepped closer, opening her robe and putting his arms around her waist. The heat of his touch blazed through the silky material. Her robe dropped to the floor as he pulled down one strap of her chemise and kissed her shoulder, his hot tongue drawing a slow circle to make her shiver.

"I doubt it would do any good." She explored his chest, feeling every muscle and curve. Forgoing the idea of going slow, she slipped her hand down his trousers and wrapped her fingers around his cock. He moaned and cupped her breasts. "I have condoms in my bedroom."

He shifted and dug into his pants and slammed a packet on the kitchen counter. "No need."

"Why am I not surprised?" She laughed.

"Zoe, tell me what you want," he said in a hoarse tone. He kissed her throat. She tensed, wanting to hide the scar, but he distracted her by rolling her nipple between his fingers. "Here, or the couch, your bed, or the shower?"

With each new suggestion, his mouth moved from her throat to her breasts, her stomach. Then he drew down her panties and licked her cleft. The deeply intimate touch electrified all her senses and directed a rush of pleasure to her core.

"I want it all." She moaned and grabbed the counter behind her. His tongue rasped across her swollen bud, drawing exquisite shivers through her body. When he thrust his finger inside her channel, she cried out and thought she'd collapse. "God, Jason. Slow down or I'll come."

He stood, licking his lips, and she reached for his zipper and yanked down his pants. His cock sprang free. Cupping his balls with one hand, she tightened her grip around his shaft with the other, then worked it up and down, tightening and releasing the pressure.

"This was what I wanted to do to you in that closet." She knelt down and took him into her mouth. He groaned and raised his hips, pumping them to match her rhythm.

"Zoe, fuck, that's good." He grabbed her shoulders and lifted her up. "As much as I'd like you to continue, I have to get inside you."

Leaning into him, she kissed his arm. "The bedroom?"

He opened the condom and slipped it on. "Do you think we can wait that long?"

"No."

He lifted her up on the counter, spread her legs wide. Pressing the crown of his cock at her entrance, he tested her slick, hot opening. "Fuck me, Jason. Now."

He drove deep in one thrust to his root. She relished the melty sensation spinning within her core, her womb as he slid back and pumped into her again. "God, yes," she cried out. Her legs hooked around his hips, urging him to pump faster, harder.

One hand on the cabinet, Jason thrust his cock deep. Zoe's ass kept bumping into the microwave, but she barely noticed. When he raised her legs, he found the perfect position. Immediately, she let go of the counter and grasped his arms. The coil of pleasure rose up deep inside her, and the most intense orgasm slammed into her. "Ahhhh."

Before the last spasm of sensation rushed through her, Jason groaned. "Ah fuck, I'm coming." He threw back his head and closed his eyes. After his body and breathing calmed down, and she felt reality returning, they collapsed into each other's arms. "That was amazing."

"Yes, very." She rested her head on his shoulder, not wanting him to see her face. Yes, how quickly they fell back into their hot and heavy sex routine.

Dexter scratched and whimpered at the back door.

"Guess he wants in." He stepped away from her and opened the door. Dexter rushed in and ran straight for his food dish.

Jason got quiet, kept his eyes averted. Was it from making love or did he have something else on his mind? The distance grew between them, and she had no idea why.

"Something wrong?" She tried keeping the edge out of her voice as she pulled the robe around herself and crossed her arms over her breasts.

He smiled, a weak one at that. "No." But he petted Dexter while he said it. "Ready for that shower? I have more to talk to you about once we get to the White House."

Chapter 8

Morning sunlight streamed through the massive Palladian window of the East Sitting Hall, filling the room with blinding white splendor. Melissa's escort brought her to the entrance, announced her presence, and waited for the first lady to call Melissa inside.

The escort, a middle-aged gentleman, gave her a nod to enter then left. Melissa stepped over the threshold. Her heart always quickened when entering this portion of the White House. It seemed intimate, private, as if she was intruding.

"Please have a seat, Melissa," Faith said. "Charlotte and I were just finishing some tea and scones. We're planning the reception for next week. It will be a small event, just a few UN officials and the foreign delegates who'll be in town that week. Small." Faith gave Charlotte a pointed look.

When Melissa's eyes adjusted to the bright lighting, she froze as she realized "Charlotte" was Charlotte Ellison, first lady from the previous administration. Her husband had lost his re-election bid. Mrs. Ellison was now working at the United Nations.

Melissa sat on a chair across from the two women everyone in the nation thought were enemies having a friendly cup of tea. At any moment, Melissa expected to see the gracious women, wearing perfectly pressed designer suits and exquisitely applied makeup and styled hair, attack each other like a couple of rabid poodles. Where was her whip when she needed it?

"Would you like some tea?" Faith picked up the silver teapot and smiled.

"Yes, please." Melissa held up a dainty china teacup and saucer while Faith poured.

Faith's hand was steady, she noticed. She was accustomed to her new role as the head of the FLC, the First Lady's Club.

"This is a last-minute reception, and we want a friendly and warm atmosphere for these most"—she hesitated, searching for the proper or politically correct word—"cautious delegates when it comes to signing the peace treaty."

"Small reception," Charlotte moaned in her stuffy Southern accent, as if Faith had no idea how to be a proper hostess. "Is there ever such a thing as a small reception in the White House?"

"I know how you love a party, Charlotte, especially in big houses, but tensions are high, and I think it would be in poor taste to have a large gala." Somehow, Melissa thought Faith was getting a dig in there. She sipped her tea, averting her gaze to the scones that looked heavenly.

"Help yourself to a scone or tea sandwich, dear," Charlotte offered.

Faith shot her a look, then quickly ignored the woman's overstep in playing hostess. "I think we have everything covered. I'll contact the caterers and give them a head count. No media will be allowed either." When Charlotte opened her mouth to protest, Faith calmly glanced at her, daring her to argue.

The woman had enough sense to know how far to push. "I understand. Small, low-key, warm, friendly and *boring* reception." She sighed then smiled in a kind manner. "Anything to put the delegates at ease and get them to sign." She stood up to leave.

Faith also stood. "I'll walk you out."

"No, no, I know my way." She smiled. "Have your meeting with your assistant."

The edge in her voice made Melissa wonder if Charlotte had guessed what type of assistant she was.

After Charlotte left, Faith walked across the room and gazed out the window. She took in a deep breath. "I do believe the East Sitting Hall is my favorite room in the White House."

"It is a beautiful room," Melissa agreed. "The lighting is perfect for the Monet." She picked up her teacup, took a sip and frowned. The tea was cold.

"Since the last administration didn't utilize the FLC, we have a lot of work to do," Faith said.

"Mrs. Ellison was opposed to the FLC?"

"She didn't agree with its philosophy," Faith stated. "If we succeed with the treaty, we can move on to other projects. This reception might allow us to line up a few more targets. The intel has been gathered. We need to make the offers."

"Let me know if I can help."

"You'll be attending the reception."

"Of course." Melissa bit down on a scone and washed it down with some cold tea. "Do you think the tapes were acceptable?"

"That was nice work last night."

Melissa sighed. "I'm glad to hear. When will we know?"

"He's having his key meeting this morning. The president was happy with the results of last night." Faith smiled. Clearly, she enjoyed going over the details of the Red Tape Room's presentation with her husband.

Melissa had heard the sex tapes were an aphrodisiac between Faith and the president. An added benefit of the FLC. She hadn't expected to make porno flicks for the president. She so didn't want to go there. If her encounters were successful for manipulating foreign policy, that's what mattered.

"With any luck," Faith said, "there might be a press conference this afternoon with some good news."

Melissa wondered if Faith was turned on by her participation, her Domme outfit, the complete scene or the potential outcome from it. Or even by the knowledge that the video would turn her husband on later. Men of power got a sexual rush when placed in a position of power. They couldn't deny it. And women from all walks of life were drawn to powerful men. This was why the FLC worked so well. This was why Faith had said she was able to persuade President Bryson to allow her to initiate the FLC.

"May I ask a question, ma'am?"

"Of course."

She lowered her voice. "How does President Bryson feel about the FLC's attempts to influence the delegates' signatures?" Melissa wasn't sure if she stepped over her bounds but figured Faith would tell her.

"If he has an opinion, he doesn't tell me. The FLC was designed so that the president knows very little and limits his participation for one very good reason." She paused for a moment. "Plausible deniability."

"I see."

The first lady frowned. "I anticipate after the reception we'll be quite busy for a few weeks. We'll need to stay in touch and plan very unique scenes. Some may be difficult for you and Alana, but you know what's at stake."

The first lady couldn't have gotten more than three or four hours of sleep, but Melissa couldn't tell. "We can handle it. When I worked as a professional, I catered to a number of well-known men and women who had very distinct tastes. And the ones who requested the most intense scenes were politicians, CEOs, and pilots. Those who are in a constant state of control desire giving up control completely and get a sexual rush from it."

"And what about Alana? How is she doing?" Faith asked.

Melissa didn't say what she really thought. Alana liked her job a little too much. "She's well-versed in a variety of fetishes and kinks. I'm sure we won't have a problem meeting the target's needs."

"Good." Faith picked up a china plate. "Help yourself to another scone or tea sandwich. The scones were made by our chef."

"No, thank you." Melissa had lost her appetite. After the reception, they'd be running a marathon in the Red Tape Room. "So many countries are opposed to the treaty. I hope this works."

Faith gave Melissa a sharp look. "Don't doubt the effectiveness of the FLC. Powerful men have excessive sex drives. Our targets have been thoroughly researched for their specific

needs."

Melissa put her teacup down and picked up a napkin, crumpling it in a ball. "I'm sure we'll all do our best, ma'am."

Faith laughed and leaned back in her chair, munching on a crab tea sandwich. "My dear, haven't you realized the power of the FLC yet? Many of the countries on our target list are religiously structured, male-oriented societies. Over the years, some have made great strides for their people and their cultures. Then a new president steps in with a conflicting agenda and threatens the stability of the country and its people. Terrorists take advantage of the instability. Many times, these leaders feel making deals with the devil is their only or preferred option."

Melissa nodded politely. Obviously, the world's situation was much more complicated than that, but Faith was explaining it in terms that a fifth-grader might understand.

The first lady took a breath. "It could take months for the United Nations and members of the Security Council to explain the dynamics. The point is, we're not going to get this treaty signed without a little push."

"I understand that."

"When I showed the president from Afghanistan the taped session with Alana, the man was terrified. I had to call in medical personnel because I feared he'd have a heart attack. Not only did he agree to sign the peace treaty, he got on his knees and begged to sign and pleaded to have the tape destroyed. If his country's officials saw that tape, a swift divorce or losing his position would have been the least of his worries. Keeping a few precious body parts was his main concern. He asked to sign right away."

Melissa folded her hands on her lap, hiding the crumpled napkin. "I hadn't realized how effective the tapes are. Sex scandals happen all the time in this country. It causes bad press, occasionally people lose their jobs and/or get divorced, but for the most part, the public doesn't care."

"A sex scandal with a foreign official with particular cultural and religious beliefs could be devastating. That's a powerful secret weapon."

"Exactly. Which brings me to why I brought you here today." Faith put her teacup down and crossed her arms, giving Melissa a serious first lady's expression. "There are horrible things the American public doesn't know. The violence is even worse than is shown in the news. In Iran, especially, atrocious things are being done to our soldiers. Their bodies, or what's left of them, are being hung along the borders as a warning."

Melissa covered her mouth with her hands. She knew the fighting was violent, but she'd had no idea how violent. The taste of bile reached her throat. "That's awful."

"I have a list of potential candidates. It's time we get our new member on board. I'll notify Julia. The president is calling a final meeting of foreign advisers in a matter of weeks. This is the last effort to push the treaty through. My sources tell me we have a few possibilities who can be swayed through the FLC. We must finish before that meeting. How is Zoe doing with her training? We need to have her ready as soon as possible."

Melissa kept her expression neutral. "I'll check with Jason, see if he needs any help. Since she's not been involved in that lifestyle, training her to be a Domme could take awhile," she warned.

"We don't have the luxury of time. A number of these foreign advisers prefer blondes." Faith smiled.

"Not Asian women?" Melissa feigned insult.

"They adore Asian women, but some don't have many blondes in their countries. They usually want what they can't have." Faith leaned back in her beautifully upholstered wing-back chair. "Zoe has been selected for our prime delegate, newly elected President Majeed Kadir from Iran. He'll be arriving earlier than expected. I understand he'll want a submissive player."

Of all the delegates on their target list, he was expected to be the most difficult, with a reputation of violence. She put her sandwich down. "What if she's not ready?" Melissa didn't want to bring up the possibility that Zoe might not agree to do it at all.

"She has to be ready. She was hired for this position specifically. The volatile situation is about to send the world into a complex war system. The US can't continue to fight multiple wars on multiple fronts. Ten thousand more US troops have been sent over to work with NATO forces, adding to the thousands already stationed there for months." Faith tossed her dainty lace-trimmed napkin onto the silver tray. "Help Jason. But have Zoe ready. She must be able to take on the role of a Domme or a submissive."

When Melissa didn't comment right away, Faith narrowed her eyes. "What is it? A problem?"

"I am concerned about Jason," Melissa said. "Will he let her do this if they get involved again, knowing what she'll have to do?"

Faith took a deep breath and stood, signaling the end of their meeting. "He's a professional. He knows what's at stake."

Melissa nodded. "I'll tell him."

"In the meantime, plan to attend the welcoming reception. Of course, wear something classy and seductive. I'll arrange the rest. It's time to play black widow again and invite a few mates into my lair."

Chapter 9

When Jason reached the stairs to walk Zoe to her office in the lower sub-basement, his phone vibrated a message from Melissa.

Must meet you today about FLC. Urgent. Can you come to W.H.?

"Hold up a second," he said to Zoe. He texted back: *Yes, I'm here now. Where?*

Press Briefing Room in 5.

K. "I'm sorry, Zoe. I'm being summoned for a meeting. I shouldn't be long. Can I meet you in your office?"

"Sure." She didn't even ask who the meeting was with. So like an ex-agent. "Hope you don't have to work this weekend."

"I'll text if I'm going to be long." He turned around and ran up the stairs.

Jason entered the Press Briefing Room to find Melissa in a daring low-cut business dress, sitting in the middle of the front row of seats.

Jason didn't know how a sexy outfit could be alluring enough to persuade an ambassador or prime minister or president to agree to a night of dangerous sex games. Apparently, Melissa knew how to pull it off. The woman was a professional in many ways. Subtly seductive, with an air of intelligence and sophistication. She was known to have been successful with her targets on a number of occasions. "What's going on?" he asked.

"Have a seat." She pointed to a chair next to hers, her face lacking emotion. The large meeting room was completely empty.

"Is there a problem?" Jason sensed he wasn't going to hear good news.

"What makes you think there's a problem?" she asked with a sweet smile he didn't trust.

He rolled his eyes. "Cut to it."

"Actually, everything with the FLC is going very well. Look for an announcement for another signing sometime on Monday.

We have to complete Zoe's training immediately. First lady's orders. President Majeed Kadir from Iran will arrive earlier than expected. I know you're not crazy about her being assigned to him, but she's his perfect type. Celia would've been ideal, and now that she's gone, it has to be Zoe."

He bit his tongue and resisted the urge to say, *No. Find someone else.* But he'd known this time would come. They were desperate for a tall, attractive blonde with a high-level security clearance. That's why Zoe had come to mind in the first place. "How soon?"

"Now. The president is organizing a reception of foreign diplomats in a couple of weeks and—"

"Weeks?" Jason jumped up and stood over her. "Are you crazy? She can't possibly be trained as a Domme in a couple of weeks. She's vanilla. Mostly."

Melissa raised an eyebrow at his outburst, but didn't look concerned. Nothing flustered her. "I thought you said she has a kinky side."

"We role-played with bondage a bit, experimented with rough sex, but nothing like this." There had been more to the kink, but he didn't want to go into details. He planted his hands on his head, interlocked his fingers and groaned.

"You've watched enough scenes to understand the power exchange between a Dom and a submissive. You can train her." She raised her hand when she saw he was about to object. "If you need help or have questions, I'll be available. And she won't be a Domme with Kadir. She'll be a submissive."

"Submissive? Great. I don't know if she'll be ready in two weeks." He shook his head. "When I was asked about her qualifications for this position, I thought it was for gathering information overseas on potentials, working undercover, not this." He knew how much Zoe wanted to do something to help stop the brutality overseas. Her brother was stationed there.

"It's too late to worry about that now. She's a professional. When she knows what's at stake—"

"I'll handle it," he snapped, holding up his hand.

"If you can't, I will," Melissa stated with the authority of the first lady. "One way or another, she will be a member of this team."

"What if she refuses?"

Melissa crossed her arms, looking angry. "I'm sure you'll find a way to convince her. National security depends on it."

He nodded, scowling at her. "Fine. I'll handle it. My way. Two weeks." And after two weeks, when she realized he'd set her up for this, she probably wouldn't speak to him again.

* * *

Zoe digitized one file then casually flipped through the folders. On several pages she read the acronym FLC. Federal Something Commission? But it didn't seem to fit in the context. Some of the documents included notations about certain events, such as a foreign ambassador having tea with the FLC and a prime minister reviewing tapes and files from a Saturday evening then providing the desired response. Other documents mentioned acceleration in communications and final international agreements that were signed promptly as anticipated. All appeared to have some significance, but Zoe wasn't sure what.

The knock at the door was a welcomed intrusion. She opened the door. Jason stood there. "Let's take a walk. Need to fill you in on some details." She followed him.

As Jason opened the door to the Red Tape Room, Zoe peeled a piece of red tape from the doorframe. "What's this?" she asked.

"I'll explain that in a minute."

Jason flipped on the lights and closed the door behind him. The antique sconces along the gray walls gave the room a dungeon-like glow. Add the Spanish Inquisition furnishings, and the effect was complete. Hard to believe what they'd watched in here the other night, what they'd done in here.

"Consider this room, and what I'm about to tell you, black

ops," he said.

Nodding, she clenched her hands around the belt of her pants. She'd been involved with black ops missions before. Those programs, if leaked or discussed with anyone, could threaten national security. A quivering inside her gut reminded her to calm and sharpen her focus, the way she did just before a dangerous mission. There was no danger here, only anticipation of something of great importance.

"Those pieces of tape are part of a code. Long pieces of red tape will crisscross the outside door when this room is occupied. No one can enter the room until the first lady rips the tape down. It's a signal to stop taping. Video recording." He looked at her with a straight face.

Her mouth dropped open. "That kinky sex scene we saw was being videotaped?"

He nodded.

She almost burst out laughing but stopped because he looked so serious. She pressed her lips together to keep from smiling. She glanced around the room. "Where's the camera?"

"Behind the walls. Six of them."

"So many?" she asked, going along with the joke. He couldn't be serious, could he? The dark tone to his words and deep crease across his brow told her he wasn't teasing. Dozens of questions came to mind. She had no idea where to start. "Who was that guy Melissa was with? Did he know he was being taped?"

"Have a seat." Jason pointed to the bed, a leather-covered mattress equipped with straps and pulleys and a padded medieval rack.

When she sat, the wooden frame creaked. Sweat beaded on her forehead.

He sat beside her and looked at her squarely. "You've been hired to be a member of the First Lady's Club, or the FLC."

She couldn't tell if he was kidding. Had they been apart that long? "Terrific. Never heard of it. Do I get to make cupcakes, share gardening tips, save neighborhood parks?"

"I'm being straight with you. Technically, your boss is the first lady. This operation has the highest level of secrecy and risk for national security. No cupcakes."

"Sorry. I'm used to working undercover with drug and arms dealers." He was serious, even scared. The last time she saw him look that frightened was when they were in Egypt together on vacation. Jason had had a decent-size camera that had vanished when they stopped at a food vendor. He saw the guy who took it and called the police. They caught the guy and interrogated him in front of them. When the man finally admitted to stealing the camera and brought it back, he apologized to Jason, claiming his son was ill and needed the money. Jason felt bad for the man. Then the police grabbed the man's left arm and, with a machete, cut off his left hand.

Jason shrieked at the guards. The man had returned the camera. They looked at Jason and shrugged. The crime was done, and the man had been punished. Why was Jason complaining?

Now, he had that pained look, not quite as horrified but as severe. "Jason, you're worrying me."

He pressed his lips together then finally spoke. "You must understand, once you're in this program, any security breach—"

"Would be considered treason, I know. And I could be imprisoned." She patted his arm. His hands tightened into fists. "Don't worry. Nothing new from our previous jobs."

"No, you don't understand. If there's a security breach, or they suspect you may consider one, they won't bring you to trial for treason, because that would expose the existence of the FLC. We have an assassin who handles security leaks."

She leaned away and leveled a hard stare at him. "Awfully efficient and barbaric. Who is it?"

"No idea."

She laughed bitterly. The mood in the room turned cool. "We'll be working together in this secret club? Was that your

idea?"

He sighed. "Partly."

"Didn't you leave Langley because you didn't want me as your partner? Or you didn't trust me."

He stood. "That's not true. I'd trust you with my life. And that's not why I left."

She glared at him. "You changed a plan during an operation and excluded me."

"Not because I didn't trust you." Jason rubbed the back of his neck. "When the missions were dangerous, I was concerned I wouldn't stay focused if I was worried about your safety. And you were never excluded completely." He touched her cheek. She saw the pain and regret in his expression.

"I'm trained. I can do the jobs. You don't need to protect me." All the emotions she'd managed to bury since he left were coming back to the surface.

"I know, I was wrong. But after Turkey, I didn't know if I could work with you again."

Zoe's chest tightened, and she didn't trust herself to breathe too deeply or the tears would fall. She placed a hand on his arm. "Why?" she whispered. "Yes, I was nervous about that mission, but it went wrong before we got into it."

He shook his head. "It wasn't you. You were amazing and kept your cool. They probably would've killed you if you hadn't. What they did to you still rips me up inside." His teeth clenched.

"Jason, I'm okay. The team got me out. I wasn't raped. I had some bruises and a broken pinkie, that's all." He lifted her left hand and gently rubbed her finger, which had a slight bend at the second knuckle. She'd told him the details of her brief capture, torture and rescue, but he never quite seemed reassured.

"I know." He released her hand and paced around the bed. "When I heard you were coming to the White House, I thought you'd be working with me overseas or as a Secret Service agent. I thought this would be my chance to show you I'm finally over that." He abruptly stopped.

"It's okay," Zoe consoled him. "You didn't think I'd be working as an archivist for top-secret documents."

"No, I thought you'd be collecting intel overseas with me. I didn't realize they had another position in mind."

"Not archivist." She hoped he didn't hear the edge to her voice. She stood and faced him. When he moved to draw her to him, she pulled away. "What then? What was I hired to do?"

He let out a breath. "To take part in similar scenes like the one you watched."

She didn't respond for a long time, because she wasn't sure what he meant. "Who was the guy? What do they do with the tapes?"

"The president from Chad," he said. "And they plan to blackmail him into signing the peace treaty."

She shoved away from him. "Are you crazy? You're saying President Bryson is blackmailing a foreign delegate with sex tapes?"

"Several foreign delegates," he said.

"You can't be serious." Hands on hips, she glared at him. "That's unethical. It's political suicide. Is it working? Oh my God."

"When you deal with unethical people who become allies with terrorists and build immense personal wealth at the expense of their own people, conventional methods of diplomacy don't work."

"Where do I fit in?" She folded her arms across her chest. Somehow, she didn't think she'd like the answer.

"You'll be one of those making the videos."

"Running the cameras?" She smiled but knew that's not what he meant. He didn't answer. "Forget it. I don't know how to do that stuff and whip someone. Why did they pick me?"

"Because you're the perfect female type they need. Blond, tall, attractive and intelligent with a high-level security clearance. The target they have set up for you likes to hire blond women, such as international lawyers, translators, economists, to work as his aides and consultants. Then he makes them his personal slaves, literally."

She groaned. "Against their will?"

"There's evidence that he's murdered some, sold others into the slave trade market, and still others are being held against their will. We intend to get them out in addition to getting him to sign the treaty. Now are you interested?" He edged closer, and she was torn between wanting to run out of the room and wanting to fall into the embrace of his arms. Either way, she wanted it all to go away.

Her stomach rolled, and she didn't say a word for a while. "I don't know this lifestyle. He'd know. If I screw up the mission, I could get those women killed."

"You're skilled at role-playing. I can train you. Melissa can help. She was a professional Domme." He took both her hands. He held her gaze and smiled. Damn him for looking excited about this.

"What if I say no?"

He squeezed her hands. "No would be a very bad choice. This is a national security issue. There will be other people in the room, so it won't get out of hand. You'll be safe."

She narrowed her eyes and studied him. "Why are you training me? Are you into this lifestyle? You weren't when we were dating. At least, you never told me." She trembled at the idea of Jason performing the acts she witnessed the other night, making her both uneasy and horny.

Seduction. The room reeked of it. Not torture. But an odd, twisted kind of kinky seduction, and Zoe felt her body responding to it. Heat rushed through her, and her breasts felt heavy. Between her thighs, she was throbbing and wet. Why was she getting aroused by this? Did this turn him on?

"What are you thinking?" His mouth twitched in amusement.

"I don't know, really. Maybe I am a little curious, maybe I missed you. I just don't want to screw up." She almost said *like last time*. What if he was thinking that?

His eyes turned dark and intently focused on her. Beneath his lowered gaze was a raw hunger, pure male sensuality smoldering behind his blue eyes, reminding her of the desperation of his last kiss. The way all his kisses were, as if each was going to be their last. That was why she couldn't resist him even though she was still pissed at him. "Good. I wasn't sure what your reaction would be."

A smile curled at her lips as she began to consider the possibilities. Striding over to the table, she picked up a whip and swung it in a circle, attempting to hit the bench but almost hitting herself instead. "Who's into this kinky stuff besides the first lady? The president? Does he make the videos, too?"

"No, he doesn't. Careful with that or you'll hurt yourself." He pulled it from her hand. "Stand over by the cross, and I'll demonstrate."

"No, thanks. I'm not into pain."

"You will be." He grasped her arm and walked her over to the cross. "Take off your blouse, and I'll give you a brief demo."

"No. Jason. Someone could walk in on us." She crossed her arms over her chest and stared at him as he swung the flogger in a circle.

"No one will come. The door is locked, and I know the schedule."

"Schedule? What schedule?" she whispered.

"Some questions will be answered later. And you don't have to whisper. The room is completely soundproof." He pressed her shoulders and back against the wooden frame.

"Can't we do this at my place?" she pleaded.

"This is where you'll be trained and where you'll give your presentation. This isn't about us in here. Go with it for a minute." His hands went to the waist of her pants and tugged on her shirt.

"That wasn't about us in the closet?" she asked.

He made a face and didn't answer.

She huffed. "Okay, okay, a little test." She started unbuttoning her blouse. "Jason, we're in the White House. You're not going to do—"

"Anything kinky? You didn't seem to mind last night. I seem to remember an agent who got horny when she was in danger."

She swallowed and glared at him. A thrill passed through her. He was right. Sex was hottest when they were in danger. Last night they'd almost had sex in the White House. "That was different. It was very late, and we were in a hidden passageway. We were spontaneous."

"We were out of control," he added as he pressed her back against the wooden X.

"Sex is always out of control for us."

He didn't argue. Tugging on her blouse, he yanked it over her head, not even bothering with the buttons.

Zoe fought to keep her breathing under control. His gaze lowered to her breasts, and his fingers traced around the lacy cups of her bra. "Pretty and sexy."

Reaching out, she gathered fistfuls of his shirt and tugged on his, too, but he grabbed her hands. "Why not?"

"Not until I say." His hands slid over her bare skin around her waist, and his lips lowered to her neck. The warmth of his breath, the hot wetness of his tongue as it glided along the delicate curve from her ear to the base of her throat was maddening. Her breasts swelled, and she wanted his hands there, his mouth there. She wanted him everywhere, now.

"Jason. Can we do the demo on the bed? This cross is kind of creepy." Her gaze widened as the clasp of her bra opened, and the garment slid off and fell to the floor.

"You have to follow my instructions without questioning them, without making suggestions." His mouth moved to her jawline, and she shuddered and let out a little moan. She leaned into him like a cat stretching out her body for a good scratch. Why wouldn't he touch her breasts? Again, she reached out to

89

him, and just as quickly he grabbed her wrists and pressed them behind her back, making her breasts stand up even higher. Her nipples were tight and sensitive now. "Keep your hands here. Don't move them until I tell you to. This is a lesson in control, power exchange, sensuality, trust."

"I'm not sure I understand."

"Go with it. You will. Because that's what this room is all about."

She nodded. "It's not about us." Her throat tightened. How could she possibly keep them out of it while she stood before him half-naked or if he touched her intimately?

He leaned back enough to look at her, and his eyes had darkened with flaming desire. His jaw flexed. Was he struggling with controlling his passion, too? Who was being tested here?

"I'll go along with it," she whispered.

"You need to do more than go along. You need to convince a Dom that you're a submissive." He kissed her mouth, deeply, slowly, but she kept her hands behind her back as he asked. When he pulled her into an embrace, crushing her body against him, she moved her arms around his neck, lacing her fingers in his hair. The kiss abruptly ended. He growled.

"What's wrong?" she asked.

"You moved your hands."

"What?" She laughed.

"I told you not to move your hands."

"Oh, come on, Jason. Can't you just tell me the plan and what I'm supposed to do? And skip all this?" She crossed her arms over her waist.

"No, it has to be done this way. Just like there's no shortcut for any other kind of training."

"Fine then." She was getting annoyed and horny at the same time. That ticked her off more.

He hesitated for a minute, gazing at the table of torture devices. "This is a lesson. Make your assessment after."

"All right." She put her arms at her sides, awaiting for his

direction.

He moved closer, taking her hands and moving them behind her back. Then he palmed her breasts, pinching her nipples until she moaned. Lowering his mouth to one nipple and drawing on it, rubbing the tip with his tongue, made her aware of the wetness and throbbing between her thighs. She couldn't refuse him anything after that.

"Tell me what to do."

"Do exactly what I tell you without argument." He stroked her bare shoulder. "If I ask you a question, answer it with a yes or no, sir."

She frowned but said, "Okay."

He stepped back. "Take everything else off and face the cross."

She opened her mouth to object but saw his one eyebrow raise, daring her to object. She stopped herself and slipped off her shoes, pants and underwear, placing everything on the floor.

"Beautiful," he said.

She felt exposed but resisted the urge to cover herself. Her nipples instantly became harder, sensitive to the cool air in the room. His hungry gaze raked over her body. Maybe they'd make love after all.

"Face the cross. Hold on to it if you like."

Sighing, she leaned against it, then spread her legs to fit into the foot rests and raised her arms. The intersection came just below her breasts so they pressed against the two arms of the structure. "Are you going to strap me in?" Her heart fluttered in her chest. Something about that excited her. She kept her smile cool, without emotion, the stoic working face she used when she was about to make a connection during a dangerous overseas operative.

"Not unless you want to be. You can just wrap your arms around the cross."

In position at the cross, she let out her held breath. "Now what?"

He didn't answer at first then placed a hand on her shoulder. He pressed his mouth to her ear. "You can stop this at any time by saying the word red. Understand?"

"Yes, yes, sir." Her body was shaking, and she wondered if he sensed that.

He rubbed her shoulders, massaging them, then her arms and back. "Relax, you're too tense."

She giggled a little. "Because I don't know what the hell you're up to."

"Fair enough." He walked over to the table, sifted through a number of items. Finally, he selected one. "I'll use the flogger and go easy on you."

"Right." A wave of sadness moved through her thoughts. What if this club was more than an assignment for him? What if he wanted this lifestyle? That would explain why he hadn't kept in touch with her when he left Langley. They weren't sexually compatible. Why hadn't he told her?

"I'm going to try a few passes across your back and see how you do. All right?"

She swallowed.

"Respond to my questions, Zoe."

"Yes, all right. Have at it." She swallowed again. How had she missed this side of him? What a fool she was. Damn it.

"That's not how you answer a Dom. You would get punished for that."

She tensed at his harsh tone. "Yes, sir. I'm ready."

The flogger bit into her upper left back with a crack, and she jumped and yelped. He paused for a moment then repeated on the other side. When she didn't protest, he struck her over and over, the sting penetrating deep. She would take as much as she could. She had to know why he needed sex this way. She partly believed him about the taping and partly believed the first lady had an adventurous sex life. Blackmailing and manipulating foreign policy seemed farfetched. Then he stopped.

His hand gently stroked the areas he'd worked. "How are

you doing?"

"Okay, I think." Her body was oversensitized to his touch. Her pussy throbbed and ached for him. He hadn't struck her there, but she wanted him to, just to see how it felt. "Should I turn around, sir?" If this was where he expected their love life to go, she didn't know if she wanted to find out.

"No, this is fine for now."

She ached for his hands to pleasure her the way she remembered, then she wanted him to take her to the bed and make love. Didn't he want her that way anymore? Her throat tightened.

He smoothed his hand over her back. "Your skin is warm and pink. Remember, you can stop anytime."

"I know. I'm not ready to stop." Her body heated up and tingled. Her nipples were ultrasensitive, and her pussy felt wet. Did their lives have to be in danger or have to incorporate hardcore kink in order for them to get turned on? Tears and unexpected emotions threatened to burst out, but she dammed them up inside. He'd said that in this room it wasn't about them. But wasn't it? He couldn't shut her completely out emotionally, sexually while doing this, could he? If he didn't care enough.

He struck her ass this time, and that stung. "Ouch."

He didn't stop. The strikes got more intense, and his breathing deepened. He groaned through a few strikes. They weren't groans of pleasure. She knew all of Jason's sounds, and he sounded angry.

Something inside her started liking the pain. After each hit, the pain rattled her, but then she rode it out like a kayak gliding over a rough wave. Again, her thoughts returned to the two of them making love. Him holding her after that bad time in Turkey, and many other times. And now this.

"Too intense?" His voice was hoarse and husky.

"No, sir." She bit her lip. The throbbing between her thighs intensified, and her clit plumped. Then the thongs whisked between her legs and snapped against her pussy. The sting made

93

her yelp, and at the same time, a mixture of pain and pleasure shot through her. God, that was good. A groan pulled from her chest. "Yes."

He swung again and smacked her.

She had to admit, it was a turn-on. Then why did she feel so emotional? Her throat tightened as tears welled in her eyes. The pain from the flogger hurt now, but a good hurt. She wouldn't stop. Maybe the pain outside would make the pain inside go away.

"Still okay?" he asked, slowing his momentum but not stopping.

"Yes, sir," she snapped. "Fine." Tears slid down her cheeks, and she was glad he couldn't see.

"No, you're not." He put the flogger down and stood behind her. "Are you hurt?"

"I told you, I'm fine." The words had a quiver to them as much as she tried to hide it.

"You've had enough." He reached around to take her hand and release her from the cross since she hadn't let go.

"Give me a minute."

"Zoe?" He turned her around, and his eyes widened. "God, no, honey. I'm sorry." He scooped her up in his arms and took her over to the bed. He sat her down and reached under the bed, opening a drawer and reaching in for a soft cotton blanket. After wrapping her in it, he took her in his arms again and cradled her against his chest. "Why didn't you tell me to stop when I started hurting you? Why didn't you call out your safe word?"

"You weren't hurting me. I'm fine," she said, tears still flowing.

"No, you're not fine. You're upset."

"I'm not sure why I'm crying," she snapped. Why couldn't she get herself together, damn it? She shoved away from him, got up and put her clothes back on.

* * *

He sat on the bed and watched her as she dressed. He'd really fucked this up. Their friendship, the job, possibly the operation. "I'm sorry."

"Just tell me one thing, Jason. When the hell did you get into this bondage stuff? We only broke up six months ago. We worked together for three years, dated a year of that. What kind of agent was I if I didn't have any idea you were into this? Why did you waste your time with me?" She picked up the flogger he'd dropped on the floor, and for a moment he thought she was going to hit him with it, or throw it at him. Instead, she slammed it on the table.

"We're trained as agents to play roles. I wasn't hiding anything."

"Were you playing a vanilla role back then?" She threw a pair of handcuffs across the room.

"No. I wasn't into BDSM when we were dating. I'm not into it now." Was that the truth? He wasn't entirely sure. He stood up but stayed out of range of flying objects. There were knives on the table.

"How can you say that after what you just did?" She spoke each word with her teeth clenched. "I know you. You were into it more than just for the job."

He walked up to her and calmly took the cane she had fisted in her hand. "Let's take a break."

"Forget it, Jason. Tell them they made a mistake. I can't do this."

Chapter 10

"There's a complication concerning the FLC, Mrs. Bryson."

Julia stood with her hands neatly folded in front of her. Fortunately, the first lady had agreed to meet with her on short notice after she discovered the news from Jason. Sunlight streamed in from the large Palladian window in a private White House parlor called the Central Hall. They were alone, and the first lady hadn't called for tea. Sunday mornings were usually Julia's one relaxing time of the week. That would not be happening this week, perhaps for a long time. "Zoe doesn't feel suited for the position in the FLC. She doesn't believe she can perform her duties."

Faith didn't blink. "Change her mind. Whatever it takes. Fighting at the borders has escalated. We're on heightened security alert. Several leaders are arriving in a couple weeks for the reception. I intend to have a full schedule for the Red Tape Room by the end of that evening."

"Zoe may have another reason for not joining our program," Julia said.

The first lady shifted slightly in the elegant chair. Her arms, resting in her lap, stiffened. "What's the problem?"

"Her brother, Damien, is Special Forces, recently reassigned to a mission in Iran. He could become a target after Zoe's encounter."

"I know about her brother, and the Iranian leader won't know who Zoe is. That isn't an issue." Faith's voice rose. The last time Julia heard the first lady's voice rise in anger had been when terrorists bombed a Norwegian cruise ship, killing two hundred and thirty-three Americans.

"Damien was in Afghanistan at the time we recruited Zoe. He only recently was deployed to Iran."

"I'm aware of his mission." Faith Bryson's brows knotted in deep furrows. "I don't want Zoe's concern for her brother's safety to distract her." She tapped a finger over her lips. "I'll look into it. Maybe he's due for an early leave."

Julia sighed and relaxed. One problem solved. "Thank you for your time, ma'am. Is there anything you'd like me to do?"

"On second thought." Faith stood, walked to the window and gazed out. "His presence there might be to our advantage."

"How so, ma'am?"

"His presence there could motivate her. Perhaps she'd be more willing to help."

Julia stopped breathing and hoped the shock didn't show on her face. Was this woman so heartless? "I…I don't know."

Faith narrowed her eyes and huffed. "I'm not the monster you may think. We're dealing with people who have no integrity, no honor, no value system or respect for human life, who be-friend terrorists, who murder men, women and children for per-sonal gain or to simply please their narcissistic nature. How can I effectively deal with them, or how can the president effectively negotiate with them when qualities of integrity, honor, morality don't exist? My methods must be harsh, bold, perverted, beyond what other nations would ever expect from us. That's why this is effective. That's why the FLC was started and why it has contin-ued successfully as long as it has."

Julia nodded. "Yes, ma'am." She understood but didn't like it. She also knew there was no arguing with the first lady when she was on a rant. She'd never approved of this program but couldn't deny how effective it was. "While Zoe's brother fights a war, she has a reason to help on this end."

"Exactly."

"I'll tell Jason. He must get her trained immediately." Julia stood.

"Another thing. Clear Alana MacKenna's schedule for the week. I've made arrangements for her to give a presentation for President Ernesto Alverez from Colombia. He'll require her particular knowledge and background."

"She'll be available," Julia said.

"If you have any problems, come to me immediately. Is that clear?"

"Crystal." Julia took a breath, but her body was still tense. They had a lot to do this week. "When should we hear the outcome from last night's encounter?"

Faith smiled. "The president was quite pleased with your efforts. Melissa's presentation went very well. He'll be meeting with the Somalian president this afternoon after I show him the video. We should have some news soon."

"Good. Melissa has another *event* later this week," Julia said. "And she wants to go over a few things with Alana now."

A flash of lightning made Julia jump and jump again when thunder followed a few seconds later. Faith never flinched. When had the clouds rolled in? Julia hadn't noticed. Rain pelted the large windowpanes, streaking the gray view of the garden and lawn.

"I'm not concerned about Melissa or Alana," Faith said, her lips pressed into a tight pout. "They're professionals. I'm confident that Zoe's skills as a CIA agent and her abilities in role-playing will make her an effective addition to the FLC. If she can handle an assignment with weapons dealers in Turkey, she can handle Kadir."

"I certainly hope so." Julia hated setting the most inexperienced member up with the most dangerous target. With a deep breath, she willed the muscles in her shoulders to relax. She performed a mini-meditation and relaxation technique her masseuse taught her. As soon as the meeting was over, she'd dab a little of her essential oil formula on her temples and wrists. The peppermint, chamomile, lavender and grapefruit oils were supposed to be good for headaches and stress and helped to keep her focused.

She would have liked to burn an incense diffusor in her office, but it would probably set off a fire alarm. "What if Alana handled Kadir instead? She could wear a blond wig or dye her hair."

Faith shook her head. "Other delegates prefer her red hair. Kadir would notice the wig. She might be a switch and could play either Domme or submissive, but she would still be too aggressive for him. Zoe knows how to manipulate dangerous men, think quickly and stay calm under stress. She also speaks Persian. I can't give details, but she can handle extreme stress. We need someone who won't crack under pressure."

"If you say so." Julia couldn't help wondering what Zoe had experienced that was so stressful. She could only imagine the worst with Zoe working with terrorists and drug dealers.

"Of the twenty dignitaries who will be coming to Washington for the peace talks, only seven are potential targets for the FLC with the type of intense sexual encounters we can provide. We expect a ninety to ninety-five percent success rate." Faith smiled. "For some reason, one of the leaders who had said he would not sign the treaty recently changed his mind. Even before any FLC contact. That's one less candidate needing our services. The others should be shot, but assassination would be a waste of time if the next in line has the same ideology. Kadir's our number one target. We can't mess this one up." A look of dread crossed Faith's features. She frowned and stared at the floor.

Julia suspected the first lady's coldness hid a heavy burden of responsibility and risk, but she still wondered why Faith looked so upset. Maybe because no matter how good a potential candidate's background looked, some men couldn't be persuaded to fall into the FLC trap. Over the years, it hadn't been one hundred percent successful. The program didn't come without risks. "You think he's going to turn your offer down?"

"I'm not sure. He won't be at the reception. I'll have to meet him alone," Faith said, her voice getting heavy with emotion.

"What can I do to help?"

"Get ready for the party." Faith stood, signaling the end of their meeting. "A funny thing about evil, narcissistic men. They fancy their pure, powerful image and will guard their honor with their life, but it doesn't take much to turn their head when it comes to sex. I'm sure this encounter will go smoothly."

"I hope so," Julia said. "When dealing with the most dangerous and evil men of the world, I don't take anything for granted."

"By the way. I'll handle Zoe. Sometimes a little first lady influence is all it takes."

Chapter 11

Zoe finished dressing, but the chill remained. How could he have thought she'd be right for this? She touched the four-inch scar on her throat. "Can we get out of here?" She walked across the Red Tape Room and grabbed her purse. The longer she remained in this room, the more closed-in she felt.

"It's more secure here for what I need to tell you."

"I got it. They make sex tapes here to blackmail influential people. Is there more?" Her cell phone buzzed. "The room isn't so isolated that cell service is blocked." She glanced at her phone and smiled.

"Melissa?" Jason's mouth twitched in a sardonic grimace.

"No, my brother. I thought he left on his mission, but he probably got delayed. He's determined to best me on Words With Friends before he leaves."

"Do you need to text him back?"

"Not right away. I'm surprised the phones work in this room."

"There is a reason for that," he added. "A necessary precaution that you'll learn about soon."

"I'm ready to get out of here." She felt drained, and her insides ached for what she thought they might've had. She'd been wrong. They'd lost what they'd had a long time ago.

"Aren't you even a little curious to see what's behind the curtain of the great and mysterious Oz?" Jason asked with a wicked grin.

Her heart swelled with that grin. "Now I'm intrigued. Fill me in." She sat on the bed and motioned him to do the same. Her body still hummed from their sexual play. Was this sex to him now? "So who besides you likes this kind of sex?" She leaned back on her hands.

He narrowed his blue eyes and took a breath. "This is more than blackmailing with sex tapes. The FLC is called in to fight terrorism and manipulate foreign and domestic policy when the usual channels fail. Members are selected for specific skills, hired as White House staff, then invited privately. You've been invited."

"Because I'm a blonde."

"Because you already have top-level clearance and can handle yourself in highly stressful situations. You've worked undercover with terrorists, and that takes a lot of skill and nerve."

She wished she was as confident in her talents as a few other people apparently were. At the foot of the bed she picked up what she assumed was an ankle strap attached to a pulley system. What the hell? She followed the pulley lines to other straps and restraints overhead in the canopy. "Interesting bed."

"It has its functions. I can show you."

"I'll pass for now." She got up and headed to the table of devices of torture. "Big D said I was welcome to come back to Langley anytime. Which got me thinking, her boss, the director of the CIA, was in cahoots with the White House security adviser about something. Does Big D know about the FLC?"

"Don't think so."

She picked up a device that she at first thought was a dildo, but it had an odd-shaped glass attachment that looked too fragile to insert into any human orifices. "He didn't seem sorry to see me leave."

"What makes you think you left?"

She put the object down on its velvet cloth and spun around. "I sent in my two weeks' notice and filled out a thirty-page application form to work as a White House staff member."

"Technically, everyone who works here fills one of those out." His eyes sparkled as he picked up the tool she had put down and flipped a switch. It hummed like a vibrator, but the glass attachment glowed violet. "Hold out your hand." He reached for it, holding it palm up.

She yanked it back.

"What's wrong? Don't you trust me?" He smiled, teasing

her.

She had to think about that. "I don't know. You left Langley without saying good-bye."

His smiled faded, and a hurt look filled his eyes. "Even after I risked my life to save you?"

She shrugged. "You were doing your job. Any agent would've done the same. You couldn't run the risk that they'd break me and get me to spill government secrets. It was imperative that you rescue me for the integrity of the mission, not because you cared about me."

He scowled at her. "When did you get so cynical?"

"When I got this." She pointed to the scar at her throat.

For a brief moment she saw the pained look in his eyes and regretted the sharp remark. He didn't give her any pity, and she was glad for that. He held the glass rod an inch above his own palm to demonstrate. "See? The wand isn't frying my skin. Now give me your hand."

She did, and he positioned the wand over it. A sensation of sharp pins and needles skimmed over her skin and spread out to her fingers. "Strange. It stings, but doesn't really hurt."

"Each of these attachments will give a slightly different sensation, especially when placed—"

"Yeah, I get it," she said.

"And there are different gases in these attachments." He held up a few oddly shaped ones. "They'll glow different colors, make different sounds and give various sensations."

She nodded. "The stimulation must be pretty intense on certain body parts." Imagining Jason hovering that toy over her nipples or her clit, she expected she would achieve quite an orgasm, if she could stand the stimulation. "Do I get to try that out?" Her voice went low and husky, and she was unable to hide her smile.

"If you like." His words sent a tremble throughout her muscles.

"Can we borrow it? Take it home with us?"

He shook his head. "Nothing can leave this room. We'll have to play with it here."

She pouted. "I was afraid of that."

His hand slid over her ass in a gentle gesture, then turned her so her butt was cradled against his hardened cock. Both hands smoothed over her hips, along her sides and to her breasts, where he roughly massaged them. "I know how much you like me to touch you like this."

"Yes." Her head rested back on his shoulder.

Slowly, he unbuttoned her blouse and eased it down her arms again, trapping her arms at her sides. Then he slid the bra to her waist without unhooking it.

Reaching for the violet wand, he turned it on, and the sizzle of the instrument came to life. "Don't move."

She gasped, knowing what he planned to do.

"Have you ever come by stimulating your nipples?" He glided the wand so the sparks tingled along her arms, across her shoulder and over the curve of her breasts.

She giggled. He couldn't be serious. "Afraid not."

He hovered the wand above her nipples, and Zoe held her breath. Then he touched her with the thin glass, and she felt the jolt. Pain and pleasure rolled through her, and she cried out. "God, Jason. That's too much."

"Relax. You'll get used to the intensity." He began moving it around her breasts, bringing it close but not touching her nipples. Just when she thought he'd reach the most sensitive place, he'd retreat to the other breast or move down to her lower belly.

As her shirt and bra fell away, and her pants slid down to her knees, she said, "Are you going to touch me there with that thing?"

He laughed huskily. "Not yet." His free hand smoothed down her hip and over her pussy, trailing a finger between her moist folds and finding her swollen bud. "Nice. And you're very wet." He thrust a finger inside, and Zoe lifted her hips and moaned. His finger circled her clit, and he brought the wand down onto her nipple again. The sensation was so intense, she jerked and her knees buckled. Jason held her with his arms. "Oh my God, I feel sparks where you're touching me."

"Electricity conducts." He held his fingertip over her clit and touched the wand to the other nipple. Both nipple and clit felt the jolt of a tiny shock.

"Keep that up and I will come," she said.

Her nipples were red and distended. The sight of the sparks in the dim lighting enticed her to hold still. "More," she begged.

At the same time, he turned a switch in the handle and held the wand a fraction of an inch above her right nipple. "Told you." His finger continued to circle her clit, sending electrical sensations through her pussy and making her inner muscles clench.

"Ow. Too much."

"Want me to stop?"

"Don't you dare." He shifted to the other nipple, and the sensation in her pussy stopped. He'd moved his hand away.

"What happened?" Damn it, she was so close.

"I don't want you to come yet," he whispered at her ear, and his lips gently touched her, sending sparks and new sensations around her ear and neck. She shivered and leaned her head back, her legs barely holding her up now. "Delayed gratification is another lesson in power exchange."

"Hmmm. Why the lesson?" she asked as he alternated smoothing his hand over her breasts, hips and abdomen and then used the violet wand. His fingers came close but didn't touch her clit, a sweet torture.

"Later. Surrender to me now, and I'll explain more later." He stroked her thighs, bringing another shiver throughout her body. Pitched on the edge of a glorious orgasm, she didn't know how long he could hold her here before she'd lose it. "Trust me to know how and when to make you come," he added.

"Yes." Her response was a husky whisper. His finger dipped into her channel, but not as deep as she wanted, needed, but she resisted the urge to ask him to go deeper. Resisted the urge to ask him to go down on her.

She was soaked. He spread her juices over her delicate folds. "So wet. So beautiful," he murmured. Then she heard the hum of the violet wand intensify. Had he cranked up the power? The wand hovered directly over her raw clit and pushed her closer to the edge of her climax.

"God, it's so intense," she said through gritted teeth. "I don't know if I can—"

"Yes, you can. Just a moment longer. If it's too much, tell me and I'll stop."

"Okay. More."

Her body trembled as the electrical jolts focused only on her clit, firing every nerve ending, then throbbed so intensely she could barely stand it, but she didn't want him to stop. The tremors suddenly thrust her into a violent climax. He placed the wand on a side table and wrapped her in his arms, stroking her until the shock waves of pleasure eased. He turned her around and brought his mouth down on hers, plunging his tongue between her lips, possessing and pleasuring her there, too.

Gasping for breath, she stepped back and gazed into his eyes. She remembered that look from their overseas operations. The desperate lust, perhaps love, that deep connection they had. Was it back? Were they back?

Then his eyebrows furrowed, and a shadow of pain crossed his face. He groaned, then scooped her up and carried her over to the bed. He yanked off the pants hanging from her ankles and quickly removed his clothes, but first found a condom packet in his pocket. He slid it on his thick shaft while studying her. "I have to be inside you."

"Finish the lesson later?" she teased.

"Fuck yes, much later."

He shoved her legs apart and maneuvered his cock between her thighs. Zoe sat up, wrestled with him, trying to get him to switch positions. "Since this lesson is over, on your back,

Merritt." She pressed his shoulders onto the bed.

He grinned. "Fair enough." She wrapped her hand around his length and positioned his cock at her slick entrance, then impaled her body on him. They both groaned, and he arched his back off the bed. Kneeling on either side of his muscular thighs, she rocked on him, slid up and down his shaft. He filled her deep with his rigid length. As she lifted up, he pressed her down again until they moved faster and faster in a rhythm neither could stop. She felt her moisture pooling around his shaft as another orgasm built.

Then she leaned back to increase the pressure where she wanted it most, and he rubbed her swollen clit with his thumb. The climax came, not as intense as the first, but it still made her cry out his name.

Jason grabbed her ass and pulled her toward him and used his hips to drive into her body with several deep, quick thrusts. His groans and shudders signaled his release, and he bolted upright, pulling her against his chest. With their arms wrapped tightly around each other, their breathing and pulse rates slowly ticked back to normal. She clung to him, her face buried in his shoulder, avoiding his eyes as long as possible. Could they have sex only when there was an element of danger of getting caught? Normal sex and normal relationships didn't appeal to him?

He shook her. "Hey. You got quiet. You okay?"

"Sure." She swallowed the large lump in her throat, but it was too late. Tears stung her eyelids. She tried to get up, but he held her back, raising her chin so she would look at him.

His eyes widened. "Oh no. Zoe, what's wrong?"

"Nothing, I'm fine." She pried herself out of his embrace, got up and began dressing. She grimaced when the bra touched her sensitive nipples. She didn't know whether to laugh or cry. Controlling her emotions was something she was trained to do.

"I can see that." He let out a long breath and leaned back on the pillows, his arms cradling his head.

She stared at him for quite some time and got the courage

to confront him. "Where did you go after you left Langley?"

He gazed up at the ceiling. "Overseas to collect intel on potential targets, then back for training."

"Training? For what we just did?"

He laughed, avoiding the question. "You were always able to get straight to the point. Yes, and more."

She tossed him his shirt and pants. "What happened to us after Turkey? What about Nevada? Can we have sex only if danger is involved or if it's kinky like this?"

He sat up and pulled on his pants. No underwear, and his dick was still semi-hard. Seeing him naked, all heavily toned muscles, wasn't helping her to stay focused.

"Yes, we had a great time in Nevada," he responded then grimaced. "Except when I woke up to see the pinpoint laser dot on your forehead."

She stared at the floor. "You can move fast. And it worked out in the end."

"I lost focus in the operation because of sex. I almost got you killed. Our relationship was putting our lives and our operations at risk. There's a reason many agents lack personal entanglements. It's not just because it's inconvenient or because they can't tell loved ones where they're going or when they'll be back. It's because the lack of focus might get them killed. Two agents who are in a sexual relationship and working on the same mission is about as dangerous as making crash-test dummies out of C-4."

"Thanks for the clarification. But I went home to visit family, and when I came back, you were gone, your desk was cleaned out and I never heard a word. You could've said good-bye."

"I was out of the country and couldn't contact you. You know the drill."

Zoe grabbed her purse and marched toward the door.

"Where are you going?"

"Home. Today is my day off."

"But we haven't finished your training." His voice changed

from personal to official.

"It can wait until Monday."

"No, it can't."

She huffed and leaned a hand on her hip. "Why the hell not?"

"I was told to explain it now."

"Now?" She was confused. "Someone knows we're here?"

He nodded.

She tossed her purse on a chair. "Fine. Fill me in." He was fully dressed now, but his shirt and pants stretched tight over firm muscles, and she couldn't help imagining him taking her again.

"I didn't say good-bye because I never officially left Langley and neither have you."

"What?"

"We've been recruited as semi-permanent contractors," he clarified. "A mission unlike any you've ever done."

She shoved her purse aside and plopped down in the chair. "I'm listening."

"Usually, they bring a new member on slowly, but the schedule has been moved up, and you need to start ASAP."

"Why?" Zoe waited for Jason to answer, but he worried his bottom lip with his teeth. Any harder, and he'd draw blood.

He crossed the room and took her hand. "I don't know. Whatever they're planning goes beyond the peace treaty and stopping wars."

Here was her chance to do something important. What if the powers that be had made a mistake by choosing her? "They need people they can count on."

Jason smiled. "Yes, absolutely. Come on. Time to see what's behind the curtain of the great and mysterious Oz."

Chapter 12

In the Mason Room, Jason reached inside a desk drawer and pressed several switches then closed and locked the drawer again. Zoe returned from the restroom looking reenergized, hair pulled back in a neat ponytail and makeup refreshed. Aside from the glow to her cheeks, no one would guess that they'd just had hot sex. Well, practically no one. His body responded to her instantly, his cock hardening again. But the adrenaline coursing through his veins was due more to anxiety than arousal. This was one mission he wasn't looking forward to.

"So how does this work?"

"Follow me." He led her behind the loose canvas wall hanging, into the narrow passage at the end of the room. This time, it was illuminated by a strip of fluorescent lights along the floor from the hidden switch in the desk.

"Didn't we almost get into trouble the last time we were in here?" she asked.

"This hallway is next to another passageway that surrounds the Red Tape Room." He slid open a hidden panel in the wall and pressed his hand against a palm scanner.

"Do I have access to this room?" she asked.

He nodded. "You will. All members of the FLC do."

She glanced at the added security but didn't mention it. "Why is it called the Red Tape Room?"

When the panel opened, they entered the narrow hall dimly lit in a red glow. Zoe eased by him, her body rubbing against him as she studied the long table of equipment, computers, servers and other electronics. He knew she hadn't quite caught on yet. "What do you see? What's your impression?"

"A control room of sorts. Monitoring system? Seems like a lot of equipment for a few sex tapes. Unless there's more." Her eyes widened. "The president?"

Jason shook his head.

"The first lady?" She held her hand to her mouth.

Jason shook his head but hesitated this time. The first lady was involved, but not like Zoe was thinking. "There's more. This room has the potential for other uses. For now it's being utilized for the Red Tape Room." He took her arm and led her around a ninety-degree bend in the passage to more equipment and yet another turn. The U-shaped room was filled with electronic machinery. Jason slid open a panel in the wall. "Look through there and tell me what you see."

Zoe gasped. "It's the Red Tape Room. These are cameras. How many?"

"Six. Two on each of three walls." He pressed a few keys on one of the computers, and a large plasma screen lit up and began playing a video.

A woman, head bowed, was naked and leaning against that wooden cross. Six screens showed her from various angles. And the man was Jason—

"Oh God, oh God, oh God. Someone was videotaping us? Who was watching?"

"No one." He fast-forwarded to them fucking on the bed. "It's automated. I set the system up as a demo."

She punched him in the chest. "Turn it the fuck off," she yelled over the noises coming from the video.

"I don't know," he said as a tease. "I'm getting turned on again watching you on my cock. You have a nice ass."

Without warning, she slammed him against the wall, her hand gripped at his throat and her knee poised at the tender location between the base of his cock and his balls. One wrong move, and he'd be doubled over, puking his guts up. Never piss off a woman trained in martial arts.

"Just a demo before I show you the real thing. Let me loose and I'll delete it."

She released her hold and removed her knee from the permanent crippling position. "Screw it. You've taught me enough about computers. I'll do it myself," she snapped, glaring at him.

Willful, confident, even a little arrogant were all good traits for a Dom or Domme, but Zoe was known to have a temper, and for this target she needed to be submissive. Once she learned what was at stake, she could handle it.

"I would've done it."

She clicked a few keys. "Deleted. Now what else is in here?" The screen lit up again, and three people were in the Red Tape Room. Two women and a man. The man stood at the cross, arms and legs spread and strapped down. He was blindfolded. The two women beside him wore fetish clothing, black leather and heels, and their faces were covered in decorative, full-face Mardi Gras masks. One woman had a cane in her hand and tapped the end along his arms, legs, chest, abdomen and all around his groin. His dick was fully aroused and bobbed with each strike. Some hits were gentle taps and others sharp raps. The man cried out with each hit. She reached between his legs and prodded his balls, and the man groaned in pleasure and writhed, tugging against his restraints.

"Who the hell is that? He's not the same guy from the night we were in the closet."

"No, this is a different time and someone else. President Kasim Rutu. We had agents in Somalia months ago collecting intel that determined he had this particular sexual taste."

Zoe gripped his thigh as she continued to watch, mesmerized. The man in the video crunched up his face. "Mistress, I'm close to coming."

"Do not come, slave. I have not given you permission." She smacked his cock with the end of the cane, and the man cried out. Zoe also cried out.

"God, how can she do that?"

"That's his kink. He likes cock torture." Jason was getting turned on by Zoe's reaction. Did she realize her hand was rubbing his dick now? Lifting her blouse out of her pants, Jason slid his hand along her back. When she didn't resist, he unhooked her bra. Her breath caught, and her hand rubbed his erection

112

harder. This kinky stuff was turning her on. Maybe he was worrying for nothing.

"And I thought the president or the first lady had a kinky side and that room was mainly for their private entertaining. I thought the blackmailing was their cover. You are serious. I can't imagine the president using sex tapes for blackmail. What could he possibly gain?"

Jason shook his head. "You have no idea what the FLC has accomplished over the years. President Rutu has a lot of contacts with known terrorist groups, but many global leaders would like to see Prime Minister Akram take over. He has good intentions for his people and opposes Rutu's policies. This video will damage Rutu's position if it's revealed. He'll do anything to keep that from happening."

"Like agreeing to specific foreign policies?" Zoe asked.

"Or signing peace agreements."

"Wow. That could anger any ties he has with terrorist groups."

"True, and hopefully weaken or destroy them."

The woman stroked the man's chest in a soothing manner. "How are you doing, slave? Ready for more?"

"I'm fine, Mistress. Yes, please, more."

"I think you've earned a prize." She removed the man's blindfold and stroked his head. "I'm going to let you watch while I torture your cock."

Rutu leaned into her hand, and his breathing became faster, as if he'd run around a track. "Thank you, Mistress." When the Domme smacked his ass with the cane, he yelped but moaned as he was enjoying it.

Zoe stopped massaging Jason's cock. She didn't take her eyes from the screen. "In the closet, I figured out who the women were. Melissa and the first lady. But the women in this video don't look anything like them, even with their masks."

"It's what they're wearing, the angle of the camera, and technical skills."

She leaned back in the chair and sighed. "This is really perverted."

Jason shrugged. "Everyone has their own kink. Sex is a powerful manipulator."

"I suppose." She stared at him for several heart-pounding moments, then dropped her hand to his crotch and massaged his hardened dick beneath the stiff denim material. Then her hand slid inside his pants, and her fingers wrapped around his shaft.

Groaning, Jason reached out and grasped her breast. Her nipple was stone-hard. "I think you are getting aroused," he teased, pinching her nipple.

She jumped, but didn't take her eyes off the screen. "Undo my blouse."

"Hmmm." He did and grabbed both breasts. In the video, the woman had slid her corset down to reveal her breasts. The man smiled. Again, she tap-tapped him with the cane, harder and harder, until the man groaned and pleaded to come.

"Now, slave. Come for your Mistress, now." He groaned, and moments later a stream of fluid spurted from his cock.

Abruptly, Jason stood, slid his pants down as he watched Zoe do the same, then rolled on a condom. She climbed over onto his lap.

The groans of the man and woman mingled with their own. Zoe rocked on his cock, wild and rough, the way they both liked. It didn't take long for her to reach her climax. She cried out, and he felt her inner muscles flex and grip him, sending him over the edge.

After they caught their breath, Zoe giggled. "Kind of like getting turned on from watching a porno movie."

"Some porno movie." He grabbed some tissues from a box sitting on a desk and wrapped them around the used condom. He handed a few tissues to Zoe. How were they going to get through training with this highly sexual atmosphere?

"What are they going to do with the video? Money? Demand the return of hostages?" she asked as she freshened herself up with the tissue.

"The primary purpose is to pass foreign policy in the US's favor."

"Quite a risk. But very effective." She didn't flinch. She had switched to CIA mode. "How did they know he'd go for this?"

"Intel. That's what I was doing after I left Langley."

"This sounds more interesting than deciphering and digitizing top-secret documents."

He let out a breath. Thank God, this would be easier than he'd thought. "I'm glad you see the importance of this operation."

She nodded. "So when do we leave?" Her remark was calm and so Zoe—straightforward.

"Leave where?" He thought he'd been obvious about what her new duties would be.

"We'll be leaving for an operation overseas to continue where you left off, collecting intel, right? Once they realize I'd be more effective in that part of the operation, they won't make me do the sex tapes. I'm trained to gather intel. I could also work this equipment. What dignitaries will we be targeting?"

Fuck. Not so easy. "Zoe, the intel has been gathered. And dignitaries are targeted."

"Then you need me to work the cameras, video?" Her voice went up an octave.

"No." He paused, letting the reality sink in.

Her eyes widened in the dim red light. "No fucking way."

"Zoe, this is vital to national security. These peace treaties—"

"No. I can't do this. I've been trained to work undercover with weapons dealers, drug cartels, not play sex games. It's not my skill set."

"You'll be trained."

"I will not." She laughed bitterly.

"It's no different than any other undercover operation. Perhaps a bit more creative."

"Forget it." She kicked one of the stools in front of a computer. "Pull a prostitute off the street and train her. I won't flog anyone's ass or whip anyone's cock to get them to sign some UN agreement. I refuse to give them pleasure in any way at my expense. Suppose it doesn't work? Suppose I'm not a good enough actress?"

"The First Lady's Club only includes members with top-secret clearance. We need someone like you, and we don't have time to bring in someone else."

"Then you'll have to work with those you have." She strode through the room and out the door, leaving Jason alone. He listened as her footsteps continued down toward the Mason Room, and a moment later he heard the door slam.

That went well. At least she didn't pull a gun.

Chapter 13

"Hello, Julia." The redhead, Alana, strutted into the press secretary's office early Monday morning, moving across the room as if walking down a Paris runway wearing the latest haute couture. She sat in the chair in front of Julia's desk without an invitation. With one hand, she swooped her wavy, red hair around her neck and over one shoulder, so the strands fell well below one breast. Julia admired confident women, but not reckless ones, and Alana was one she had to keep an eye on.

Alana rarely wore her hair up, unusual for most women working in the West Wing. Proper business fashion didn't seem to occur to her. "I got the message it was urgent." A wicked smile curved her glossy lips, and her sea-green eyes had that wild look, making Julia think, *Serial killer.*

Mrs. Bryson insisted that Alana was the best at her particular skills. Of all the members of the First Lady's Club, Alana MacKenna scared Julia. She was a brilliant, beautiful, charismatic attorney and much too arrogant. Alana's no-fear attitude was a risk to the secret organization, and to Alana. One day they all might suffer for it.

"You're scheduled for a presentation tomorrow." Julia glanced down at her notes, avoiding Alana's eyes and prepared for the objection. Julia could tolerate her role in the FLC when she had plenty of time to prepare.

"Tomorrow? Oh. I thought you were going to tell me tonight. Not so urgent then." She sounded disappointed.

Julia let it drop and continued, "President Turi Aleid from Chad has agreed to your established limits: no needles, no knives, no fire play, no permanent scars. He does want Prime Minister Miron Gerard present. Our intel says they're lovers. Let me know now if you have a problem with that or any other hard limits."

"No problem." Alana casually picked up the crystal, water

globe paperweight sitting on Julia's desk and shook it, then held it up to the sunlight coming in through the large window. She watched the bits of colored crystal drift down around the tiny Earth. "I have a high threshold of pain and don't mind seeing small amounts of my blood as long as my partners are skilled and I trust them. Generally, I wouldn't be opposed to knife play, but with these monsters, I don't want some amateur slicing my arteries by mistake, or for the fun of it. Secret Service can't move fast enough to stop a knife. And if I'm bound, I won't be able to stop it, either."

"You won't be bound. He will. He wants to play the submissive. I'm not sure what role his prime minister will be playing."

"Interesting." Alana grinned, the evil side emerging. "We'll work it out. Not unusual for a submissive to be their preference."

Julia didn't quite understand. "I suppose. They get a break from making huge decisions, enormous responsibility. As a sub, they can let someone else take control. Can you imagine the stress these leaders go through?"

Alana snorted. "Oh, I feel so sorry for them, all right, considering how they treat civilians, especially women. From what I hear, President Aleid doesn't give a hoot about his people, only his own ass." Alana crossed her legs and swung her red-heeled foot.

Julia didn't agree or disagree. That point wasn't relevant. "Melissa will be in the room, Secret Service outside the door." Julia paused. "I should tell you, our sources believe he murdered his wife."

Alana shook the globe again, not blinking an eye. "Motivation for my presentation, don't you think?"

"Absolutely. I like your enthusiasm. He's been called a sadist." Alana's calmness chilled her. She had to make FLC members aware of the dangers.

Alana laughed low in her throat. "That won't be an issue

since he'll be bound."

"Our intel said he's a masochist as well."

"That is interesting," Alana said. "He likes giving and receiving pain. I'll be sure to work him over good and keep sharp, shiny objects out of his reach." A smile spread across her beautiful face. She looked manic, as if she was getting turned on by the prospect.

Could a masochist also be a sadist? Julia rubbed her forehead. She never got this whole scene.

"Headache, Julia? You should try a flogging. It'll take your mind off the pain in your head."

"No, thanks. I prefer a couple acetaminophen."

"Anything else?" Alana asked. "I should get a few items together and make a plan for my session with Mr. Aleid."

"Yes, this man is living in one of the most volatile countries in the world. His friends and neighbors are terrorists, arms dealers and white-slave traffickers. Be careful. Don't let your confidence get in the way of common sense. Don't turn your back on him or let your guard down for a second."

* * *

Zoe stood in line in the small cafeteria, waiting for her second cup of coffee. Her lids were drooping from her lousy night's sleep. Jason had tried calling and texting her for days, and she'd refused to answer. At first, she was surprised he hadn't shown up at her office, but the first lady was busy with speaking events, and he was traveling with her. Zoe hadn't handed in her resignation yet, hadn't decided what to do. The idea of quitting, failing another mission, was making her physically ill.

Jason had set her up in this insane program. What gave him the idea she'd be interested in that perverted plan? And the nerve of him not asking her first. These thoughts racked through her head over and over, a barricade that blocked a peaceful night's sleep.

"Hey, girl," Melissa said from behind her. "You look like

hell. Must've been a great weekend. Hot date? I'm jealous."

"No, just didn't sleep well." Zoe got her coffee and decided to drink it black this time. She never drank it without loads of cream and a sugar substitute. Sitting at a small table, she curved her hands around the cup and sipped while she watched CNN news.

Melissa sat beside her. "So you hung out at home all weekend?" Melissa didn't make eye contact, but she did keep checking the news.

"I did some work at home." Which was a lie. She couldn't bring her work home. In the background, Zoe heard the words "breaking news," followed by: "The White House has just released news that Turi Aleid of Chad has returned to his country, but not before signing the UN peace agreement. Chad has been one of the key countries in this long, drawn-out effort for…" Other employees stood around the television screen watching, giving cheers.

"He signed?" Zoe exclaimed. "How the hell did that happen? When?"

"Julia had a press meeting a few minutes ago," Melissa said. "I just came from there."

"But Chad was set against this treaty."

Melissa frowned. "Did you and Jason talk this weekend?"

"Yes." Zoe opened her eyes wide as if the caffeine had sent a jolt through her system. She lowered her voice and glanced at the television then back at Melissa. "Was that you?"

"How do you mean?" A satisfied smile slowly quivered at the corners of her mouth.

"That room," Zoe whispered. "You made it happen. The signing."

"Now you see the importance of this operation." Melissa leaned close and whispered, "So you're ready for your first presentation?"

"Hell no." Zoe shoved her coffee away. "I told him I wasn't interested." There. It was out.

120

"What?"

"I'm not into that crap, and I'd do a lousy job faking it."

Melissa flattened her hands on the table. "National security, the world's security for that matter, depends on this program. You can't say no."

"I already did. I told Jason. I just haven't given my notice yet."

Melissa shook her head. "You don't give notice, or resign from the FLC." Her eyes held fear.

"I'm happy to work in another aspect of the program, not the sex-game part."

"Why? It's just a role. You could be saving thousands of lives." Melissa smacked her hands on the table, drawing the attention of a few people at neighboring tables. She ignored them, and they politely turned away. Obviously, she had expected Zoe to be thrilled to be part of this warped secret society.

"Lots of reasons. For one, I don't think I'd do a good job since I'm not familiar with that lifestyle." *And dark, dangerous sex destroyed my love life once before. I don't want to risk it again.* Zoe stood and tossed her cup away. "I need to get to my office."

Chapter 14

At eight p.m., the West Wing looked deserted. Rather odd for so early. Zoe's footsteps echoed more loudly than usual without the muffled voices on the main level. Hours ago, a few people had come down the stairs briefly, but returned after about a half hour.

Zoe closed the third folder of the day when her phone buzzed with a text, Twitter or Facebook update. Normally, she'd ignore it while at work, but her brother being in Iran made her nervous. Her blood pressure maxed out every time she heard the phone now.

The text was from Jason. Her pulse quickened. The ache for him was deep, just when she'd thought they were meant to be together. But after what happened over the weekend, what chance did they have? Work had always gotten in the way of their relationship.

Meet me in the Red Tape Room now. Door is open. Please. We need to talk.

She stared at the message for a while and considered ignoring it, sending a message saying, *Forget it*, or telling him to come to *her* office. But maybe what he had to say was black ops again and that room was more secure than her office.

Whatever his reason, she wanted this over with. Maybe he had a suggestion on how to avoid a resignation. *Fine*. She'd meet him.

Marching directly to the Red Tape Room door, she tensed. Jason was excellent at problem solving, but she knew there wouldn't be an easy solution. There must be something she could do to help without wielding a whip.

The door was ajar. A sliver of light showed through the crack. Slowly, she opened it and stepped inside. Jason stood at the far corner by the St. Andrew's Cross with a serious expression. Seated in a medieval-looking chair with elaborately carved wood and leather cushions was a woman. She was turned away from Zoe, her head down as she studied the clipboard in her hand.

"What's going on, Jason?" Zoe asked, ignoring the woman for the moment.

He stood straighter and gave a slight nod toward the seated woman.

"Have a seat, Zoe." Facing her, the first lady pointed at the leather bed beside the chair.

A rush of air left Zoe's lungs as if someone had hit her in the chest with a sledgehammer. Sweat broke out all over her body, and she felt cold and hot at the same time. "Mrs. Bryson. I'm sorry to disturb you. Please excuse me." Zoe turned for the door.

"Have a seat, Zoe. I'm the one who asked you here. I told Jason to set it up."

Zoe sat on the bed, where Jason and she had made love. The bed with restraining straps and pulleys. And she was here, about to have a conversation with the first lady. "Yes, ma'am." She folded her hands in her lap and sat up straight.

"I understand there's a problem."

"Problem, ma'am?" Hot chills raced through her again. She hadn't been working for the White House for more than a couple of weeks, and already she was screwing up.

"Do the duties of the FLC disgust you?" Mrs. Bryson was calm, straightforward, not judgmental. A simple inquiry.

"It's not that, ma'am. I don't feel I'm…qualified to perform." Zoe cleared her throat. "To be effectively convincing. If I don't fool these dignitaries, the consequences—"

"Could be horrific," Mrs. Bryson agreed. "Call me Faith."

"Yes, ma'am. Faith."

"Consider this your intelligence briefing," Faith said, taking a deep breath. "The FLC, or First Lady's Club, is a secret program initiated only during desperate times, and the world has been going through very desperate times, especially since

9/11. Hardline opposition, economic sanctions, military pressure, bargaining, and other foreign policy tactics become useless against foreign leaders who are convinced that their ways and beliefs, no matter how violent or detrimental to their own people and culture, are the only way. They're so resolute in their thinking that they'd rather kill thousands or even die themselves than change." She paused for a moment, as if letting that sink in. "Sometimes they mean well, but mostly they're interested only in personal gains of power, wealth, resources."

"I don't understand how sex tapes can manipulate these men," Zoe said.

Faith smiled. "Men from different cultures, religious backgrounds, in a variety of locations, have been fighting the same war for centuries. Men start wars because they want more power and control than their neighbor. With all their differences, there are a few things these leaders have in common. Basically, men are aggressive creatures. They're competitive and have strong sex drives." Both women glanced at Jason, and he gave a wry smirk.

"Can't argue," he said.

"Perception, honor and trust are very important for a successful career and also for a man's self-worth. Even among terrorists. They have their own strong sense of honor and trust among their followers. If honor and trust are compromised, the leader will lose respect, control, and he'll not just be forced to resign, but he may lose his life or be maimed to set an example. In some countries, even today, a thief will have his hand cut off."

"I understand that," Zoe said.

The first lady continued before she had a chance to add more. "If we can't negotiate with them through peace talks and the United Nations' influence, how can we discredit them among their followers? We destroy that honor and trust on a basic level so their followers stop following or take them out of their position. The FLC creates scandal with our tapes."

"Can't these dignitaries claim these tapes are fake?" Zoe

asked.

"A photo can be faked. Several high-definition videos cannot. At least easily. Experts can examine the recordings and see they haven't been tampered with."

"You've found the FLC to be effective?" Zoe didn't want to question the first lady, but she wanted to know.

She smiled with pride. "Very. We've managed to get treaties signed, recovered hostages, and ended wars."

Zoe sat up straighter. "End wars. You mean, more than one? Which ones?"

Faith studied her for a while and glanced at Jason, who stood at his straight Secret Service attention again.

Zoe glanced back and forth between the two. What did Jason know that he hadn't told her yet?

"What wars?" Zoe said softly.

Faith raised her chin, extremely serious now. She paused for a moment. "For one, the Civil War."

Zoe jumped up. "What?" She pressed her hands to her mouth, glancing at all the equipment in the room. The furnishings and sex toys were not very old.

"This room has been updated since then, of course, and they used photography, not video," the first lady said. "There's a cave in Kentucky that houses some very old files, including letters from Mary Todd Lincoln to her Pinkerton agents, who helped her arrange meetings with key officials. There's also an outfit she wore, sealed in a container to preserve it."

Zoe huffed and made a face. "I'm sorry, but Mrs. Lincoln? Really? That's ridiculous." As soon as she said the words, she regretted them, because Mrs. Bryson slowly stood, narrowed her eyes and pinched her mouth together.

"Sit down, Ms. Summers. This is not a joke."

Zoe complied.

"Mary Todd Lincoln did a heroic deed, and she'll never be honored for it. When thirty thousand British soldiers were perched on the border of Canada, awaiting orders to invade the

United States, her husband feared he'd have to fight a war on two fronts. If that happened, Lincoln would've lost the war. Out of desperation, Mary stepped in. Foreseeing this future outcome and the consequences, she had shopped in New York City well before the war got out of hand and organized the Pinkerton agents to investigate Lincoln's enemies, trying to protect him.

"The Pinkerton agents helped Mary set up the Red Tape Room and arrange a rendezvous. She called it Mary's Parlor for Tea, where she wore an outfit that looked like a cross between a saloon moll and a dominatrix. She wielded a riding crop and wore a black mask and riding boots. Behind a privacy screen, photographers had cameras set up. After the British prime minister's assistant was photographed in a compromising position, Mary threatened to send copies of the photos throughout Europe. The British are a very formal and proper people, and political positions are handed down through generations. Perception, honor, and trust are severely guarded. One photograph is worth a thousand words. An indiscretion like that could have destroyed the reputation of a whole family and a country. British soldiers were pulled out, and the prime minister's assistant quietly resigned, claiming an illness contracted while preforming his duties in the United States. The invasion never happened, and Lincoln could focus on ending the war between the North and the South."

"The FLC has been going on since then?"

"Yes. Not all first ladies have initiated its functions or taken part directly. Sometimes they appoint someone. I chose to take part."

"I understand the importance of this program," Zoe said. "But wouldn't it be best to have someone familiar with the BDSM lifestyle? I don't think I could fake it and be convincing enough. I'm sure there must be someone else better qualified."

Faith nodded, and for a moment Zoe thought she'd say, *Okay, fine, forget we asked. You can go back to your job at Langley.*

Faith stood and paced to the middle of the room. Zoe

stood, too, out of respect.

"Sit, Ms. Summers."

Zoe sat and crossed her hands in her lap again.

Faith tapped a finger to her lips, as if thinking. "Consider this. Would you have slept with Hitler if it could've prevented the Holocaust?"

Zoe's mouth dropped opened. *What do you say to that?*

"How about Bin Laden? Would you have played his Domme or his slave for one night if you knew that videotape would've prevented 9/11?"

Zoe didn't know how to respond. The heat in the room rose, but her body felt chilled.

"We'll help you prepare, and you won't be alone," Jason added, his tone guarded.

The first lady narrowed her eyes. "Men like this don't know what civilized is, don't know what the meaning of integrity is. They're pure evil. They hunger for supreme power and control. That's why we have to warp our logic when dealing with them."

Zoe stiffened but attempted to keep her nerves intact. "The FLC kicks them in the balls, but not literally. Discredits them and drops them to their knees with a sex scandal." Did she just say that to the first lady?

Faith smiled. "Zoe, you're a professional. You're trained to remain calm when dealing with terrorists, drug or arms dealers. Am I right?"

"Yes, but I'd be more effective in the field," Zoe argued.

"This is the field. It takes months to find people and establish top-level security clearance. You have the physical appearance our targets are interested in—blond, young and attractive. The FLC must never be made public under any circumstances. You will complete your training with Jason and Melissa by next week."

"Next week?"

"There's a reception planned a week from Friday, and a number of the delegates will be attending, including President

Majeed Kadir from Iran."

"Nice guy." Zoe tried to keep her tone light.

"Our intel determined he's a sociopath," Jason added. "He's worse than what you've read about in the news. His latest feat was attacking a group of British soldiers. Kadir staked twenty of the murdered soldiers' heads on spikes and lined them along the border."

Zoe pressed her hand over her heart and felt nauseated. "My brother's in Iran right now. Won't I be putting him at risk?" She lowered her gaze, fists clenched as she tried to grasp the horror of what she was getting into.

"I've known about your brother," Faith said. "Kadir won't know who you are. There will be no connections made between you and your brother."

"Good. Then it'll be my pleasure to whip that SOB's ass. Sorry, ma'am."

Faith smiled. "Don't be. But he's not a sub. He's a Dom and a sadist. He'll want a submissive. He prefers slaves, actually. You'll be his slave for the session."

Zoe let out a breath and shot Jason a look that meant business. He returned an innocent shrug. "I guess we better get busy." Heat rushed to her face. She knew what busy meant.

Faith walked toward the door. "Welcome to the First Lady's Club, Zoe. You're officially our newest member."

Tyler Kirkwood, a Secret Service agent who had the demeanor of a Marine, was waiting to escort the first lady back to the residence. He closed the door behind her.

Chapter 15

The Master must stay in control in all situations, especially when an inexperienced sub struggled with her emotions and desires. Zoe stood in the middle of the room, head lowered, hands at her sides, and body shaking. All Jason wanted to do was take her up in his arms and walk away from all of this. That couldn't happen. Duty came first. Wasn't mixing emotions and duty what nearly got them killed in the past? They could get through this. It was early evening. After this session, he'd take her to dinner.

"Zoe, I know this job isn't what you expected." *Crap.*

When she raised her head to look at him, tears sparkled in her eyes. "You really think I can do this?"

"Yes, I know you can. It's not what either of us expected. Missions change. We can do this."

Except for her sharp tone, she blanked her expression. Not only was she in agent mode, she was drawing away from him. Would he lose her when this was over? His chest tightened. He refused to believe that. Zoe was good at hiding her emotions, though she had a couple tells.

"Get it over with now and tell me what you really think of me. I know you're pissed," he said. "Get it out of your system now so we can get to work."

"How do you know I'm pissed?" Her tone was calm and even, not giving away the storm of fury he guessed was building inside.

"You're trying not to cry. You cry only when you're really angry. And you're tapping your hands at your sides, a nervous twitch."

She stopped the tapping. "Yes, I am pissed." She shrugged at that. "So now what? You spank my ass, and I say, 'Yes, Master, more'?"

"You call me, sir. I'm not your Master."

"Let's get on with it." She unbuttoned her pale gray suit

jacket, but left it on. Beneath it, she wore a pale green blouse, scooped low enough to reveal the swell of her breasts. The skirt was tight along her hips and thighs and stopped a couple of inches above her knees with a back slit and pleat, revealing more leg and a hint of lacy thigh-highs.

His groin responded to the rim of lace. He reminded himself he needed to stay in control during this session. Her life and the lives of those involved in the FLC were at stake. How could he do this while she was upset? "Have a seat. We're not going to do this when you're not mentally prepared."

She breathed in through clenched teeth. "I'm fine. Really. I want to do this. Finding out ahead of time probably wouldn't have helped."

His gaze followed her slim legs to the pencil-thin heels. How did women walk in the damn things without breaking their ankles?

"Okay, you're about to get a crash course in dominance and submission." Jason stood in front of her, toe to toe, his nose almost touching hers, as if he was about to interrogate a prisoner. "It's more than just putting up with an asshole, withstanding some pain and humiliation. You must be utterly convincing. So much so you believe it yourself. You have to convince yourself you're the slave of a monster. Willingly."

Zoe opened her mouth to speak. He raised a finger and shook his head. She stopped and lowered her eyelashes and nodded.

"Do not speak while I'm giving you instructions. When I'm finished and you have a question, you may ask, but you must say exactly, 'Sir, may I ask a question?'"

He paused a moment to see if she would argue. When she didn't, he continued. "I will push you to your limits emotionally, physically, spiritually. You may find you love it or hate it. You may find you love me or hate me." Did he see a flicker of sadness in her eyes? "Do you understand so far?"

"Yes, I understand."

"You must watch your expressions. A Dom and Master can see defiance in your eyes, a pout, tension in your muscles. You must be aware of every mannerism, every sigh or roll of your eyes."

She nodded.

"While you're in this room, you are my slave and will do my bidding without hesitation unless you have a valid question. And it better be a valid question or you'll be punished. While you're in this room, you'll refer to me as sir. Or any other male who I say has claimed you as his slave. Discipline or the power exchange is not an easy concept if this is not your world. Couples who are in this lifestyle agree to a pace that's right for them. This is a different situation. Our goal is not a loving BDSM relationship. It's to bring down a monster. Do you understand?"

Zoe sighed and wet her dry lips. "Yes, sir, I get what you're going to do will probably seem cruel, but what happens when it becomes too much? If it's more pain than I can handle?"

"I will give you a safe word. Someone else will always be in this room with you. Myself, another Dom or another Secret Service agent. If it becomes too much, before you call out the safe word, you take a deep breath and consider whether you can take a little more. Think about taking part in bringing down an evil man, possibly stopping his connections to terrorism by withstanding some pain and discomfort. But I don't want you to be injured, either. Your safe word is red. If you can't speak, raise your left pinkie or blink your left eye. Those will be tells to me that you've gone beyond your limits. And I'll stop it. Promise."

"Okay."

Just like old times, they were planning a mission together. He was feeling that rush of adrenaline, but not in a good way. They were in a fortress of security, but he didn't feel good about this one. There were no guarantees it would go down the way they planned or achieve the result they intended. "You understand we can't predict how the target will behave. You have to prepare yourself for anything."

"I understand that. Rarely is a mission flawless," she said. "I can handle it. At the worst, I'll end up with a few bruises on my ass." She gave a nervous laugh, and he knew she was trying to show her support for this project. A look passed between them. They also both knew any mission could turn to shit at any moment no matter how simple it might seem.

"I need to ask you if you have any health issues. I don't think you do. But I haven't seen you in a while. Haven't broken any bones lately, knee injury, blood pressure, heart condition? Anything I should know about?"

"No, I had a recent checkup and work out regularly, including my hand-to-hand combat training."

"You won't need any martial arts while on your knees," Jason said. "Make sure you don't get pissed and try a few jujitsu moves on our target."

"May I ask one more question, sir?"

"Of course."

She looked him squarely in his eyes. "What about us? How will this affect our relationship?" Her voice cracked a bit, giving him a kick in the gut. She was right. Their relationship was shaky as it was.

His insides balled into knots. "I don't know, Zoe. What we have is outside this room. Not in here. We can't let our relationship interfere with this project."

She nodded and glanced down at the floor. "Projects interfered in the past. Don't you think this one will, too?"

He shrugged. "That's up to us. The stress of this type of job has consequences. But I won't let anything happen to you." He cupped her chin and kissed her tenderly. Her lips were soft and hesitant, but soon she opened her mouth for him and urged him on. When she moaned and gripped his arms, he knew she was getting turned on, and so was he. He broke the kiss and stood back. The swelling of his cock was a warning. He had to stay in control, not get overly aroused. Her life and the success of this project depended on it.

"Let's get started, sir."

He raised an eyebrow at her, and she clapped a hand over her mouth, realizing her error. "Sorry, sir."

"That could be a fatal mistake. Submissives give up control, surrender to it. They never give orders." He ran his hand through his hair. Did he have enough time to break her of old habits? "First lesson. Remove your skirt and underwear slowly and place them neatly on the chair. Then bend over the spanking bench from the opposite side so the pad is at your waist and your hands are gripping the kneeling pad. Keep your shoes on and spread your legs."

The vulnerable position would elevate her ass at the perfect height. When was the last time he'd fucked her from behind? She had the sweetest ass, and he remembered she did enjoy sex like this with a little prompting. No way could he halt the raging erection now. Even the pending mission with the psychopath wouldn't distract Jason's libido. This was why he and Zoe shouldn't work together. Was he making another mistake?

Zoe expected her lessons in dominance and submission to be awkward, embarrassing, even painful, but she hadn't expected to be a little turned on by this. Her reactions to Jason would be different than to Kadir.

"Don't ever hesitate," he said brusquely.

And don't give orders or suggestions. When she was on a mission, she had a methodical mind-set, especially if she was in charge of a particular aspect. There was no time for discussion. That came in the planning weeks before a mission. In the field, orders were given and carried out, adjustments made if needed. She'd have to bite her lip to keep from trying to take control of the scene. When it came to sex, she was too accustomed to telling her lover what she liked or didn't like while making love. *A little faster, slower, I want you inside me now.* Being a submissive was a whole new world.

Naked from the waist down and feeling self-conscious,

133

even though she was with Jason, she bent over the bench as he ordered. With her legs spread, everything between was exposed. Cool air tickled the tender folds of her pussy. She was wet and quivery anticipating his next move. Her leg and ass muscles tightened, expecting to feel the strike of his hand or a flogger.

Surprisingly, she wanted to feel the sting of that sensation again.

"While I'm training you, no pleasuring yourself. Leave that collection of vibrators in your drawer at home. I will know. Because I will ask you each time, and you better not try to lie to me. Your pleasure and your orgasm are mine to give, as well as your pain and punishment."

Her body heated up as he walked over to the table of implements, picking up various toys, floggers, and canes then placing them back down. Glancing over to her, he saw she was watching him, frowned and ordered, "Eyes front and down."

Gripping the pads on the knee rest, she kept her gaze on the floor in front of her and tried to stop the trembling. She'd rather be completely naked than be naked from the waist down. Something about wearing her business jacket and blouse and this position made her feel embarrassed and ashamed. It was demeaning, but at the same time, why was she feeling wet and her pussy clenching, aching to be filled with his cock?

Jason stroked her hip and ass. "I'll start off light then increase the intensity. You'll need to build up your tolerance to this and a number of things."

"What things, sir?"

"You'll see. Keep your legs spread and your ass high." He shoved her blouse and jacket up higher. Then the thongs of the flogger brushed over her skin like a velvet caress.

She arched her back, sighing. The first strike caught her off guard, and she cried out. "Ow, fuck."

"No swearing, slave." He struck her again.

"Sorry, sir." She bit her lower lip, preventing the *fuck you* response. Each time the flogger lashed her butt in a different spot, moving up and down her thighs in rapid succession. After several hits, he stopped and smoothed the tender areas. His hand felt cool on her burning skin.

"How are you doing?"

"Okay, sir. It stings, but I'm trying to get used to it."

"Good girl. Let me know if it becomes too much." A knock at the door made her jump, and she tried getting up. He pressed a hand to her back. "I didn't tell you to get up."

"But someone—"

He stared her down with a scathing look, and she stopped. "You'll be punished for arguing with me." He took a black cloth from the table and covered her eyes, tying it behind her head. She couldn't see anything.

"I'm sorry, sir. I forgot, but we're in the White House. It was a reflex."

"No excuses. As your Dom, you must put all your trust in me, completely surrender." He walked over to the door while he was talking and opened the door. "Come in, we're just getting started."

Zoe strained to hear a response or listen to the shoes on the wood floor. A woman or man? She wasn't sure. The footsteps sounded like boots or heavy shoes, so maybe a man. If so, who? They wouldn't have her be Kadir's slave so soon, not when she wasn't trained yet. There was too much at stake.

"We're having some difficulty with discipline. She's being defiant. I blindfolded her for punishment."

She felt a hand on her arm. "Stand up, Zoe," Jason ordered. "I want our guest to finish undressing you. Don't resist, or my punishments will get more severe."

"Yes, sir." She stood on shaky legs, feeling humiliated, knowing whoever was in the room could see her bare bottom and pussy. She shaved her pussy, and the moisture there was probably visible, too. Resisting the urge to cover her sex with her hands, she placed her arms straight at her sides.

The stranger slowly unbuttoned her jacket, slid that over

her shoulders and placed it nearby, then she felt tugging on her blouse as buttons from the bottom up were unfastened. The silky material fell away. She shivered as the cool air hit her skin.

"Nice," Jason commented. "Now the bra."

She felt fingers at her back. Were they a woman's or a man's? She couldn't tell. Then a click and the bra dropped away. Her nipples tightened from the cool air, but also because she knew she was being observed, completely exposed to the unknown stranger.

"Isn't she beautiful?" Jason said. "Her bottom is slightly pink from the flogger. I think she can take more of that, but I have something in mind for her in a moment."

Zoe waited for a response, but there was probably a nod.

"Zoe, clasp your hands behind your back. I want our guest to touch your breasts."

Zoe opened her mouth to protest, but bit her lip instead.

"Is there a problem with that?" he asked.

"No, sir. I would love for our guest to touch my breasts." She tried to sound sincere, but her tone was anything but.

"Do it," Jason ordered. "And make her nipples hard and raw in any way you like. Zoe is trying, but she's not convincing."

The stranger was gentle at first, cupping her full breasts, squeezing them and pinching the nipples, then Zoe felt a tongue over the tip of one, rubbing and flicking. By reflex, Zoe pulled back.

"Don't resist." The hoarseness in Jason's voice made her cringe. She felt like a child being scolded. "And watch the expressions on your face. Later, we'll work on how to look at your Master and be convincing." He smacked her with something hard and stiff across the backs of her thighs.

"Oh," she moaned.

"Yes, I know that hurts. It'll be a reminder when I see you make a face, press your mouth together in a defiant pout, glare at me in anger. All these reactions will be noticed easily by Kadir. You're supposed to be a compliant submissive. Our intelligence

gathering discovered that one of his subs, who decided to get a little smart-assed, was sold to the white-slave market."

She heard a smacking sound and suspected he was hitting a cane against the palm of his hand. Would he strike her with it again? Her muscles flinched, anticipating the sting, and surprisingly, she craved it.

Teeth tugged at the tender tip until Zoe cried out. Pain shot through her breast. Then fingers rubbed the sore tip until the pain eased. It was unnerving not knowing who the person was. The fondling began. Stroking her breasts, her back, hips and ass, but not quite touching her pussy. The caresses felt good, Zoe couldn't deny it, but at the same time, how could Jason watch? Did he like it? Did she like him watching her with another man? Or woman?

"Sir?" Zoe whispered hesitantly.

"Yes, slave. You have a question?" Jason asked. "Go ahead."

"I don't understand the purpose of a stranger…touching me." She almost said molesting, but that would certainly get her a whack from that cane. "If you would explain the purpose of what you're doing, maybe I'll be able to adjust easier, and it'll help motivate me."

He whacked her right thigh, and her knees buckled. "Your purpose is to be a compliant slave and exhibit unconditional surrender. Questioning every order, chore or test with logic is not in your realm as a slave unless you don't understand the specifics of what I expect you to do or you fear a certain aspect."

"I'm sorry, sir." She still didn't understand what was expected of her and felt uncomfortable with the situation, but for now she'd go along for the ride. Maybe he'd allow her to discuss it after.

"Bend over the bench," Jason ordered as he pressed her back down. "Spread your legs and brace yourself with the knee pads."

She did as he asked, and her ass and everything were exposed again. The sound of a vibrator clicked on, and Zoe squeezed her eyes tighter, knowing what was going to happen next.

"You're nice and wet," he said as he slowly slipped the thick shaft into her pussy. The thickness and vibration got her aroused even with the stranger's presence. "Hold this in place," he ordered the stranger. "Don't come, Zoe. I have a bit more training for you. It might be a little uncomfortable, but it's necessary. Kadir may want to do this. So try to take as much as you can."

Zoe heard some rustling at the table of tools, and a moment later, he spread her ass cheeks. *Fuck*. She felt something cool and wet dripping between her ass cheeks. Then something hard, stiff and slick pressed at her tight opening. "Relax and breathe." He pressed the hard butt plug slowly into her ass.

Her stomach muscles clenched as the pain and burn zinged through her. She whimpered, but didn't want to protest. Sooner or later, she'd have to do this, wouldn't she? She tried taking her mind off the pain and focused on the vibrator in her pussy, which was pressed at just the perfect position. If she focused on it for too long...

She gasped and tightened, trying to slow the swiftly rising build of an orgasm, now so close to the edge. She whimpered and groaned.

"Are you in pain?" he asked.

"A little. But I might come, too."

"Good," he said. "Don't come." He removed the plug and replaced it with a larger one. It had to be larger, because she felt the wider spread, and it hurt more.

She swore under her breath.

"Excuse me, did you say something?" he asked.

"No, sir." Trying to relax her ass and tighten her pussy to prevent an orgasm was torture of a kind she'd never experienced before. Sweat beaded across her forehead and across her back, and her body quivered.

If the vibrator moved a fraction, she'd come, and nothing would stop her. Her nails dug into the pads.

"You're close, aren't you, slave?" he asked.

"Yes, sir."

"Not yet." He pressed the plug in deeper, and by doing so, he moved the vibrator against her G-spot. She was done for. Her legs shook so violently, she didn't think she could stand much longer. "Okay, slave, come for me now."

"Oh God," Zoe screamed, and her knees flexed and her back arched. The orgasm ripped through her, every muscle completely out of her control, convulsing, pulsing in the most violent and wonderfully intense climax that she'd ever had. The two objects slipped from her insides, and she hung limply over the cushion, unable to move.

The door opened and closed, then a minute or two later, opened and closed again. She felt a warm wet cloth over her shoulders, down her back and buttocks, then between her legs, cleaning her. Strong arms swept her up and carried her over to the bed and laid her down. A soft blanket covered her.

The blindfold was removed, and Zoe looked up at Jason and Melissa. Anger and embarrassment swelled in her chest. She liked Melissa, so why was she so angry? Would she have preferred one of the Secret Service guys to work with Jason?

She sat up and began dressing.

"You need to rest a bit. A session like this can disorient you," Melissa said. "You did well."

"I'm fine," she said sharply.

"Melissa's right. Sit for a minute. Have some water."

Zoe glared at Jason. "Lesson's over. I'm going home." She grabbed her purse and stormed out of the Red Tape Room, slamming the door behind her.

Chapter 16

"Well, that wasn't so bad," Melissa said, her hands on hips and her mouth in a sarcastic pout. "Keep at it. She'll come around." She picked up two floggers and began swirling them in rhythmic, alternating circles against the wooden cross in a Florentine pattern. Normally, Jason would've been impressed with her technique.

"I pushed her too fast." He kicked the spanking bench, and it slid a few feet. "You forget I'm not that experienced as a Dom."

Melissa stopped swinging and held out one of the floggers to him. "Here. Practice. I'll work with you. Then you can show Zoe."

He rubbed his forehead, trying to avoid the headache building. This would never work. "I should check on her."

"No, she's fine. She never reached subspace because she was analyzing everything you did. You made progress, though. She did come. If she wasn't into the submissive role, she never would've responded so well." Melissa dropped the floggers on the table. She placed a hand on Jason's shoulder. "There could be another reason for her apprehension."

"What's that?"

"She's conflicted about you training her, how it'll affect your relationship." Melissa paused for a moment. "You're sure you two didn't practice a little BDSM when you were dating?"

"Mild role-playing, tying each other up and some other kinky stuff."

Melissa grinned. "Really? I'm intrigued. What kinky stuff?"

Jason glared at her in silence.

"Seriously, tell me. It might help. Maybe we can use that somehow."

He gave a long sigh. "Fine. When we were on a long stake-out, watching a house where there were known drug cartels, she liked to get busy. We could be in a car, a van, an empty building. If we were alone and the element of danger was there, she was horny."

"Sounds like she or both of you are addicted to sex."

"That might be true if we'd continued to do it when we were home," he said. "I think it was more of an adrenaline rush and fear that we might not live to see the next day. Emotions run high when you think this might be the last time."

"All the more reason to keep emotion out of this and have Tyler train her." Melissa was back to her uppity attitude.

"No fucking way."

"How are you going to handle it when Kadir or any other target is controlling her, mastering her, flogging her?"

Jason bit his lower lip until he tasted blood. "That's different. It's a job, a mission. She'll do what she has to. Tyler's only interested in another sexual conquest."

"Stop worrying." Melissa handed him a spray bottle of disinfectant and a roll of paper towels. Then she straightened the items on the table for the next presentation. "She needs some time alone to acclimate. Call her tomorrow."

Jason took a breath. "I don't know if she'll be convincing. What if Kadir suspects?"

"He won't. She'll be fine."

What choice did she have? Or he?

"The problem isn't whether she can handle Kadir," Melissa said. "The problem is whether she can respond properly as a slave if he gets intense. She can't break her submissive role. And you can't interfere."

"I'll work with her, and I won't interfere," he said as he neatly arranged the items on the table, as careful as a surgeon setting up a tray of surgical instruments. The sex toys he'd used on Zoe were wrapped in a towel. He'd take them to the restroom to clean and sterilize in a minute.

Melissa crossed her arms over her chest and shook her head. "You shouldn't be dungeon master on this one," she continued, her voice lowered. "Not even to observe. Your relationship with her complicates this program and can compromise it."

"That monster is not getting his hands on her without me close by to protect her."

"Which is exactly why you shouldn't be in the room. You're too close to her. Maybe even in love with her?"

No, he wasn't in love with her. Was he? He glared at Melissa. For a petite woman, she had balls. He wasn't budging on this. He could be as bullheaded as she was.

Her body relaxed, and her sudden smile didn't look forced. Jason didn't trust her change in attitude. The woman was a trained Domme and knew how to use psychology, emotions and subtle manipulations to leverage her control. "We'll talk more about this later. I have to prepare for a presentation tomorrow night. I need to walk Alana through a few things."

"The Red Tape Room is getting popular," he said.

"It's about to get even more so." Melissa squeezed Jason's arm. "Don't worry, Zoe will do fine. She did great for her first time as a sub. I think she has submissive tendencies."

He gave a hoarse laugh. "I doubt that."

Melissa shrugged. "Then she better be good at faking it." Her phone buzzed. She checked it and frowned.

"Everything okay?" Jason asked.

"Alana. She's asking to see me right away in Rowland's office. It's urgent."

Crossing the room to grab her purse and jacket, Melissa continued to text. Then her phone buzzed again and again.

"Sounds serious," Jason said.

"Eric Rowland. And he just ordered me to get to his office." Melissa texted a message back. "What the hell is going on?"

"Isn't the president attending a function at the Capitol Building? Shouldn't Rowland be with him?"

"You'd think." She put her coat on as the phone rang. "Hello, Melissa Tadeshi." She stood straighter. "Yes, ma'am. I just got the text. I'm on my way now."

Jason waited for her to speak, if she could fill him in. "What's up?"

"Got to go. We have a problem."

* * *

Zoe marched so fast out of the White House, she got a few strange looks from the guards at the exit. If she hadn't been so sore, she might've walked all the way to her Georgetown town-house. After Jason had worked her over with the flogger, she had a tender behind and back, and her muscles ached, more from tension than from the flogging. During the drive home, she could hardly keep her eyes open and it was only eight o'clock. By the time she got home, she was exhausted, and her ass burned. Anal play had never been a big thrill for her.

A hot bath and a cup of tea sounded like a good plan. She hadn't eaten yet. But when she got to the porch of her town-house, Mrs. Snyder called from her door.

"Zoe. Hold on." She crossed her small yard and ran up her steps. She was wearing a yoga outfit. "Just getting home from work?"

"Yes, Beth. Long day. I'm ready for a bath and bed." She hoped her nice neighbor got the polite hint she was too tired for an evening of neighborly gossip.

"I just wanted to let you know the FedEx guy was here with a package. I let him in only so he could leave the package inside. I signed for you." She handed her a paper. "It's from your dad."

Zoe smiled. "How did you know?"

"Because the return address is from a John Summers in Ohio. I know you have family in Ohio and only have one broth-er, and he's in Afghanistan. So it must be your father."

"Good guess. You're right. You could've been a spy." Zoe laughed. "I bet it's apples and cider. My dad said he was going to visit my uncle in Pennsylvania. He lives near an orchard and cider mill."

"Mmmm. Fresh apples," Beth crooned.

"I'll bring you some tomorrow. Better yet, I'll bake a pie later this week."

"Thank you. I'd love either. Go inside and get some rest." Beth waved and jogged back to her house.

Inside, Zoe found the large box in her foyer. After she let Dexter outside to pee, she picked up the box and carried it into the kitchen, placing it on her island and her purse on one of two barstools. With a knife in her hand, she cut open the box as her cell phone buzzed.

Putting the knife down, Zoe dug in her purse and checked her phone. Her brother had posted another word to their game. She checked the update. DEATH was placed across the word TEAL, which she'd played.

A chill crept up her back, and her heart pounded so loud it reached her ears. In a rush, Zoe raced through the first floor, her kitchen, dining room, living room and turned on all the lights. Then she picked up the cell phone and sent a text to her brother.

Damien? U ok?

She stared at the screen, expecting an answer instantly but knowing he wouldn't. She turned on the tea kettle for tea. Her hands shook. While the water heated, she picked up the knife again and finished slashing through the clear strapping tape. Then she removed the bubble wrap. She got a whiff of fresh apples, and the tension in her body eased.

Inside were at least eight quarts of two different types of apples—large golden skin Mutsu and smaller red Romes. Both were great for eating or baking. Also in the box was a gallon of cider. She grinned. She could hug her dad for going to the trouble.

She rinsed off one of the large apples and bit into it. Sweet and tart, the juice ran down her chin. Her phone buzzed again. She snatched it up and read the text from Damien.

Fine, why? Don't like getting beat again?

She sent a text back. *You scared me. Don't use words like death.*

Sure you're ok?

I'll be home soon. Having a party. Can't wait to see Ohio. Don't worry.

Having a party was his way of telling her things were bad. And Damien hated Ohio. He was saying they were really bad. Now she was worried. The first lady had said she'd see about trying to get his team out, but if the fighting was bad, Zoe doubted Damien's team would leave.

Be careful. Love you.

L U 2

She let Dexter back inside and gave him a big hug. The dog licked her chin, then squirmed to be released and charged for the living room to play with a toy. Zoe turned off the tea water and poured a small glass of apple cider instead, adding a shot of cinnamon schnapps. Dropping down on one of the barstools, she took a sip. Whatever happened, she'd do this FLC thing with Kadir even if he beat her to a bloody pulp.

Her doorbell rang, and Zoe reached for her gun, then realized she wasn't carrying one. Reflexes and old habits never die. Damn, she was jumpy. Acting like she was on a mission.

She was, if they hadn't fired her. Right now she'd prefer the West Bank and Gaza Strip during the Israeli-Palestinian conflict to the Red Tape Room.

Dexter raced to the door, barking. Peering through the peephole, she saw Jason, holding two large paper bags. Her body heated from lust and embarrassment. Her nipples still felt raw and sensitive, her butt tender and her cleft slick with desire. Her lesson had riled her up and irritated her at the same time. How could they possibly have a sexual relationship, any kind of relationship, when they planned to use sex as a weapon for blackmail and manipulation?

She opened the door, her jaw tight. "If you have floggers, dildos or any other similar devices of torture in those bags, turn around and leave."

He held up one bag and smiled. "Subs from Bozzelli's

Deli?"

Her mouth twitched in a grin, and the tension in her body eased a little. "Bozzelli's?" She opened the door wider. "Get in quick before someone mugs you."

He strolled inside. "You live in a nice neighborhood. It looks like a Stepford Wives neighborhood, where the yards are small but neat, the houses freshly painted, and the wives are baking cookies all the time."

"Funny. There isn't much upkeep for the yard, but I do bake cookies sometimes. Pies this week, since my dad sent fresh apples. Want one?" She pointed to the box on her island as she brought out plates for the sandwiches.

"Later. Apple pie sounds good."

"I'll make one right now," she said sweetly, teasing him. "I'm not a Stepford wife. Not happening." She grabbed the bag of sandwiches. "I'm starved. What kind did you get?"

"Prosciutto and mozzarella for me and turkey and Havarti cheese for you."

"Ah, I love a man who can order deli. Cider, beer, wine?"

"Beer." He studied her while opening his sandwich and taking a bite. "Are you okay?" His voice was gentle now.

She took a bite. "Mmmm. Let's take these in the breakfast room." He left the other bag on the kitchen island, and she didn't ask about it yet. The sandwiches smelled too good, and something told her she didn't want to know what was in there. Had he cleaned out her desk? Had she gotten fired and kicked out of the FLC?

They grabbed their plates and sat down at the dinette table off her kitchen. Wide windows looked out onto a small private garden lit by small solar lights. "I'll be okay. I needed to catch my breath."

Jason sighed as if he was relieved. "We thought you were going to back out."

"I thought you came here to tell me I was fired."

"No. Just checking in on you. I also have some intel to

share." He took a guy-size bite of his sandwich and smiled.

"Is that what's in the other bag?"

He nodded. "After we eat. Right now, it might spoil your appetite."

"It won't bother you watching these monsters do this bondage stuff to me?"

He stopped eating and put his sandwich down. He took a sip of beer. "It bothers me a hell of a lot, but it's the results that matter."

"I don't understand the psychology. What if this Kadir realizes I'm not a true submissive? How can I possibly be good at this in a few days?"

"You're playing a role, just as if you were working undercover on any other mission. Except in this one, there's sex involved. BDSM is about trust, but also about a power shift, surrendering control."

She covered her face with her hands. "That's the problem. It's against every natural instinct to give over my power, surrender control to an evil person who murders to advance his position and wealth and claims to have God's blessing."

"The war on terrorism is being fought in unusual, subtle ways. You'll be a hero, but the world will never know. Do you know how many heroes there are in the world that the general public doesn't know about?"

"I don't want the glory. I want to stop the bad guy." She pounded her fist on the table.

"Let me help you."

"All right." She leaned back in her chair and stared into her antique light hanging over the table. Her thoughts were in a tailspin. "What about my brother? I just got a text. His code says it's bad over there."

Jason made a face. "It is bad, and it might not be a good idea that's he's texting you."

"I know." He didn't press it, and she was grateful. "Promise me we'll be okay when it's over."

He got to his feet and pulled her up. His hands held her face as he looked intensely into her eyes, his brows furrowed in deep lines. "This is a mission against terrorism and a means to prevent wars, to at least maintain some element of stability in the world. It has nothing to do with our relationship, as complicated as it becomes. You mean everything to me. I won't let any harm come to you."

She smiled and nodded, although her smile felt a bit weak. He hadn't said he loved her, never had. Even though they weren't working CIA anymore, relationships hadn't gotten any easier. "I think I can do this if you're present."

He made a face again. "They don't want me in the room."

"Too bad. I want you there."

"They feel it will distract you and Kadir will sense our connection."

"I'll tell them you have to be there." She sat back down and picked up her sandwich.

He sat. "We'll talk to them." When he finished his sandwich, he got up and placed his plate in the sink, then grabbed the other bag. He took out a manila envelope and opened a folder that contained photos and a printout of information. "Intel collected on Kadir."

Zoe picked up photos of a man with two women who were naked and lying at his feet. The man held a bullwhip high in one hand. He was bare-chested and had on a pair of loose-fitting pants. His feet were bare.

"How do you know this is Kadir?"

"It was taken by cell phone at a distance, so the photo isn't clear. The computer printouts are of a number of hard-core S&M sites he's visited recently on his laptop, home and work computers. We confirmed his IP addresses."

She flipped through twenty pages of URLs and IP addresses. He used a number of computers and his cell phone to search and download photos from these sites. "I see a few kiddie-porn sites. Now I hate this guy even more."

148

"There are thousands of these sites, but many are tracked. It's not hard to pick out which foreign dignitaries are potential targets for the FLC by monitoring these sites. We like to have numerous criteria met before we make a decision. A lot of men search porn sites, not a big deal. We want the world leaders who are sexually obsessed with a particular lifestyle that their people and peers would find extremely offensive."

He shoved the photo of the two women back to Zoe. "Study that photo and tell me what else you see."

She looked closer. "Oh God. There are crisscrossing lines of blood all over their backs. He was whipping them that hard?" A shiver went through her as she imagined the severity of that pain.

"What else?"

"Oh no. Is he standing in a pool of blood?"

Jason's expression grew grim, and his voice lowered. "Yes, blood from the two women. He slit their throats. See the knife sheathed at his hip?"

"Yes." Zoe felt sick.

"One more item to notice in this photo. Look closely."

She studied it again, then threw the photo onto the pile. "He has a fucking hard-on."

Jason collected the folder and stuffed it back into the envelope. "Ready to meet me tomorrow for another lesson?"

"No. I'm ready now."

"I had a feeling." He reached inside the bag and slowly pulled out a long rope. After seeing those women tied and murdered, Zoe felt a wave of nausea pass through her.

"What are you going to do with the rope?"

"Give you a lesson in power exchange and surrender. Do you trust me?"

***

Melissa heard the shouting coming from the office of Eric Rowland, chief of staff. Rowland's voice bellowed at an unknown victim. She was smart enough not to walk in on that. "What the hell is going on?" she mumbled to Alana, whose doe eyes had widened. "Who's in there? Doesn't Eric know we have a presentation in a half hour?"

"Are they calling off my presentation?" Alana sounded disappointed, stuffing her hands deeper in the pockets of her trench coat. "We've been preparing for weeks."

"I doubt it. There's too much at stake," Melissa said. "He better make it quick. I still need to get changed."

"I don't want to stand in the hallway dressed like this." Alana opened her coat for a second so only Melissa could see her outfit.

"Very nice." Beneath Alana's trench coat, she wore a green lacy camisole with matching thong, garter, sheer stockings and spike heels. They would use a private office, previously arranged for these events, so they could change, walk through the scene they had planned, and get mentally psyched. Melissa had a leather corset, thong, and thigh-high boots stuffed in a tote bag slung over her shoulder. They were both part of this particular presentation.

"Not sure if you want to go in there," Tyler said. He was the other FLC member who was involved with this presentation and was waiting outside the open door to the office with his stern Secret Service expression.

"Is the first lady in there?" Melissa asked.

"Not yet. She should be arriving soon," he said.

Melissa waited a few moments, hoping the arguing would settle. It didn't. Alana's eyes held troubled concern. Melissa motioned Alana toward the office. "Before your two guests arrive, let's see if we can stop this pissing contest or whatever it is." Tyler followed them.

"I don't like the sound of this," Alana whispered to Melissa as she opened the door and they walked in.

"It's a bad idea. Aleid and Gerard are terrorists in training." Rowland pointed his finger at Julia, who glared back at him with her arms crossed. "We can't trust them. The FLC should be shut down. It's outdated and should not be used for manipulating foreign policies or fighting terrorism. It's an insult to this administration, to say the least, and a major risk to national security. Never mind how this type of thing could destroy our reputation and credibility as a nation if it ever became public." He lowered his voice, glancing at the three at his door but continuing. "The first lady is out of control if she thinks these sex stunts and videos will change the world."

"You prefer to fight wars that never end," Julia argued, her voice equally low but severe.

"No, I'm saying the FLC doesn't work. It was set up by Lincoln to keep his wife out of his hair while he tried to save a country from collapse. He wanted to make her think she was doing something important."

Julia shook her head. "That's not what's in the FLC's recorded history."

Rowland growled and slammed his hand on his desk. "Recorded history can be interpreted in a number of ways."

Melissa had never seen Rowland so angry.

"I have to agree with Rowland," security adviser Frank Phillips said in an even tone as he stepped into the room. "Fucking your enemy into submission isn't the best method to direct foreign policy. The military is prepared to handle this if the peace talks fail."

Melissa opened her mouth. Two against one wasn't fair, and she had to say her piece. These men were way off base. She wasn't about to let them undermine a program that had proven results, especially when they were ready to proceed with a target in a matter of minutes. "Military action can work to a point. Sometimes other options are necessary," Melissa said. "It's easy to recognize a military man. They tend to prefer the military course of action." Eric Rowland might appear to most to look like a college professor with his large-framed glasses and slightly wavy hair. But he'd once served as a helicopter pilot in the National Guard prior to getting into politics.

Frank grinned, not in a pleasant way. He walked up to Melissa and got in her face, nose to nose. "In your last job, were your johns a lot of military and ex-cons?"

She didn't flinch. "I was a Domme, a professional, not a prostitute, and I graduated from Harvard. Where did you matriculate?"

"West Point."

She nodded, conceding a little. "Nice. Then you should have better manners."

"Enough of this," Julia said. "If you have a problem with the FLC, you can talk to the president or the first lady in the morning. Right now we have two guests arriving any minute. To back out now would raise suspicion."

"I'll do that," Eric snapped.

"Excuse me, Julia. Would you like Alana and me downstairs?" Melissa asked.

Julia's cell phone rang. She held up a finger to Melissa, putting a hold on her question, and answered the phone. "Yes, ma'am. Thank you. I'll meet you." She clicked off. "They're here. The first lady just met them in the hall. Yes, Melissa. You and Alana get ready in the Red Tape Room. Tell video it's a go. Masks on."

When Melissa left the chief of staff's office and entered the main hallway, she glanced toward the front entrance. The first lady was greeting two young black men and General Terrence Guzman, secretary of Defense.

"What the hell is he doing here?" Alana asked.

"Hang on a second. Let's see." They stopped and watched the first lady talking to the general with a tight smile. She pointed to Frank and Tyler. The excuse was that the first lady was giving President Turi Aleid and Prime Minister Miron Gerard a private tour of the White House during the cocktail hour at the Capitol Building, since the delegates from Chad wouldn't be able to stay long. The general tried unsuccessfully to speak but was repeat-

edly interrupted by the first lady. Finally, he nodded and left.

"I have no idea what that was about," Melissa said, "but I'll bet Faith is annoyed. Let's go. We have a party of our own to give, and the guests have arrived."

Chapter 17

Zoe walked into her living room wearing nothing but black heels and a tailored blouse, unbuttoned, no bra or panties, as Jason had instructed. She fought the tide of fear and uncertainty. Her body quivered with need for him, but this wasn't about them. This was about using her body for manipulation. How was she supposed to keep the two separate? Jason knew the more dangerous the situation, the more frantic their desire for each other became. Didn't he realize that by working together in the FLC, he'd put them in the middle of a minefield?

In the center of the room, Jason had cleared away the coffee table and stood holding a length of rope coiled in one hand. Wearing only jeans, he looked hot, but she couldn't read his expression. CIA agents were skilled at hiding their emotions. She wished, just this one time, that she could read his.

The room had a soft glow with the lights dimmed, a lemongrass candle burning on a side table. He didn't move. Heat smoldered in his eyes as he looked her up and down. Her pussy gave a twitch, and her nipples tightened as the seconds ticked by. She knew if she tried covering herself, he'd scold her. The longer he looked at her, the more nervous and turned on she felt. Was this part of her lesson?

"Is this all right?" She glanced down at her shirt and shoes, holding the shirt open a little wider to show she wasn't self-conscious, even though she was.

His mouth quirked slightly, as if fighting off a grin. "Is this all right, what?"

She took in a breath, suddenly realizing her mistake. "Sir. Is this all right, sir?"

"It's perfect. Tell me what you're thinking right now," he said. "I sense your mind is struggling with something."

"I'm not struggling. Maybe a little apprehensive, because I don't know what you have planned. I realize this isn't about

us. It's about understanding and getting a lifestyle routine down right."

He frowned and stared at her, as if she'd said something wrong and, like a child, was waiting for her to figure it out. "Don't overthink."

She looked up at him indignantly.

"By the time we're done, it will be about your sexual exploration. Whether you decide BDSM is something you enjoy or hate, it will be difficult to leave your emotions out of it. Trying to go through the motions by responding in predictable ways like an automaton is a very bad idea. Your target will know. You don't have to like it, but you have to connect with your Dom and the pain, his discipline on a deeper emotional level."

"How can I do that when I know who he is?"

"Live in the moment and know you have people there who are protecting you. You have the power as a submissive to stop it at any time. He will know that. That is a rule in the Red Tape Room. Do you understand?"

"Yes, sir."

He walked up to her, placed his hand under her chin. "That defiant tilt of your chin you did a moment ago? Don't do that again to me or to your target during a scene or expect a severe punishment."

She lowered her eyes.

"It's sexy as hell, but that type of defiance is not typical for a submissive," he added as his mouth came down on hers. The kiss was sensuous and slow at first, then his tongue thrust into her mouth, and her whole body responded with tiny shivers. He broke the kiss the moment she tried leaning into him.

"Now, kneel on the floor and sit on your heels, back straight, palms flat on your thighs." He'd taken the throw blanket from the sofa and stretched it out on the floor.

She did as he instructed, then waited. He placed the rope on the floor in front of her, then he took several items out of his bag. A flogger, a vibrator, nipple clamps, lubricant and a pair of scissors. She frowned at the scissors. He noticed.

Holding them up, he opened and closed them in a cutting motion. "If I need to punish you, I do some cutting. You didn't say you were squeamish about blood."

She stared at the scissors, not sure what to say. A chill raced through her. He wouldn't cut her, would he?

He laughed. "No, I won't cut you. That's what they call a mindfuck. The scissors are a precaution, so I can cut the rope if I can't untie the knots. Or for a quick release."

"Oh." She smiled, relieved.

"Some of what I'm going to do, I'll explain, some I won't explain because you need to learn to guard your responses and expressions. A trained Dom will be able to read the slightest muscle twitch. In the lifestyle, it's a good thing. In our situation, not so much. If he suspects you're trying to fake it…"

"I understand, sir."

Jason tied the rope around one wrist, testing to make sure it wasn't too tight, then made her lie on her back on the floor, knees up. "A completely neutral expression won't work either. Our target doesn't want a robot as a submissive."

He tied her wrist to her ankle, then wrapped a length around her thigh so she couldn't stretch out that leg. He continued up along her side and bound her breasts in a snug figure-eight pattern. Jason slid the rope meticulously over her skin, tying small knots to create a delicate lacework.

Zoe relaxed, intrigued by his sensual movements. With each knot, she lost a little more mobility and became more aroused. Her knees were up and legs spread, exposing her pussy. Her breasts swelled from the restraining ropes and also her arousal. When his fingers brushed over her erect nipples, she gasped and felt her clit throb.

The sensual demonstration continued until he ran out of rope and Zoe was completely restrained. Her arms and legs would not move, and she couldn't sit up or roll to her side if she tried. "This feels so strange—"

"Shhh," he scolded her. "I didn't give you permission to speak or ask you a question."

She frowned and made a face. He smacked her bottom with a cane, and she cried out.

"Watch your expressions."

"What did I do, sir?" She cast her eyes down to show him she wanted to know.

"You gave me an annoyed expression and a frown. Not that a submissive wouldn't show signs of annoyance once in a while, but your Dom would have to punish you for it. We just got started."

"I understand, sir. I'll be more careful."

"Are you comfortable? Feeling any discomfort anywhere?" he asked. "The ropes aren't too tight?" He checked them again.

"No, sir. I feel fine. A little strange but okay."

"Strange how?"

She didn't answer right away. How did she tell him she kind of liked it? He smacked her ass with the cane, and it really hurt. "Ow."

"I asked you a question. I expect an answer."

"Yes, sir. I'm conflicted."

Jason's voice softened. "Conflicted about what?" He stroked her thigh in a non-sensual way.

Zoe wanted him to touch her breasts. She was so turned on right now. She'd even liked the flogger earlier. The cane, too, was getting her hot and wet. How would she get through this training? "What if Kadir wants to fuck me?"

"It's rarely about the sex. It's about the control. Can you handle it if that happens?"

"Yes, sir."

He tightened nipple clamps on each peak, and she cringed from the instant pain. "Learn to ride through the pain," he told her. "Kadir may work you over pretty good, but don't be afraid to call your safe word. Targets understand their play partners have limits and the Red Tape Room will honor them."

He rolled her back enough to expose her ass and swatted her with a paddle several times. The burning sting traveled like sharp jolts. She moaned and tried to ride through the pain as he suggested, but it hurt like hell. Then he smacked her hard. "Ow. Sir. That hurts."

"Such a wimp."

She opened her mouth to deliver a few choice words and tell him to let her give him a go, but she noticed he was watching her closely. "Yes, sir."

"Good girl." He put the paddle down, thankfully, and picked up a smaller flogger. She almost laughed because it was so small. "Did you know some people can have orgasms while experiencing the pain of a flogger?"

"No, sir. That's hard to imagine."

The mini flogger came down on her pussy. Her clit was swollen, and if she hadn't been tied up, she would've pulled away. Zoe sucked in a breath and tried not to cry out.

He stroked her hard with the flogger, then soft, over and over. The muscles of her vagina contracted, anticipating each strike. Through the pain, the sensation of a building orgasm coiled inside her, drawing her closer to a release. She let go, following the pain and pleasure toward what promised to be a glorious release.

Then he stopped. "I think you were beginning to enjoy that. That's a good sign. But I'm not ready for you to come yet."

She glared at him. *Fuck.*

"Wipe that look off your face."

She stiffened. Slowly, he untied the ropes. She wasn't ready yet. She wanted more, wanted to come like this.

"It's not good for your circulation to be tied too long." He massaged her arms and legs and breasts as he removed each knot. The clamps were still tight, and she wasn't ready to give those up yet. "I'll take those off in a second."

She nodded.

As he removed one clamp at a time, Zoe yelled from the

sharp pain. Jason gently rubbed her nipples until the pain subsided. "On your hands and knees. We're almost finished."

She did as she was told. How would she tell him she liked this, that she wasn't faking it? She'd never known she was interested in this lifestyle. Once Jason found out, they were done. He was adventurous in bed, but not BDSM adventurous.

Jason was very impressed with how well Zoe handled this scene. He needed to go a little slower, explain the lifestyle. Training her was more difficult than he'd thought. Fighting his own arousal was a losing battle and getting painful. It took all his control not to fuck her right now. His groin tightened at the idea. He had to think of her safety, think of the mission. If he took it slow, she'd be cool and adjust. Too much too soon was why she'd freaked out in the Red Tape Room. She would be ready in time. He hoped.

If she could keep her cool when dealing with a drug cartel or terrorist, she'd have no problem with a dignitary with a warped sexual appetite. He wasn't sure if he could watch her with Kadir, but he couldn't bear to leave her with him alone.

With the large flogger, he stroked her back and ass. Not very hard, enough to see her skin turn pink and make her feel a little more pain. Push her a bit more.

Melissa and Faith had warned him of the consequences if Zoe wasn't trained properly. He had to push her limits, because Kadir would. Who knew that the bondage and discipline scene would turn him on? He'd always been a straight-sex kind of guy, open to the adventurous side, but never imagined stepping into a completely different lifestyle.

"Spread your legs."

She did and sighed. He wasn't sure if the sigh was of pleasure or weariness. He directed the thongs between her legs, lightly at first, then harder and harder, until she moaned. If he hadn't known better, he would have thought Zoe seemed to be enjoying it. Was this her practiced fake or was she really getting off?

"Do you like this?"

"Yes, sir."

"Do you want me to keep going?" he asked. Damn, he was getting harder, thinking she might be enjoying it.

"Yes, sir. Keep going." Her voice sounded strained, and her body was quivering. From pleasure? Weakness? *Fuck*. Damn, he wanted to take her. His cock was so hard.

He dropped the flogger and got down on his knees. "Zoe, are you all right?"

"Yes, sir.'"

He growled. "No more calling me sir for the night. We're finished." He turned her around and pulled her into his arms. "Are you hurting?"

She was taking in gulps of air. "No." She took a deep breath. "Jason, if you don't fuck me now, I'm going to scream."

She eased backward onto the floor, pulling him down with her in slow motion. His hands fumbled for his zipper, tugging his pants down. He pulled a condom out of his pocket and placed it on the floor beside them.

He made a sound between a growl and a sex-crazed moan. Kicking off his shoes, he managed to remove the rest of his clothes in a matter of seconds. His body settled down between her legs, the wetness of her pussy bathing his cock. It took all his control not to slam deep inside her sensuous body. If he did, it would be all over.

Bending down, he took one of her nipples in his mouth, rolling the tip with his tongue. Her body jerked, and she whimpered. "Still sensitive?" he asked. The nipple clamps had been on for a while.

"Yes, a little, but it feels good, too."

He moved to the other nipple, and she arched her back, moaning. Before he got rough with her tender breasts, he moved lower. She let out a soft whimper that got him more aroused. She raised her hips as an invitation, and he teased her by moving slowly to her pussy. His thumbs parted her folds, exposing her most sensitive places, and generously worked his tongue and lips on her swollen bud.

Zoe cried out and lifted her ass off the floor. "Damn, Merritt, if you tell me I can't come until you say so, I will kill you."

He laughed into her pussy and thrust a finger deep into her channel. She had to be on the edge of an orgasm by the way she was shaking and moaning. "Go for it. I can do this all night."

"You won't need to. God," she shrieked as her body thrashed beneath him and her hands gripped his head, holding it.

He lapped at her juices and plunged deeper with his finger, pressing her G-spot, drawing another yelp out of her. When her cries began to subside, he slipped the condom on and thrust inside her. He thrust slowly at first, easing into her tight passage, feeling her slick and hot depths. When her hands gripped his ass, he lost control and moved like a piston, quick, hard thrusts as he stared down into her eyes. The look of desperate passion raised his hunger and need for release, but something also wedged deep in his chest. "Damn, Zoe. I can't slow down."

She laughed. "Would it help if I said you must ask for permission?" She grabbed her breasts, lifting them up. She knew damn well that got him hot.

"Fuck no." He pumped into her hard, tensing his body, trying to hold back his release. His balls ached as the pressure built.

"I have the willpower. I guess you don't." She smiled in a teasing dare. Her hand slid down to finger her pussy.

He groaned. "Cold, heartless." He held back his climax. Damn it. If she could, then he could.

"Keep fucking me like this, and I'll come again." She rocked her hips in a perfect rhythm.

He was battling between proving he could hold off and enjoying the most intense orgasm he'd had in a long time. Then her legs wrapped tight around his waist, and she rode the next wave. The ache for release was more than he could bear, and he spilled into her with his cock buried deep. "Fuck yes." Spasms raged through his body. The scent of sex, the scent of her stirred his senses, making him lightheaded. "Ah, fuck yes," he groaned again.

She looked up at him as he slipped from her body and collapsed beside her. "Hold me," she said.

"All night," he promised as he pulled the blanket around them. He'd get up in a minute to clean up. Right now he had to feel her close. He pressed her head into his chest, stroking her hair. That wedge was still stuck in his chest, a sensation of emptiness or worry. He finally figured out what it was. "I don't want you to do it."

Chapter 18

Melissa lifted the coffeepot, held it up and frowned. "Empty. Probably a good thing. If I drink any more, I'll be awake for three days," she said to Tyler.

She paced the press secretary's office. Waiting was the worst, more than when she was leading a presentation. Tyler, however, could have been at home lounging by the pool for as stressed as he looked. He sat in a delicate Victorian-style chair, his hard body overly male and sexy in contrast to the cream-colored print fabric. The top button of his tailored white shirt was open, his tie loosened. He sat sideways in the chair, head back and eyes closed.

"Hmmm," he answered, not opening his eyes. "Julia said we could go home."

"Go home then." She stuffed the pot back on the hot plate and turned off the machine. The kitchen staff had brought in a cart with coffee, sandwiches and cookies for the late meeting. Melissa sniffed at a sandwich and put it back down. Julia had gone home over an hour ago. Normally, Julia hung in her office until the presentation was over and she got word that the target had left the White House, but this evening she'd gone home with a migraine.

The first lady, Alana, Clay Stewart, a Secret Service agent and also part of the FLC, and several other Secret Service agents and video technicians were currently engaged in the presentation with two representatives from Chad. "I don't like last-minute changes."

Tyler narrowed his gaze and lifted his chin. "You don't like the Chad delegates choosing Alana over you. Don't take it personally." He closed his eyes. "I think the two delegates would've preferred to have the room by themselves without Alana."

Melissa hadn't considered that. If they were lovers, what a rush to get it on in the White House. "Maybe you're right."

"I'll leave whenever you do."

"I'm not leaving until it's over." Melissa sat on Julia's desk. She was too tired and too worried to care. "Alana's done threesomes before, but not with the likes of these two men."

"What's the deal with these two? I know they have ties with terrorists, and there're rumors they've given these groups safe refuge. But most of the action is in the Middle East."

Melissa nodded. "After the president of Chad and his wife were assassinated, the new president, Turi Aleid, stepped in and quickly appointed Miron Gerard as his prime minister. Chad then became a new hotspot for terrorist groups. Julia said they believe these groups can centralize there and move their focus outward like a spiral."

"Blackmailing these dudes might get them out of the picture one way or the other, but how are you going to get the terrorists out?"

Melissa rubbed her face and expected her eye makeup was smudged beyond repair. "The ultimate objective is to blackmail these guys into gaining some damaging information about these groups first, then take them out of office. If the terrorists find out, Aleid and Gerard may not live long enough to step down. President Bryson or the UN advisers should have someone in mind to help Chad with the transition, if not a recommendation for a new president."

"That's a lot of ifs," Tyler said.

"I know. Sometimes this whole setup scares the hell out of me. It's like we're building a house of cards. One wrong move, and everything collapses." Melissa checked her watch. "Damn it, it's after one. What's taking so long? Alana doesn't like an audience, but I'm worried. The first lady should never have agreed to both delegates from Chad for Alana's presentation. They're both bastards. I've read their files. Aleid, especially. He prefers to carry a machete and dagger instead of a sidearm."

"Weapons are not allowed in the White House," Tyler reminded her. "The metal detectors would light up like a Christ-

mas tree."

"I'm going to check on her." Melissa got up and straightened her skirt. "Coming?"

"She's fine. You can't get in there anyway. The door's sealed. Clay Stewart is in there. The guy could strangle both of them with his bare hands."

The Secret Service agent had a powerful presence. Narrow-hipped but tall, barrel-chested with large biceps and hands. His military-cut dark hair had a squared-off shape, as did his angular jaw and cheekbones. The only soft features on Clay were his hazel-green eyes and full lips. He would tower over the two delegates. Knife or no knife, they wouldn't attempt anything, Melissa hoped.

Melissa smiled. "He probably could flip over a small European car with one hand."

"Relax, Miss Control Freak, they should be done soon."

"I'm not a control freak. Alana's my friend."

"Not a control freak? So you didn't try to stop Jason from training Zoe? I thought I heard you discussing this with Faith and Julia."

She glared at him. "That's different. I'm the best person to train her. I'm a Domme. Jason isn't in the lifestyle."

"You did train him, though," he pressed. "Weren't you thorough enough with him?"

"Screw you, Tyler."

"Anytime. I might even allow you to tie me up, if you'll let me do the same."

Melissa leaned against the doorframe, folded her arms and rapidly tapped her toe on the carpet. "I know and I don't care. Coming?"

When they got to the basement, they moved slowly and silently down the hall. The two Secret Service agents came to attention and blocked the hallway but eased their stance when they realized who they were. One raised a finger to his lips, signaling them to be quiet.

They both nodded. Melissa noticed the red X of tape stretched across the door leading into the Red Tape Room. Tyler pointed to the adjacent Mason Room, showing the other agents where he and Melissa were going. One guard cautiously nodded his approval.

After Melissa and Tyler entered the dimly lit room, she quietly closed the door and eased around the tapestry and into the tunnel. When they entered the video room, Melissa noticed two men engrossed at laptops. The technicians glanced up at them, alarmed at first, but recognized them and turned back to their work. Video cameras were clamped on stands at various heights, pointing through slits in the wall.

The narrow hallway-like room was mostly soundproof, but the people inside wouldn't take the chance to talk or move around too much. Melissa looked over one technician's shoulder at the laptop monitor. The picture on the screen was of the inside of the Red Tape Room.

Alana stood to the side of the St. Andrew's Cross with a flogger in hand. Clay stood beside her. Since when did the Secret Service guy stand so close during a scene? As a switch, she was prepared to act as a Domme or submissive, depending on the needs of her clients or targets. Apparently, she was engaged as the Domme, but she was practically uninvolved with the scene.

Prime Minister Gerard was totally nude, facing forward and strapped to the cross, arms and legs spread wide. His dark, mahogany skin gleamed with a fine sheen of sweat. He was quite aroused, his cock hard and pointing straight up. The president of Chad, Aleid, pointed to Alana, and she swung the flogger in an arc and smacked the back of the cross. Gerard jumped and yelped. Melissa suspected she hadn't even hit him. Was it a playful act?

Aleid turned and Melissa saw the knife gripped in his hand. She planted both hands over her mouth and stifled a scream. The tech gave her a warning look and half-smile. Were they crazy to allow knife play? That usually wasn't allowed. She

glanced at Tyler's deep frown.

Alana wore an under-bust corset in black with black lace thigh-high stockings and red suicide-spike heels. Aleid, also nude, had his back to the camera but occasionally turned enough so they could clearly see his face and hard cock. Melissa nodded to Tyler, referring to the clear shots of video. He looked worried, even though the scene appeared to be under control, except for the naked delegate and the president gripping a knife.

Hadn't they filmed enough for a successful blackmail recording? Melissa wished this scene would end. Her insides knotted, and a wave of nausea passed through her. Alana's flogger struck the cross, not Gerard. Then Aleid brought the knife up to Gerard, close to his face. Clay tensed. The knife edge slid over his chest, making the tiniest of score marks, then lower to his abdomen, a couple of scores, and still lower, toward his cock.

Gerard's cock was still hard. Either he trusted Aleid that much or he was crazy. Aleid held the knife at the base of Gerard's shaft then removed it. Smiling, he kissed the bound man and put the knife down. Everyone in the room let out their breath.

Faith stood to the side, in the shadows, her face hidden by a decorative masquerade mask and her body carefully blocked by furnishings, standing wall dividers and hanging tapestries. Madam first lady knew exactly where she could and couldn't stand. If she accidently moved into view, the video could be edited. From what Melissa could see, Faith wore a slight, humorless smile as she observed the scene. Her body language didn't show signs of stress. Then Alana approached the table of sexual implements, and the first lady's smile widened.

Alana selected a handful of nylon straps off the table and fitted them around her hips, securing them tightly. Her back was to the table, and the men from Chad watched with complete fascination.

"Oh my God," Melissa whispered.

One of the technicians glanced a warning at her to be quiet.

Tyler glared at her. *What?* he mouthed.

Watch. Melissa pointed to the screen. This was about to get interesting. *Bravo, Alana.*

Alana turned so that those taping could see she had a strap-on dildo sticking out from the straps at the level of her pubis. In one hand, she held a bottle of lubricant gel. She stood in front of President Aleid and pointed to the floor in front of the cross.

"Bend over," she ordered, and he complied without hesitation. "Now, pleasure him."

Aleid took Gerard's cock in his mouth and began sucking. Alana used the gel on Aleid and positioned herself behind him, her slick dildo pressed between his cheeks. She thrust into him, and Melissa couldn't tell which delegate groaned louder. Melissa glanced at Tyler, who had his eyes closed and mouthed the word, *Fuck.*

Satisfied that Alana had everything under control, Melissa took Tyler's hand and led him out of the video room, the Mason Room, and back up the stairs to the West Wing. "Can we go now?" Tyler asked. "I think I've been scarred for life." He laughed uneasily, but there was a note of teasing.

Melissa laughed. "Too much?"

"I can watch pretty much anything in a porno movie, but when it's someone I know and foreign delegates I've seen in the news, somehow it's hard to watch." He sighed, the exhaustion evident in his eyes. "Should we go back to Flynn's office?"

"No, I'm tired. Alana's okay. She's almost done. The video will be amazing."

"Cool. I'll walk you to your car." Tyler placed a protective hand on her shoulder. How nice to get a Secret Service escort.

"That scene didn't turn you on, did it?" she asked.

He grinned. "Hmmm. Perhaps."

* * *

The next two days, the White House surged with visitors and meetings. Zoe had received only a quick text or two from

Jason, early this morning. She sat in her dark, windowless office, poking at a cranberry muffin and sipping black hazelnut coffee she'd bought at Ebenezers Coffeehouse. She hadn't felt like herself since that night with Jason. She kept replaying the scene over and over again. He knew her intimately from when they'd worked at Langley, but did he realize how much his training session had turned her on? During their year together, they'd had sex in the most unromantic of places while on missions—the back of a van, a warehouse at night, a boat dock, a storeroom in an office building that was under surveillance. She closed her eyes, recollecting those times and how hot she and Jason had been for each other. But never had they crossed into bondage or the whips and chains stuff.

Her body heated up thinking about what he'd done to her. She didn't think she'd ever had such an intense orgasm before in her life. How much was training for her presentation for her target and how much was their own private exploration? He wanted her to turn them down, drop out of the FLC. He had to know it was much too late for that.

She stared down at her schedule of meetings for the day. Muffin crumbs dropped on the memo she'd found in the interoffice envelope that morning from Julia. What time did the woman get to work?

She had to meet with Julia, Melissa and the first lady at noon to discuss details of Zoe's upcoming presentation with the president of Iran, Majeed Kadir. At two, she'd meet with security adviser Frank Phillips about her personal safety. Zoe laughed at that. What could he teach her that she hadn't already learned at Langley? Phillips was an ex-Marine scout sniper who retired early after shrapnel damaged his eye. He claimed he could still shoot as well, but the military had forced his retirement. Besides the glasses he wore and a one-inch scar slashed over one eyebrow, there were no other physical signs of his injury. Zoe wondered about the non-physical ones.

The pounding on her door made her almost spill her coffee. "Hang on, I'm coming." Zoe got up and opened the door. Alana stood there dressed in a professional business suit, quite a change from the Domme outfit she'd seen her wear. Zoe hardly recognized her. The young woman was huffing and puffing from running down the stairs.

"Hurry. You've got to see this for yourself." Alana grabbed Zoe's arm, but Zoe ran back inside to pick up her keys and locked her office before racing up the stairs behind Alana.

"Where are we going?"

"The Oval Office." Alana giggled. "Aleid and Gerard are getting a personal viewing of the video from the other night."

"We can't go in there," Zoe warned.

They reached the hallway, and Alana slowed to a professional pace, the fast walk that everyone in the West Wing did. "No, we can't, but we can watch as they come out."

"Alana. Are you crazy? Those men can't see you," Zoe said.

"Don't worry. I've done this before. I love to see the looks on their faces. Powerful, evil men defeated in a matter of seconds. Pure bliss." Alana's eyes glinted like a wild woman's. She talked faster and faster. Even more than normal. Coming from Ohio, Zoe had discovered that people in major cities like New York, Washington, DC, and Los Angeles talked fast. And those with high IQs were very fast talkers.

"Why do you keep doing this? Come on, let's get out of here before they leave." The only reason Zoe was up here again was to keep Alana out of trouble by changing her mind. She grabbed Alana's arm. "I can give you a list of reasons on why this is a bad idea. One is keeping your job. The other is never do anything stupid to jeopardize an operation or your life."

"No." She yanked her arm back. "This is my payback against Mr. Miller."

Deep breath. This wasn't supposed to turn into an argument. "Who the hell is Mr. Miller?"

Alana gave a snort. Her face wrinkled up in a frown. "My high school calculus teacher who also happened to be the football coach. He said women didn't need math and managed to flunk me out of his class. It ruined my final grade point average. When I complained to my father, he told me, 'Prove him wrong.'"

The knot in Zoe's stomach was growing. "What does an asshole math teacher have to do with a foreign delegate with connections to terrorists?" She rubbed her face.

Alana smiled as if she was finally getting her point across. "Statistical significance."

"What?"

"Neanderthals like Mr. Miller and the Chad delegates are predictable. They're blinded by their egos and don't see that their actions will have consequences. Statistically, they're perfect for this type of sting operation because they never see it coming. My payback with Mr. Miller will be when I graduate with my doctorate. He'll never know, but I'll know in here." She pressed her hand to her chest. "Each time I see the devastated looks on these men, knowing they've been humiliated and defeated through the efforts of the FLC, I imagine it's Mr. Miller. I lost a scholarship because of him, but I'll make it anyway. I'm grateful my father didn't come to my rescue."

Zoe squeezed Alana's hand. "I understand, but it's not worth the risk. Never take unnecessary risks."

Alana rolled her eyes. "After what I had to do with them, I deserve this. You do, too, considering what's up for you soon."

A number of people hovered around the doors to the Oval Office, including Secret Service and Chad's security. Inside, Zoe could hear loud voices but couldn't make out what was being said or who was shouting. Alana looked pleased, but Zoe didn't like the sound of the shouting. "What if they say no?" Zoe leaned over and asked Alana.

She gave a small laugh. "Never happens." She pulled Zoe to a position adjacent to the front entrance to the Oval Office but far enough away they wouldn't be seen by those coming out. They were also far enough away that the Secret Service agents

171

weren't getting bent out of shape.

"I still think this is a bad idea," Zoe said, pulling Alana a little farther away from the entrance.

Alana made a tutting sound with her tongue. "It's your CIA thing. Really. I've done this before. I grew up in a tough neighborhood outside of Boston. These guys don't scare me."

There was a loud commotion in the office next to the Oval Office, the office of Eric Rowland, the chief of staff. "Now what?" Zoe asked.

"Rowland must've gone in to assist."

"President Aleid, please come back inside, and we'll discuss this," Rowland said calmly. They were in the chief of staff's office.

"No, we're done here," a man with an accent answered. Probably Aleid or Gerard.

"Oh shit." Alana turned and tried walking down the hallway, but a Secret Service guard stopped them. "They're coming out of Rowland's office. They'll pass right by us," she whispered to Zoe.

The two Chad delegates barged into the main hallway. Jaws tight, they lashed out with angry words at everyone in the crowded hallway, partly in English, French and Arabic. Thankfully, the hall was crowded with staff, Secret Service and Chad representatives. Zoe pulled Alana against the wall and attempted to block the delegates' view. The guards shoved through the crowd like a plumber's snake working through a clogged drain, clearing a path for the two angry delegates.

Zoe quickly turned her back when the men reached her and pulled out her cell phone, pretending to make a call. Alana had her back turned and head down. At least her common sensed prevailed over her arrogance. With any luck, the mob would pass and march out of the White House.

Then the group stopped and voices fell silent. A chill went through Zoe. Slowly, her hand reached for her gun. No gun, of course. An instinctual move. She tried telling herself there was

172

no reason to be concerned. They were in the White House, the most guarded and safest place in the nation.

Suddenly, she was shoved away, and a man, one of the Chad delegates, slammed Alana up against the wall, his hand at her throat. Alana tried to fight him, but one of the African security guards yanked her off her feet, pulling her away from President Turi Aleid.

"It's you. You bitch," Aleid shouted at Alana as he glanced at her badge. A second later a Secret Service guard pulled Aleid away. Secret Service grabbed Alana and Zoe and rushed them into Rowland's office, while the two Chad delegates were rushed away in the opposite direction, escorted by Secret Service and their own security. Aleid shouted, "Ms. MacKenna, I know who you are now."

President Bryson stood in the doorway between the chief of staff's office and his own. "What the hell was that all about?"

Rowland pointed to Alana. "She was in the hallway when Aleid came out. He recognized her, saw her badge."

The president scowled at all of them. "Terrific. In my office. Both of you." Zoe doubted the American public had ever had the chance to witness that sharp tone of his voice.

Zoe and Alana walked in with their heads hanging low, like two puppies who had gotten caught chewing up the new sofa.

"Sit," the president ordered. "What were you two doing in the hallway? Nevermind, I can guess. You wanted to see the looks on their faces after I showed them the video?"

"Yes, sir," they both said together.

"Stupid. Do you know how dangerous these men are?"

Zoe nodded. "I've heard, sir." Alana also agreed.

He rubbed his face. "What a fucking mess."

"Yes, sir. Sorry, sir." Alana stared at her shoes.

The president sat on a sofa next to Rowland, his mouth pressed so tight that Zoe feared she'd start hearing his teeth crack. Rowland invited Zoe and Alana to sit on the sofa across from the president.

"Shall I tell Mrs. Bryson to put a hold on future FLC scheduling?" Rowland asked as calmly as possible. If Zoe hadn't known better, she would have thought he looked pleased that this had happened.

"Relax, Eric. The FLC is Faith's project, and I'm not about to stop it because of this. Chad signed the peace agreement. Set up a meeting with Frank and General Guzman. I'll arrange to have Frank keep a twenty-four-hour watch on Ms. MacKenna and have Terrence see how Chad progresses after the news is released."

"I understand, Mr. President. Right away," Rowland said as he left the room.

"Mr. President, would you like me to contact anyone from Langley to ask them to keep track of the Chad delegates?" Zoe offered.

The president smiled. "Thank you, Zoe. That won't be necessary. Our security can handle this."

She nodded. "I understand."

"Until further notice, Ms. MacKenna, you'll no longer be connected to the FLC."

"Yes, sir." Alana lowered her gaze.

Zoe cringed. That was an interesting way of saying Alana had just gotten fired. Would she be next?

"I don't see any reason to stop the operation of the FLC. The benefits override the risks," he added. "As I understand, Ms. Summers, you're targeted for President Majeed Kadir in a week."

"Yes, sir," Zoe tried to say firmly, but the words came out a little weak.

The president leaned forward and lowered his voice. "Do not fuck this one up."

Her lips trembled. "No, sir. I won't let you down."

Chapter 19

At the top of the stairs, Zoe opened the door leading into the West Wing. Jason was waiting for her, or on his way down to meet her. She checked her watch. Ten minutes before noon. "I can't talk now. I have a meeting with Julia."

He shook his head. "No, you don't."

She gasped. "What do you mean?"

Jason stared back at her, no emotion on his face. He nodded to the stairs. "It's been rescheduled for one. Let's talk."

Shoulders slumping, she let out a breath, spun on her heel and marched down the stairs. Somehow, she knew this was going to be bad news.

When they entered her office, he closed and locked her door. Silence thickened the air between them. His expression shifted from stiff business to a scowl she couldn't interpret. "What's wrong, Jason?"

His eyebrows shot up, then he frowned. He opened his mouth to speak, then closed it and shook his head. He mumbled something, swore, then, without warning, grabbed her and shoved her against the desk.

Desperation and hunger flared in his eyes. "Damn it, Zoe." He drew her to him, cupping her face to lift her mouth to meet his. The kiss melted their bodies together. She heard his intake of breath as he deepened the kiss. She sucked on his tongue, feeling the awakening desire flow through her. Trembling fingers dug at his shirt. She had to feel bare skin and hard muscle. When her cool hands found contact with his heated skin, he groaned in pleasure. Small kisses played at her throat and jawline then took her mouth again. She could hardly breathe but didn't care. He crushed her to his chest, his hands roaming over her back, sliding under her breasts.

She savored this moment as if it might be their last. What would happen after her encounter? Their missions had a way of screwing with their love life. Was that why sex was so good? They each thought it might be the last time?

"Jason?" she whispered.

"I know." He breathed by her ear as he tugged on her blouse. "We shouldn't, but I couldn't stop thinking about you the last couple days. I want you." Both of them fumbled with her buttons, opening the blouse to reveal a black lace bra. In the back, he searched for the hook.

"A front one." She laughed and opened the catch in the front. Every inch of skin was flushed and sensitive to his touch, her nipples already erect. Arching her back, she cried out as his teeth gently clamped over one peak, and then his tongue rubbed the tender skin. She groaned. "That's so good."

Maybe they were crazy for doing this now, during daytime hours in her office, but neither of them could stop. "You like to take risks?" He reached under her skirt and yanked hard on her pantyhose. She heard the tear and gasped. He hesitated for a moment, checking her response, and she grinned.

"Yes, and so do you." That was all the encouragement he needed. He ripped the hose down to her knees and lifted her up on the desk.

The skirt was up around her waist. The heat of desire had her wet. He slid a finger inside her passage, and she leaned back and spread her legs. As Zoe fumbled with his jacket and shirt, he had to stop pleasuring her long enough to remove them. This was how sex was when they were on a mission, hot and desperate. "You want it like this?" he asked.

"Yes." Then she reached for the waistband on his pants, but he pressed her back on the desk and knelt between her legs. She glanced at him and bit her lip. Skilled fingers played with her sex, teasing her. She opened her legs wider, but the pantyhose restrained her.

"Good. We're going to play a little."

She laughed. "We can't play much. What about my meeting? You said it was rescheduled. I should find out for when."

"It's scheduled for one. Don't worry. I'll take care of it." He pulled her shoes off and ripped the pantyhose into two pieces. Then he tied one piece around one ankle and attached it to a leg of the desk and did the same to the other ankle, stretching her legs wide. "That's a start."

"Jason, what are you doing?"

"Getting you worked up for what's coming later." He removed his belt.

She stiffened. "Are you going to hit me?" The idea made her anxious and her clit throb.

He glanced at the belt, and the corners of his mouth curved up. "Nope. I have another plan. Lie back." She did, and he moved her hands to one side. He slipped the belt through the buckle and tightened the loop around her wrists, then attached the belt to the arm of the chair.

"Now what?"

"Enjoy," he said. "And don't make any noise. Someone might walk by." He began by massaging her breasts and pinching her nipples, then sucking them. She was so hot, she ached for him. "Jason, make love to me."

"Not yet."

If someone had a key and walked into the room right now, they'd see her spread wide in all her glory. His hand worked her cleft, teasing her and thrusting his finger in and out as if he was fucking her. Then he knelt between her legs and used his mouth. Sweet torture. "Are you close?"

"Yes," she whispered. "I can come like this."

"Good." Just as she was about to orgasm, he stopped. "I'm not ready to let you come yet."

"Bastard. What time is it? It must be close to one," she reminded him.

He checked his watch. "So it is."

She jerked on her restraints. "I can't be late."

"Zoe late for a meeting?" he teased. He started getting dressed.

177

"Jason, what are you doing?" She struggled, but he had tied her down good. She couldn't get free.

"Going to my meeting. I'm meeting with Julia, too." He unlocked the door.

"Jason, you bastard. Get back here. You can't leave me like this." She laughed with hysteria rising as she yanked on the belt that held her wrists. Twisting and tugging only made the cinched belt tighter.

"Yes, I can." He opened the door wide. Anyone outside could have seen her exposed.

"Jason," she whispered. "This is serious. You'll get me kicked out of the program."

"Maybe that's what I want to do." He walked out and closed the door behind him.

Zoe kicked and squirmed on the desk top. The belt was secure, and the stockings were knotted so tightly she feared only a knife or scissors would get her out. Did she have a pair of scissors in the desk? How the hell was she going to get free? She couldn't cry out for help. Swearing through clenched teeth, she gave up the struggle and relaxed. How long would it be until the guard found her like this? How was she going to explain this when he did?

"Damn it. Now what?"

The door opened, and Jason stood there, his face serious. He walked in and closed the door behind him. He did have a slight smile, but he wasn't laughing. She glared at him. "That was called a mindfuck, and Kadir may use it on you."

"Was this a lesson? FLC training?" She turned her face away from him. "Bastard."

He strode over to her and caught her chin with his fingers, turning her to face him. "Yes, partly a lesson. Kadir is not a nice guy. You'll have to be prepared for the unexpected. If you're a submissive who shows surprise or defiance at every order, that will give you away. On the other hand, you can't be completely compliant. That won't be believable either. Do you understand?"

"Yes." She inhaled, not self-conscious anymore and at the same time not able to look at him. Her wetness saturated her folds, revealing her arousal. There was no denying how turned on she was. Fear continued to invade her thoughts. How could she tell him what she really was afraid of? After all these months, they'd found each other again. The stress of the job had torn them apart last time. Would it happen again?

"Zoe, what's wrong?"

"Why can't you just explain various aspects of the submissive and dominant roles? Why do you have to be so dramatic?" She was still mad, and she didn't try to hide it.

He nodded. "Because being told something and experiencing it are two different things. And we have a time element."

"Fine. I get it. Is class over?" she snapped.

"No. One more exercise." He took out a penknife and cut her stockings, releasing her ankles, then untied the belt. She sat up and pulled down her skirt and covered her breasts with her blouse then rubbed her sore wrists.

"Did I tell you to cover yourself?" he scolded her.

His harsh words jolted her. "No."

"No, what?"

Realizing her mistake and what he was getting at, she lowered her gaze. "No, sir."

"Now, stand up and remove all your clothing then stand in the middle of the room, feet shoulder-length apart and hands clasped behind your head."

She looked up at him and frowned, then quickly remembered she had to be wary of her expressions. Reluctantly, she removed her skirt, blouse and bra, placing them on the desk, then stood in the middle of the room as he described. She checked the door, but couldn't see if it was locked.

"Don't worry about the door. I take care of all details."

With him fully clothed and her naked, she'd never felt so exposed.

"Remember not to make eye contact unless your Dom requests it. Don't answer these questions, just think about them. How does your body feel right now? How is your breathing? Do you feel nervous, shy, vulnerable? Turned on maybe? Does this seem silly? Is your mind drifting to other things, like will you be late for that meeting?"

She nodded at that.

"I told you I'd take care of the details. You don't have to worry. Trust me."

"Yes, sir."

"Good girl." He stood directly in front of her. "Now, if I was Kadir doing this and he decided to touch you, could you handle it? Could you disconnect enough so you could surrender to him?"

She nodded. "Yes, sir."

"Close your eyes." She did, then he touched her breasts. Gentle strokes with both hands. Then his fingers slid over her cleft, spreading her juices all over her delicate folds. Zoe gasped. "Imagine I'm Kadir touching you."

She tried. Her breath quickened, and her heart rate shot up. The idea of Kadir touching her made her uncomfortable. Knowing it was Jason turned her on. So damn much. Savoring every moment, she floated into a new level of sensual delight. Caught between desiring Jason's touch and wanting to learn how to fake enjoying the touch of an enemy, Zoe fought between desire and disgust.

What shocked her more than anything was how aroused she was right now. She wanted to press her thighs together to ease the throbbing there. Why should she be turned on?

As if sensing her turmoil, he stopped touching her. "Now tell me what you're feeling. I see your body is shaking."

She hadn't noticed, but it was true. "I'm not sure." Tears welled up in her eyes.

"Yes, you are. Tell me what you feel physically and emotionally. This is more than an exercise, this is a necessity." She started to put her arms down, but he stopped her. "Not until

you tell me."

She took a breath and let it out. "Frustrated. And I'm nervous about Kadir, but part of me likes this. Likes the rush and danger. I'm so horny right now, too. I don't know if it's because of you or because of what I'm about to do. But I'm afraid, too." Her phone chirped.

Jason stopped. "Is that important?"

"No, the ringtone indicates it's a minor news alert."

He took her wrists and brought her arms down to her sides, then grasped her hands. "What are you afraid of?" he whispered.

She had to tell him. "What this is going to do to us. What if I decide I like being a submissive? What happens after this mission is over?" Her voice cracked, because the memories of what had happened before came back.

He took her in his arms. His clothes rubbed over her sensitive skin. If only she could feel naked skin against hers. "It'll be okay." He leaned back and looked at her with troubled eyes. "I won't let our mission stand between us. We can handle it."

She nodded, still unsure. "Okay." She forced a smile. In the back of her mind, something dug away at her confidence and trust. He'd never said he loved her. "Class over?"

"Yes, class is over." His words were smooth and gentle. It didn't help.

"Then why are you still dressed?" she asked, tugging at his pants.

He leaned closer and lowered his voice. "How quickly you step out of the submissive role. But you have a meeting. We'll have to finish this later."

She glared at him, then the laugh rolled up inside and she burst out in giggles. "Merritt. I will kill you, but not today."

"Good. I get a running start." He kissed her tenderly on the mouth. Fire blazed in his eyes again.

He helped her dress, minus the pantyhose.

Her phone chirped again. She checked. "I was right. It was

a fire. A car fire." She clicked on the link and read more, then read a text from Melissa. "Oh my God, Jason. It's Alana."

* * *

Zoe's gut clenched as she waited in a chair in front of Julia's desk for her to get off the phone. Jason grasped Zoe's hand and gave it a squeeze.

"Let us know if there's any change," Julia said into the phone then hung up. She took a breath and held her hands to her mouth, then gently placed her palms flat on the desk. "Alana's in critical condition. The burns are minimal, but the concussion from the blast is their main concern."

"The blast? I thought her car caught fire," Zoe said, her voice strained.

"That's what the media are saying. What the police and FBI told them they're allowed to say. It was a car bomb that luckily went off early."

"Luckily?" Zoe clamped a hand over her mouth to keep from shouting. "Aleid. It was Aleid, wasn't it?"

"We can't prove that," Julia said. "That's what we suspect. He hired someone."

"I should've stopped her when she wanted to see his face in the hallway." Zoe hung her head, shaking.

Jason patted her arm. "She's been in the FLC the longest. She knows the dangers and ignored the guidelines. No contact with the targets after a presentation." He looked at Julia. "Are we canceling the other presentations?"

"Cancel? Why?" Zoe shifted in her seat and stared him down. As much as her stomach rolled every time she thought about playing slave to that madman Kadir, the FLC was working and she would be doing something important. This program affected the lives of many people and could make the world less violent. "A number of other countries have signed the treaty because of the FLC, countries who swore they wouldn't sign. We can't stop now."

"We're not canceling anything." Julia held her face in her hands. "In fact, as you'll see in a few minutes, we're upping our schedule." Extra chairs had been brought into the room. Julia must be having another meeting after theirs, or were others joining in this meeting?

"What do you mean?" Jason asked. "After an exposure like that, aren't we taking unnecessary risks continuing?"

"It was dangerous in this case because we did something foolish," Zoe argued. "It won't happen again."

"You mean like Turkey?" Jason asked his tone even. He wasn't letting this drop. Why was he determined to undermine her? Hadn't he gotten her this job?

Turkey had been her fault. She'd lost her nerve during the deal, and the dealers had sensed that. They would've killed her eventually, after they'd all had their turn and tortured her for as much information as they could. The image of the head man ripping her clothes off and three others holding her on the cold concrete floor flashed in her mind. Then Jason and the team had been yanking bodies off of her, bullets and blood flying, and it had all been over before she could crawl for cover. They'd had to blow their covers and the mission to rescue her. They'd failed to stop the deal for bombs and other arms from going through. The same weapons were linked to a bombing attack a month later in London.

"This isn't Turkey," Zoe argued. "This is too important to quit because of a little risk."

"I'm glad you think that, because with Alana out, we'll need you to do another presentation with the Algerian vice president. The president is seriously ill, and the vice president has stepped in for him."

"What?" Jason snapped.

Julia raised her chin. "Vice President Qadir Muhunnad was going to be scheduled with Alana. She was his submissive until the accident. Melissa does not do submissive."

"That's fine," Zoe said. "Fill me in on the details or have

Melissa do that."

"I don't know if this is a good idea," Jason said. "There's no time to plan."

Zoe glared at him. Was he going to challenge her participation at every turn?

The press secretary ignored them for the moment as she flipped through a manila folder, slamming each page or photo on her desk. The scent of fresh potpourri drifted through the room. Without moving her head, Zoe spied the crystal bowl filled with the dried flowers on a bookcase. Every object in Julia's office was meticulously placed, like a staged house in an upscale real estate sale. And Zoe's coworkers teased *her* about being OCD. The bookcase also held a small Zen sand garden with the tiny rakes and smooth stones and a Newton's cradle, those silver balls that bounce in perpetual motion. Had someone given these to Julia as gifts because they thought she needed to chill? In the two weeks Zoe had been there, she'd never known Julia to chill.

Julia closed the folder, picked up her cell phone and punched out a text. Finally, she looked up at Zoe and locked eyes. "Jason is right about your presentation with Kadir probably being the most dangerous." Julia held up the file.

"I've seen it," Zoe said, unperturbed.

Julia sighed, clenching a pen in her hands, then pointed it at both of them. "Don't get a false sense of security just because you're working in the White House. Treat this project as if you're on a mission in a highly volatile area."

Zoe nodded. She couldn't argue with that. Had her boss ever spent time in a jungle overrun by guerrillas? "I understand."

"Fine. Alana's in a lot of danger. She's under twenty-four-hour guard."

"Good," Zoe said.

Julia leaned over her desk and lowered her voice. "I'm sure we won't see a repeat of this morning's fiasco." She continued to stare, waiting for Zoe's answer. The woman's lower lip trembled, and her hands shook. Zoe couldn't decide if it was fear or fury.

184

"No, ma'am."

Julia shook her head and gazed up at the ceiling.

"No more mistakes. Stay focused on the project. I'll give you updates on Alana. No one is to visit her."

"Why not?" Zoe exclaimed.

"I'll explain in a moment," Julia answered. "Now, I hope your training is completed."

The door to Julia's office swung open, and General Terrence Guzman stormed in with Julia's administrative assistant frantically following behind. "I told you, Julia, this type of operation should not be run by civilians. This is a catastrophe."

Julia waved a hand to her panicked administrative assistant. "It's all right, Heather." Julia narrowed her eyes at the general. "Thank you for coming, Terrence. Have a seat, please."

He glowered at her. "This operation must stop now, before any other—"

"Sit down, General," Julia ordered. "We have a lot to cover."

He took a deep breath, and Zoe expected him to explode, but he didn't. He sat.

Heather, the young administrative assistant, who had long dark hair and intelligent eyes, stood patiently by the door. "Excuse me, Ms. Flynn. The others are here. Shall I send them in?"

"Just a minute." Julia held up her hand, making the girl wait. "Is she ready for her presentation?" she asked Jason, glancing at Zoe.

"Yes, she's ready. Melissa and I will go over a few more details with her. But she'll be ready," Jason said.

"Good." Julia looked at Heather. "Yes, send them in, thank you." The other members of the FLC, at least those whom Zoe had met, entered the room, and each took a seat. Melissa, the three Secret Service agents in addition to Jason—Tyler Kirkwood, Clay Stewart and Johnny Vargas—Frank Phillips the security adviser and Chief of Staff Eric Rowland. By their expressions, Zoe expected they'd heard about Alana.

"Any more news about Alana?" Melissa asked. "I keep calling the guard on duty, and he keeps hanging up on me."

Now Zoe folded her hands on her lap to keep them from shaking. She swallowed. There was no turning back now. Julia was right. They had to remain focused. Too much was at stake. She shifted uncomfortably in her chair.

Jason reached over to give her hand a squeeze then rubbed his thumb over her wrist. When she looked down, a physical pull yanked her insides. Red marks encircled both wrists, and he'd noticed them.

A wave of heat slid over her skin. Were there red marks around her ankles, too? Had Julia noticed? Zoe pressed her thighs together. Her body was still worked up from their scene in her office. She shot Jason a warning look and hoped no one else noticed the marks.

Julia leaned back in her chair. "Thank you for coming on short notice," she said after her assistant closed the door. "We're about to increase the schedule of our presentations right after our welcoming reception on Friday evening in the White House. Many of the targeted leaders will be attending, except the president from Iran." The group remained quiet, waiting for Julia to continue. "But there's a problem. We have to be on high-security alert because we cannot rule out the possibility of a leak. We suspect the secrecy of the FLC has been compromised."

Chapter 20

Adrenaline has a taste, and fear could shift the atmosphere of a room. Jason picked all that up when the members of the FLC entered Julia's office and heard her words of a possible leak. Jason had suspected something more was up, since Julia rarely called these meetings.

"You probably heard about Alana's accident," Julia said. "She's in critical condition. The doctors are hopeful for a recovery. At this point we believe this is an isolated incident. But we can't rule out sabotage of the FLC by a mole."

"How can you be so sure?" General Guzman asked.

"Because of what led up to the bombing," Julia said.

"Aleid saw Alana coming out of the Oval Office and recognized her. It wasn't long after that that the bombing occurred. We know Aleid has ties to terrorist groups, but it doesn't prove he was responsible. Other terrorists could be linked to the car bomb," Guzman said, crossing his arms.

"Zoe saw him glance at Alana's badge," Julia added.

The room fell silent.

"I appreciate the work the FLC is doing," Chief of Staff Eric Rowland said. "But aren't you getting in over your head? Doesn't this put the first lady in jeopardy?"

"I have to agree," Frank said. "But the first lady won't back down. I've tried talking to her."

"It's too late for that now anyway," Julia said. "With all of the targeted delegates in town, we need to move up our schedule. Melissa, Zoe and I will be taking on the additional presentations. As needed. There will be a private reception in the White House on Friday evening for the delegates. The first lady will be giving tours to the Red Tape Room."

Jason held back from whistling. Julia never participated. And tours during a party were very risky. They must be desperate. "What about the media? If they notice the first lady wandering off, they may try to tag along," Jason said.

"No media are allowed."

"That's a relief," Tyler said. "What about Zoe and Melissa? Should they not attend?"

"No, they should. It'll give them a chance to study their targets in person. Avoid speaking with the delegates, if possible. No badges after you enter the White House. If you speak to the delegates, don't give them your real names, and if asked, you work as White House staff, nothing more." Julia looked around the room, as if expecting more arguments.

"I don't like the idea of Zoe meeting Kadir ahead of time," Jason said. "The man is highly intelligent and brutal."

Julia smiled reassuringly. "Don't worry. He won't be there. Zoe won't have to worry about anyone other than Kadir. The Algerian vice president is a secondary concern. Kadir's a huge player in the success of the peace agreement. We want her to be focused mainly on him."

Jason nodded. Kadir was the worst of all their targets and the most challenging. One madman was enough.

"Mrs. Bryson is meeting with the Algerian vice president tomorrow. The Iranian president will be in on Saturday. Expect to do your presentation by the beginning of the week, Zoe."

"Yes, I'll be ready."

Jason didn't make eye contact with anyone. He heard his breathing and concentrated on slowing it down. This was going to happen, and he didn't think there was any way to stop it.

"Nothing can go wrong or this project will collapse and the world could be tangled in wars for decades." Julia pressed her lips tightly together then rolled her shoulders back. "We have a serious problem."

"Bad timing for a leak," Johnny said in his New York accent. "Who do you think it might be?"

Julia's fists were clenched on her desk. "The FLC has been a vital part of this nation for over a hundred and fifty years, having to deal with very difficult issues. It will continue. If there is a leak, trust that it will be dealt with in the most severe way possible."

* * *

After they finished dinner, Jason cleaned up the kitchen while Zoe put on a pot of coffee. Dexter had eaten and was curled up in his bed in the dining room. "I think he likes you," Zoe said, her heart swelling. She took out a couple of mugs and placed them on the island.

"Dexter? How do you know?" Jason grinned. He'd asked if he could take him for a walk the moment they got to her house.

"Because he doesn't bark anymore when you come over."

"I found the trick." He wagged his eyebrows.

"What trick?" He was teasing her.

"I picked up some dog treats." He pulled them out of his pocket and showed them to her.

"Cheater." She play-punched his shoulder. "So was there a trick with me?"

His face turned serious. He tossed the dog treat into Dexter's bowl and took her into his arms. "No trick." He pressed her head to his chest and stroked her hair. "I know I left without saying good-bye. After Turkey, I needed time to think. Working together was going to eventually get us killed."

"It has nothing to do with working together. We work in a dangerous field," Zoe argued.

He held her back at arm's length to look at her. "But we're distracted by our feelings for each other, and that puts us at a higher risk."

"I disagree. You're blaming the distraction of our relationship for a failed mission. It was just a failed mission. It happens." She pulled away from him and walked into the living room.

"Zoe." He didn't follow. A few minutes later, he came in with two cups of coffee. "Cream and one sweetener, right?"

"Right, thanks." She took the cup and didn't argue when he sat next to her. "Who's Celia Aldridge?"

Jason's eyes widened only for a second, then he shook his head. Rarely would he be caught off guard and show emotion like that. Either he was over-relaxed by being in her house, in her company, or Celia Aldridge had some significance. "A previous FLC employee," he said warily. "How did you hear about her?"

"I found an old ID badge of hers in my desk. The badge still works. It opened the Red Tape Room. Do you know her? What happened to her?" Zoe pressed.

Jason rubbed the back of his neck and stared at Zoe, hesitating. "I knew her briefly. She was killed."

"Killed how?" Zoe glared at him.

He groaned. "You have to understand. The existence of the FLC cannot get out to the general public. That's why its members are carefully selected. If there is risk of exposure, that risk must be eliminated."

Zoe stiffened. "What happened to Celia?"

"She was in the FLC as a Domme and a researcher. She wanted out, but they decided she was too valuable to let her out yet, so she decided she could sell her information to the media for a lot of money."

"She was going to tell the media about the FLC? Oh my God." Zoe gasped.

Jason nodded. "Frank overheard her making a contact during a reception at the Kennedy Center. They had her phones, computers, every movement monitored. She made other contacts. She was looking for the highest bidder."

Zoe cradled her stomach. She knew where this was leading. "Where did it happen?"

"Outside her apartment." Jason held up a hand to continue explaining. "She was on her way to one of her contacts and was found dead with two shots to the head."

"By an assassin."

He nodded. "The media said it was a random shooting, but the closed file said two bullets struck her."

"The assassin in the FLC?" she asked.

"Probably. At least one. The file doesn't mention if the bullets were of the same caliber." He took her hand and squeezed it. "She was a threat to national security."

"I know." She nodded. This was a typical conversation between two intelligence agents. Normally, she would easily accept it, but in this case, Zoe was really bothered. "Okay. I get it. I won't mention her name at a meeting." A look of fear crossed her face. "I understand they didn't want her exposing the FLC, but I can't believe they would kill her."

"Stranger things have happened. Before my aunt died a few years ago, she gave me letters she'd saved from my uncle. He was in the Secret Service when Kennedy was assassinated. JFK and my uncle were friends, and my aunt recalled phone calls from JFK to the house in Florida. When he and his fellow agents were on the road with JFK, my uncle would write to her, telling her about their adventures. Quite a few interesting stories. Days after JFK's death, my aunt received a call that my uncle had died of a sudden heart attack. He was only forty-three and hadn't had any health issues. She tried contacting authorities to make arrangements to have his body returned to Florida for a funeral. After two days of calls, a coroner called and said he had been cremated."

Leaning forward, Zoe put her mug down on the coffee table. "Cremated? Did your aunt request that?"

"No. My aunt insists there was no record in his medical files or any files requesting cremation upon his death."

"Sounds suspicious," she said. "Did you or your aunt ever find out what happened?"

"It's not unreasonable to believe someone in the government felt my uncle was a threat to security and had him killed. We can't prove it."

"Do you think the FLC had anything—"

"No, I don't think so," he continued. "This proves the government will go to extremes to protect secrets."

"Where are those letters now?" She smiled, curious. What

secrets had they thought they were burying by killing his uncle and cremating him?

"Hidden. A safe place."

"Good." She leaned back and closed her eyes.

"What's wrong?" He rubbed her shoulder.

The hairs rose on the back of her neck. "Can we never leave the FLC? Does anyone leave?"

Knowing what he knew, hadn't he considered that? He laughed. "Don't start getting all paranoid on me. Of course, people leave. With every new administration, a new first lady takes over."

Zoe gave a wry laugh. "I can't imagine Charlotte Ellison having anything to do with the FLC."

"She didn't. She appointed someone, although not much happened during that administration."

The doubt remained, no matter how much she tried to ease the worry. He took her hands in his. "Hey, be honest with me. Do you want out? If you do, I'll figure out a way to get you out safely. Tell me now."

She groaned. "No, I want to do this. I believe in what the FLC is trying to accomplish, even though the methods are extreme. We can survive this, can't we?"

Shaking his head, he drew her across his lap and bent his head to kiss her. The kiss, deep and slow, melted away the worry. All she wanted was him, now, in every way. She opened her mouth for him as the kiss heated. Breathless, she gripped his shoulders as her pulse quickened. She wanted to forget the past, the present and their obligations for the future.

"Nothing is going to happen to us," he said. The tip of his tongue glided across her jawline to her ear, and he tugged on her lobe with his teeth.

She shivered. "I believe you. What should I do with Celia's badge?"

"Give it to me. I'll give it to Frank."

"Okay, now can you tell me why the president doesn't at-

tend our FLC meetings?" Zoe asked, sitting back up.

"Plausible deniability."

She shrugged her shoulders. "I guess that makes sense in light of what's going on. Who could possibly be the leak? If there is one."

"No clue. I was talking to Frank about it. He's started an investigation of each FLC member."

"Terrific. Right in the middle of an operation? I guess I expected that." She sipped her coffee. The hint of cinnamon cleared her head. "Time to stop talking about this."

"I agree." His tone perked right up. "What would you like to talk about instead?"

"Actually, I'd like to show you what I bought." She stood up and walked to her bedroom. "I'll be right out."

"Hmmm. I think I'm going to like this."

* * *

Several minutes later, Zoe came out of her bedroom. She leaned on the doorframe with one hand, a leather flogger dangling at her side in the other. She wore a shiny leather or pleather corset outfit with silver studs and lacing. Ankle boots, thigh-high stockings and a studded collar. Jason felt himself get hard.

"Do you like it?" She spun around, and the thong showed off the cheeks of her ass nicely.

He swallowed and heard his pulse pounding in his ears and felt it down in his dick. *Fuck.*

She dropped her arm and pouted. "You don't like it."

"No, no. I do like it. It's hot. I'm blown away. Wow." He stood up and looked at the flogger.

"I thought I'd wear this with Kadir. Melissa said I needed an outfit. She helped me pick it out. So you think I'll look okay for the scene with Kadir?"

He didn't answer right away. "It'll work," he said stiffly.

She laughed a little. "Jason. Remember this is a role to take down a monster."

"I know. I was remembering his file. The guy is certified." He picked up the flogger and slid the tassels through his hand. The idea of another man, let alone a madman, using this on her ripped him up inside.

"And I'll be surrounded by Secret Service. He won't be able to hurt me."

"You will give the safe word if he goes too far, right?" Jason touched her cheek.

"Yes, I will. Stop worrying."

"Okay. I'll trust you." His hands roamed over the tops of her breasts. "This is nice. It's turning me on." Did she get turned on by the BDSM routines?

"Can I ask a favor?"

"Name it." His hands smoothed over her ass and squeezed. She moaned and went up on her toes.

She handed him the flogger. "Here. I want to see how much I can take."

Chapter 21

Zoe held out the flogger to Jason, but he wouldn't take it. The lustful look in his eyes suddenly turned dark. She had to admit, she wanted to practice more of the BDSM techniques at home to see if they'd both become aroused. When he'd restrained her in her office, they had. This was a new side to their relationship she had to understand. "Jason, come on. Help me here."

"Why? You know as much as you need to know to play a submissive to Kadir. Melissa will go over a few things this weekend. Etiquette, what else is expected of a submissive during a scene, what else is expected of a Dom, safety, hopefully anything that could happen."

"I want to know my pain limit. The reception is tomorrow, and Kadir is coming Saturday. I can have my presentation at any time. If I quit after three lashes, he'll know I'm not a true submissive." She took his hand and smacked the handle into his palm. "Let's get this over with."

"Fine." He didn't sound happy.

She knelt on her hands and knees on an area rug in the middle of the living room. A sandalwood candle burned with a sweet earthy scent, and the lights were dim. She took a deep breath to relax. "My safe word is red."

"Okay. Don't push yourself too far," he warned. "I will stop if I feel I'm injuring you."

"Not unless I say the safe word," she argued.

"The Dom always must protect his sub. His partner may be in subspace, too dazed to register that the pain is at a harmful level. As your Dom, I will stop before you call your safe word if I think I'm injuring you."

"That's your call, then."

She waited there, on her knees, expectantly. The whoosh of the leather thongs circled in a figure-eight pattern. Jason cracked the tips of the flogger in the air. "I love the outfit, but it has to come off. Stand up and remove it for me."

She stood, facing him, and unfastened the front hooks. The back laces were tied tightly to fit her curves, and the garment had hooks in the front to make it easy to put on and take off. Melissa had pointed that out when they were shopping.

Her nipples puckered when the cool air brushed them. She dropped the corset in a nearby chair.

"Now the panties," he commanded. "And don't forget to respond when given an order."

"Yes, sir." She had forgotten, caught up in the moment. A chill went through her, and her pussy throbbed with need.

"Now kneel again."

"Yes, sir." She did and was thinking about the party the next night, how turned on she was getting, wondering if Jason was getting hard, when the first strike hit her shoulder. Zoe wasn't expecting it because her mind was everywhere but in the moment. The leather bit into her skin, and she yelped.

"Stay focused."

"Right." Lesson one for the evening: *Don't let your mind drift during a scene*. He continued to lash her shoulders, back and buttocks with light and hard strokes, stopping at times to smooth her skin.

"How are you doing?"

"Okay, sir." Her skin felt tingling and heated but not too bad so far.

"Kadir may be harder on you, and he may not check in to see how you're doing. Don't be afraid to ask for a break."

"I understand." She was wet and so freaking hot. What would Jason think of her if he knew pain got her excited?

"You're stiffening up. Too much?" He stopped swinging the flogger.

"I'm fine. Don't stop. You're not hurting me."

"We'll take it up a notch and try something else." He slid his hand between her thighs and shoved her legs apart, then slid his hand to her pussy. "Wow, you're getting wet."

196

Heat rushed to her face. She laughed awkwardly. "That's because I'm naked, and you're not. And I'm thinking about what we're going to do later."

"Focus on the now, Zoe."

His sharp words stung. The flogger caressed her skin gently this time. Then he swung it like a pendulum between her legs, the thongs stroking her swollen clit. She groaned and raised her ass. If he continued, she'd come like this. No, she didn't want to come. But a coil of sheer pleasure stirred deep in her belly, and the rhythm of his strikes continued. She couldn't bear it any longer. "Jason. Slow down."

"What? Are you giving me your safe word?"

"No, not yet." Too late, she cried out as the orgasm slammed into her. He must've realized what was happening, because he dropped the flogger and knelt beside her. His hand slid between her legs, and a finger slipped inside her channel, thrusting in and out until her cries subsided. Pulling her into his arms, he held her close.

He half-laughed and kissed her. "Hmmm. I guess you were enjoying yourself."

"You don't think that's weird?" She searched his eyes and wasn't sure what she saw.

He shook his head. "Just the opposite. I couldn't see doing this twenty-four/seven, but I don't mind mixing our love life up a bit. As long as you're not turned on when you're with your targets."

Her stomach churned as reality gripped her. "I won't. Don't worry."

"Hey." He lifted her chin and brushed his lips over hers. "Don't worry. I'll be there."

Did she want him there, or would she be too self-conscious? She picked up the flogger and handed it to him. "This time don't hold back."

* * *

"Since this will be a cocktail party, we don't have to worry about seating arrangements," Faith said to Julia and Melissa. Rarely did the first lady show signs of fatigue, but bloodshot eyes and slumped shoulders made Melissa think she hadn't been sleeping well. This evening she was serving coffee, not tea, in the East Hall.

"What would you like us to do, ma'am?" Julia asked delicately. Melissa sensed Julia also noticed Faith's worn state. "When do you expect the delegates to arrive?"

Faith took in a long breath and let it out slowly. "By eight p.m., security will be stationed outside to keep the media away. Secret Service will be inside. I've asked General Guzman not to wear his uniform. We want the delegates to feel at ease, especially the ones I plan to pull to the side for a private tour. A few of our most attractive interns will be invited. They've been instructed to be friendly and make the delegates feel welcome, although these young women have no idea I'm using them to stir the men's interest."

Melissa rested her cup in her lap. "Would you prefer Zoe and I not engage with these men?"

Faith nodded. "I'd rather you observe them from a distance, let the interns talk to them. But don't ignore them if they speak to you."

*　*　*

Red marks crisscrossed Zoe's back and buttocks, and yet she still hadn't called the safe word or even for a break. Every time Jason stopped to check in, she moaned for more and harder. Her skin was heated, and she wasn't even flinching when he struck her. She had to be in subspace, drifting through the pain. He reached her limit and beyond.

Something inside his chest twisted in a knot. Was she pushing too far again? Getting too immersed in her role? Was she going to put herself in danger again? He cursed under his breath. Damn it. She hadn't learned. A black and blue mark appeared at

her right shoulder blade. *Fuck.*

He tossed the flogger on the chair. "We're done, Zoe." He tried to keep the anger out of his voice. Gently, he stroked her hair back from her face. "Are you with me?"

"Did I call my safe word?" she asked like a drunken person.

He groaned. "No, you did not." He regretted his harshness when he saw her cringe. He picked her up in his arms and took her into the bedroom and gently laid her down on the bed, covering her with a blanket. Then he went into the kitchen and brought back some water. He held the glass to her lips so she could drink. "Slowly."

She took the glass and looked up into his eyes, a little dazed. "I got it, thanks."

"I'll be right back." He went into the bathroom and started a bath, testing the water to make sure it wasn't too hot. On a side shelf, he found some bath salts and thick towels. The tub was an old-fashioned free-standing tub with claw feet. While the water was filling, he went back into the bedroom to check on her.

To his surprise, she was sitting up, looking tired but alert. "Are we taking a bath?" she asked with a sultry smile.

Warmth slid down his spine and soothed all his tense muscles. She was okay, thank God. "You are. The bath salts will help soothe the lash marks and bruising." He helped her into the bathroom and grimaced when he saw the ugly purple bruises on her back and shoulders. "I had no idea I was hurting you so badly, Zoe. I'm so sorry." He stroked her shoulders and back.

Looking at herself in the mirror, she gasped. "Wow, I felt it, but it didn't seem to hurt so badly. Guess it's like walking into a cold lake. You go in up to your ankles, then your knees, and by the time you're up to your waist, you don't feel the cold."

"The last thing I wanted to do was hurt you." Seeing the bruises made him sick inside. He should've stopped sooner. How could he let her do this?

She touched his cheek with her fingertips. Then she kissed him, her lips featherlight at first, then hard, opened wide to tease his lips apart with her tongue. He deepened the kiss until they were both gasping for breath. When they parted, she gazed up at him. "I'm okay," she said. "Thanks for not holding back. I needed to know my limits. I expect my scene with Kadir may be rough, so I wanted to be prepared."

He could tell she was still half out of it, still in subspace. Her eyes had that faraway, glassy look. Melissa had told him about this. She held on to his arm as she stepped into the tub and slid into the warm, scented water.

"You have to remember not to let it go that far," he said, sitting on the edge of the tub. "Don't trust Kadir to be a thoughtful Dom to stop a scene."

"I know," she said, patting his leg.

"You seemed to enjoy it." The idea that she enjoyed the bondage role-playing made him even harder. Since when did he get off on this stuff? He watched porn, watched some of the bondage flicks. What guy didn't? But he hadn't thought he was interested in that lifestyle. He smoothed his hands over her shoulders and back, careful not to press on the bruises.

She shrugged. "Would that worry you if I did?"

He didn't answer right away. Would it? "I don't know."

She stiffened. "Well, don't worry. It's all for the FLC."

He turned on the hot water to keep the water from cooling. "I know. We have to take this guy down."

"I can do it. He won't harm me with Secret Service around."

"As long as you don't get reckless like Alana."

She furrowed her brow. "I'm smarter than that."

He thought about it. She was right, but he was damn well going to make sure she didn't get overconfident. On a shelf, he found a thick sponge. He soaked it and added a ribbon of shower gel and smoothed it over her back, shoulders, and arms. He was tempted to move to her breasts but waited for the moment. This was sweet torture for him. She was so beautiful.

"Hmmm. That feels good," she murmured. "I'm going to do this, and we're going to have a successful mission."

"It'll go just fine," he agreed, but inside he hoped Kadir turned the offer down.

"Could you come in here with me?"

He blew out a breath, thinking how much she meant to him. He did love her, damn it. But telling her now might distract her. "Sure, baby, I can try." He got out of his clothes and slid into the tub.

She spun around and faced him, hooking her legs over his and around his back so his cock barely touched her pussy.

"Better?" she asked, grabbing the sponge from his hands and adding more gel to it.

"Much. It's a decent-size tub." He grinned. Then he sighed as she soaped up his chest and groin. The water was up to his ribs, so areas below the water level received more of a good rubbing than a soaping. "If you keep working my cock with that sponge, I'll come in the tub."

She laughed and dropped the sponge. "Not yet, I have plans."

"Which are?" As she got more playful, he got harder and hornier.

She sighed and ran her hands over her breasts, pinching her nipples, then slipped one hand between her legs and stroked herself. She was killing him slowly, softly, and he fucking loved it. Then she put her hands behind her and arched her back. "Touch me."

"Where?"

"Everywhere." She groaned. Her eyes sparkled with lust. His body reacted, forgetting the anxiety of the FLC, wanting nothing more than to bury his cock deep inside her.

He reached for her breasts, kneaded the beautiful globes. With the flat of his thumb, he flicked her nipples until they pebbled, then he leaned forward and sucked one. She cried out. He tugged, drawing the nipple out and sucking it harder. Then his fingers parted her folds between her legs and found her swollen clit. He pinched it with his two fingers, and her body jerked.

201

Then he teased it, lightly touching, knowing he was making her ache. "You want more?"

"Yes, harder. Please."

"I thought so." He pressed on her clit, and she shouted out his name as his fingers shoved inside. "Like this?"

"Yes."

"Hmmm. I can feel how wet and hot you are."

He wasn't expecting it when her hand clamped around his cock, and she stroked him. Damn, she felt so good. "Tell me what you want," he said.

"Make love to me." She looked at him with pleading eyes. And his heart burst. He loved her. How could he let her go through with the plan?

"I'll help you out of the tub."

"No, right now. We've both been tested and immunized for everything on the planet after getting this job, and I'm still on the pill, so no worries." She shifted so she was on her knees and straddling him.

He should be making this comfortable for her, instead of doing it crunched up in a bathtub. "You sure?"

"Hell yeah, Jason. I want you now." She held his cock in position, and he felt her moist heat touching the tip of his cock. Then, a second later, she impaled herself on him.

They both groaned. He grabbed her hips and rocked into her as best he could, considering she was on top of him and the tub was unyielding.

She ground her hips in a rhythmic thrust, and by the sounds of her moans he knew she had to be close to her climax. Using his thumb, he rubbed her clit, making her go wild. He loved it when she was like this. "Come for me, baby."

She moaned then. "Ahhhh!" Her body shuddered and jerked, and he continued to thrust into her, harder and faster.

"I'm going to come," he warned. The first pulse was so intense he gripped her shoulder, then the next several pulses ripped through him. He closed his eyes, drifting on the pure

high of pleasure. Slowly, he tumbled back down and pulled her into his arms. Her head rested on his shoulder.

He'd come so hard, his head was spinning. He kissed the tip of her nose. They held each other close until the water cooled. "Hey, Sweet Pea. Let me get you to bed."

She nodded. "Only if you stay." She tried standing but needed Jason's help. "I feel drunk."

"I'm not surprised." He drew the towel around her and dried her off.

When he opened the door, Dexter was standing there, whimpering. "Aww, Dexter. I'm okay." Dexter wagged his tail when Zoe came out of the bathroom in Jason's arms.

"It's all right, bud. She's fine." Jason carried her to the bed and pulled the covers over her. Dexter lay down on the floor near Zoe.

"Hurry back. I think I'm ready for round two," she said, giggling.

"Where are you getting all this energy?" Usually after a BDSM session, a submissive would want to sleep. They'd be thirsty, even hungry.

Jason used the bathroom then drained the tub. After he hung up the towels, he walked back into the bedroom, and Zoe was sound asleep. Soon she'd have to kneel before a maniac and be his submissive for the greater good.

How could this peace agreement help cure violence and terrorism in the world when fighting had been a part of life for several centuries? He sat on the edge of the bed and brushed strands of hair back from her face. She'd sleep for hours now. In the corner, curled up in his dog bed, Dexter's puppy belly rose and fell. His little paws twitched as if he were running in his dreams.

She'd bought a townhouse. He smiled at the irony. She'd adopted a dog. The woman who didn't want to settle down, who wanted the freedom of mobility. He didn't even know if she liked kids. And here she was a homeowner with a backyard and a dog. Everything had changed. She was making a future for herself, and it ripped a wide hole inside of him knowing she'd planned a future without him.

It was his own goddamn fault.

Walking around the other side of the bed, he crawled in and eased up next to her. After all this was over, he'd take her on a vacation someplace warm and sunny. His phone buzzed, and he checked the readout. The hairs on his arms stood up. *No fucking way.* There had been another attempt on Alana's life.

Chapter 22

Jason arrived two hours early to the cocktail reception. All the White House staff and FLC members attending had been instructed to do so. A quartet, which was warming up, played orchestral music in the entrance hall. The caterers and wait staff rushed in and out of rooms with glasses, plates, carts of food and bottles of alcohol. No one would know the level of heightened security inside and outside the building. Extra security had been added after Alana's attack.

Many of the world's most powerful leaders would be attending, those in agreement with the peace treaty and those adamantly against it. Jason wanted to see how the president was going to keep a world war from starting within the walls of the White House tonight.

"Whose idea was this again?" Tyler asked as he stood beside Jason, wearing a more formal suit.

"The president or first lady. I'm not sure," Jason said. "Frank is going to have his hands full keeping the media away. Someone leaked info about the reception. News vans are lined up outside."

Tyler made a grunt. "Frank already has his hands full assigning extra security to Alana's room. FBI has stepped in to investigate. They want to know how someone managed another attempt on her life when she was under guard. No one is allowed near her room without a security escort."

"Any chance the FLC's assassin has targeted her because of the scene with Aleid?"

Tyler frowned. "I doubt it. I hope not. She's loyal, not like Celia. The FLC had been giving Alana special training in martial arts, weapons and computers for future undercover assignments outside the Red Tape Room. The FLC has plans for her."

"If she recovers," Jason added.

"They moved her out of Intensive Care. She's off the critical list."

The news eased Jason's mind a bit. Still, someone wanted her dead. "Zoe and Melissa are driving Julia crazy because they don't have permission to see her."

"It's too much of a risk right now."

Jason heard some commotion by the entrance. "The UN officials are here. A bit early, aren't they? They were told no one would be admitted to the parlors until after seven thirty."

Tyler checked his watch. "It's six o'clock. Secret Service will have them wait in the Grand Foyer."

Jason laughed and shook his head. "Guess who's with them? Mrs. Charlotte Ellison."

Tyler nodded. "She probably wanted an early start to criticize Mrs. Bryson's party. She's a piece of work."

"I'd have used a different word."

"Good evening," Julia said from behind them.

Jason turned and gave her a polite nod. "Good evening, Julia. You look amazing." She wore a flowy green dress that showed a bit of cleavage. Quite a change from her conservative business suits.

"Thank you." Julia even smiled, but only briefly. "Mrs. Bryson wants to see all the FLC Secret Service agents upstairs in the East Hall immediately."

"Is there a problem?" Tyler asked.

"Not exactly." She glanced around the room at the preparations. "A change in plans, I believe."

* * *

Jason studied the nine men in black business suits who stood at attention before the first lady in the East Hall. They were all elite team members, handpicked for their intelligence, physical strength, covert and/or military training and also for their sense of loyalty to the country and the first lady. These nine were her private miniature army to aid her in the FLC business. The adrenaline rush tensed his muscles. He always liked that thrill right before the start of a mission, but he couldn't shove aside a sense of foreboding.

The first lady stood and walked toward her men. She looked elegant in her red dress, her signature color the media always commented on. This dress was elegant and classy, and she'd worn it before. Jason smiled. The media spent more time talking about the clothing and shoes of celebrities, or who was sleeping with or divorcing whom, than life-or-death current events. They spent more airtime discussing how the first lady wore the same dress in public more than once rather than focusing on one of her projects.

"A situation has come up." Faith paused until she knew she had everyone's attention. "Blake just informed me that Majeed Kadir will be arriving early and attending the reception after all."

Jason glanced at Tyler. The leader's arrival made the reality of the impending nightmare all too real. He hated the idea of that madman touching Zoe.

"During the evening, I'll be inviting the target delegates over to the West Wing for a tour and then to a viewing of the Red Tape Room. These tours must be private. It will be your job to station yourselves at various points to stop anyone from passing as I conduct these tours." She waited until the men nodded. "Use the excuse that it's for security reasons."

"What about the media?" Johnny Vargas asked. "How the…how did they find out about the party?"

The first lady made a face. "We're looking into that."

"What if you don't get these men to agree to a session this evening?" Jason asked.

"Then we fail," she said. "Besides Melissa, Julia, Zoe and other FLC members, we'll have a number of non-FLC White House staff women attending who are quite attractive. These men have been away from their lovers and wives for several weeks during the stressful peace talks. A little temptation of beautiful women should help maneuver them right where we need."

There was agreement and nods among the men. "Anything else you need from us?" Johnny asked.

"Any other concerns?" Blake added. The clean-cut former military intelligence officer with his hands on his hips looked like he should be wearing camouflage and combat boots instead of the nice business suit. As Frank Phillips' assistant, Blake didn't need a badge identifying him as security.

"Keep the UN officials out of the West Wing during the tours. Especially Charlotte Ellison," the first lady said.

* * *

Zoe entered the Blue Room with her heart pounding so hard she swore everyone in the room could hear. A champagne cork popped, and she jumped.

Melissa squeezed her hand then released it. "Relax, will you? Didn't you used to go undercover with really bad guys?"

Zoe took a breath and let it out slowly. Her pulse slowed down a bit. She laughed nervously. "Yes, but never dressed like this." She smoothed the royal blue chiffon dress she'd bought the other day. The material was so light it fluttered when someone walked by. The dress draped over one shoulder and was decorated with a large jeweled pin. Melissa also wore chiffon in an A-line black dress with a beaded bodice. "The bad guys I've dealt with never dressed so nice either." Delegates and their officials and aides or bodyguards stood around in small groups, drinks in hand. When she spotted Jason across the room, she relaxed. The warmth in his smile made her insides soar.

He marched straight across the room. "Wow. You two look gorgeous."

"So do you," Zoe said. She wanted to put her arms around him and kiss him, but even a friendly gesture wouldn't have been appropriate in this setting.

"You look handsome, too," Melissa said. "Make sure you keep your eyes on our targets and not your beautiful girlfriend." She scanned the room and frowned. "Looks like Miss Charlotte

already has monopolized the party."

"Where?" Zoe asked. Mrs. Ellison sat in a Victorian chair, wearing a formal gown. The party had been announced as being an informal meeting. Around her, several dignitaries, including a couple of the FLC's targeted presidents, hovered, intently interested in her flamboyant conversation.

"My, my," Zoe said. "Doesn't she look like Scarlett in *Gone With the Wind* during the barbecue at Twelve Oaks, entertaining all the single male guests?"

"Faith will have a fit when she sees that," Melissa said.

The music from the musicians shifted to playing *Hail to the Chief,* but a short, understated version without the usual flourish. Considering the hostilities and tensions during the peace talks, grandstanding would have been in poor taste. The president and first lady entered the Blue Room to a round of applause. Anyone who was seated stood. Zoe noticed Mrs. Ellison was the last one to stand. For a woman who bragged of Southern manners, she was spiteful and rude.

The president gave a short welcoming speech to the honored guests and visitors and thanked them for their patience and persistence during the efforts with the peace talks. When the music returned to a soft classical piece, the guests continued with drinks and hors d'oeuvres. The president and first lady began their rounds, greeting visitors. Faith went directly over to Charlotte.

"This should be interesting," Melissa said. "Watch this."

Charlotte grinned as the first lady approached. With a sweep of her hand, she waved toward a chair, inviting the first lady to sit beside her as if the room and party were hers. Faith shook her head and spoke to the men without showing any sign of annoyance. Charlotte hadn't even gotten up when the first lady approached. The dignitaries greeted Faith graciously, shaking hands and nodding politely. She said a few words, smiled at Charlotte, then turned to walk into the Green Room. The men followed, leaving Charlotte sitting by herself.

"Show's over," Zoe said, giggling. "Champagne?"

"Excellent idea," Melissa said.

"Behave yourselves," Jason said, grinning. "I'll make my rounds. Catch up with you later." Jason met up with Tyler, and the two men went out into the Cross Hall and headed in the direction of the West Wing.

"Let's take a walk," Melissa said. "Seems as though all the targets have been herded into the Green Room."

The musicians began playing a waltz, and a few guests started to dance. When the first lady entered, the president strolled out with two United Nations diplomats. "Did you notice that?" Zoe asked.

"Yes, I did," Melissa said in a hushed tone. "I'll bet those two won't be in the same room all night."

"With all these people around, I don't know how she's going to pull this off," Zoe said, taking a sip from her champagne flute.

"You'll be surprised." Melissa leaned against Zoe. "You see the man with the short beard and black-framed glasses standing to the right of the first lady?"

"Yes. Who is he?"

"Vice President Qadir Muhunnad from Algeria. The president isn't well. He's been in the hospital for four weeks. Why he's there has been kept a secret, but we believe he has terminal cancer. Alana was selected to be Muhunnad's submissive before her accident."

"I know. Julia wants me to take Alana's place." Zoe studied the man and tried imagining herself as his sex slave. Her stomach turned, and she fought the urge the run from the room and outside, where the cool October air would revive her, or make her numb. This mission should be easy compared to the others. She'd have to kneel for these men, strip for them, and allow them to touch and flog her. Other than embarrassment and a little pain, the assignment wasn't hard. Unlike dealing with an arms dealer, who wouldn't think twice about slitting her throat

or torturing her.

Melissa patted her shoulder. "Don't worry, you'll do fine. Someone will always be with you."

A number of guests streamed out into the Cross Hall. Voices rose. Melissa grabbed Zoe's arm and went into the hall, too. Coming into the front entrance was General Terrence Guzman and, along with Secret Service and foreign bodyguards, the president of Iran, Majeed Kadir.

"He's early," Zoe said. "I thought he wasn't getting in for another day or two."

Melissa shrugged. "He has a private plane. What I don't get is why Guzman is with him. The general hates Kadir. I'm surprised the president arranged for him to escort Kadir from the airport. Secret Service would've done fine."

President Bryson led the Iranian leader into the Blue Room, but the first lady remained in the hall, talking with some guests. After a few smiles and handshakes, the first lady directed the Algerian down the hall, slowly, pointing out historical paintings along the way. It wouldn't be obvious to most, but to Zoe, who was trained to notice subtle clues, the first lady and Muhunnad were discussing more than paintings and history. "I think we're seeing Faith in action."

"She's been working the targets the moment she walked in the door," Melissa added.

Faith and Muhunnad strolled toward the West Wing. Zoe's mouth went dry. "I think I need something to drink."

"Zoe, I think you should switch to soda."

"I was planning on it." She grabbed Melissa's glass. "I'll ask the bartender to add club soda to our flutes, while you find some yummy hors d'oeuvres."

Back in the Blue Room, Zoe sipped her soda while holding Melissa's glass.

Melissa walked up to her with a plate of bite-size snacks. "Zoe, you have to try these crab puffs. I'm going back for more."

Handing Melissa her flute, she popped a couple of puff

pastries into her mouth. "Hmmm. They are good." Melissa headed over to the hors d'oeuvres table.

"How's the champagne?" asked a gentleman with a strong Middle Eastern accent.

Zoe smiled when she faced the man she feared. "Excellent, but I've switched to club soda. Champagne headaches are the worst." She held out her hand. "It's a pleasure to meet you, President Kadir."

"And you, my dear." He smiled and held her gaze with silver-gray eyes, chilling her from the inside out. If it hadn't been for his violent reputation, he'd be a handsome fortysomething man. He had thick black hair, dark brows and a trim beard. "And your name is?"

"Jennifer Brown."

He narrowed his eyes and smiled. "No, it's not. I heard your friend call you Zoe. I guess Brown isn't right either."

Heat rushed over her face. Had he been that close, watching her when she was supposed to be watching him and the other delegates? She'd been paying more attention to how the first lady worked her targets. Bad mistake. "A nickname," she explained.

He didn't seem convinced. "No matter, I could easily find out if I wanted."

What the hell was that supposed to mean? She glanced toward the snack table, but Melissa was too far away to pick up on their conversation. "Would you like to dance?" he asked.

Her mouth dropped open. Dance? How could she say no? "Of course, sir. I'd be honored."

Another waltz started, and Kadir slid his arm around her. His hand tugged on the silk scarf she wore, and she tensed, hoping it didn't slip. He drew her around the dance floor. There was no way out. How could she turn him down without being rude? He was an excellent dancer, but held her closer than she would've liked. "And I thought this trip would be boring," he said, glancing down the front of her dress.

212

"How long will you be staying?" she asked. "Maybe you'll get a chance to see some of the sights in the city."

"Maybe you will be my guide," he said.

"I'm sure the White House has guides who know more than I do."

"Yes, I'm sure they do," he said, then added a few words in Arabic that she translated in her head: *Not as beautiful as you, my dear.*

Zoe frowned, pretending she didn't understand. "Excuse me?"

"You don't speak Arabic?"

She gave a short laugh. "No. It wasn't a requirement in law school. I do know a little Spanish."

"Really? How little?" He seemed amused.

She smiled back as if she were dancing with a businessman and not a world leader with known connections to terrorists. "Enough to ask where the bathroom is and order a beer."

He laughed out loud. "You're a delight." Across the room, Jason stood beside Faith, and both stared at her with tight expressions. They didn't look amused. *Crap.* When would this song end?

"You're a lawyer?" he asked, not taking his gaze from her face.

How quickly she leaped into a role. As long as she didn't overdo it like she did in Turkey. That's what had gotten her into trouble. "Yes, international law. I have the degree but never practiced because I was hired here as an aide." Zoe did her best at showing innocent pride in her job. The lie was partly true. The music was ending, and Zoe hoped the musicians didn't start right into another piece. She needed a graceful exit.

"I'm sure you'd have made an excellent lawyer." He studied her face and frowned. "How did you get that scar on your neck?"

Zoe held her breath for a half second then smiled. "I was in a car accident when I was nine. Broke my arm, too."

His face relaxed. "I bet you were a handful as a child."

She shrugged. That lie was nowhere near the truth.

He glanced at the entrance to the Blue Room, where four of his aides or bodyguards stood, giving him impatient looks. Kadir sighed. "My dear, regretfully it appears I'm being summoned on business. Thank you for the dance. I hope to see more of you, Jennifer-Zoe. Whatever your name is. I will find out."

The music ended, and Kadir stopped dancing but still held her in his arms. "Enjoy your stay, sir."

Jason was still at the door, not far from Kadir's aides or bodyguards. The first lady had moved to another room.

Kadir smiled. "I'm sure I will." He glanced around the room. "I must say good night to the president and his first lady." He gave a slight bow and walked into the Green Room.

Tremors shook Zoe's body, and a cold sweat dripped down her back. She had just had a pleasant dance with a man said to have murdered at least two of his mistresses and known to cut off the heads of enemy soldiers and stake them on spikes as a warning. She felt nauseated. She needed a breath of fresh air.

Heart pounding, she marched for the Cross Hall and the exit. Jason stood in the doorway. He took her arm and pulled her down the hall to a quiet corner away from guests.

"What the hell were you thinking?" Jason whispered. "You're not supposed to take unnecessary risks."

"He asked me to dance," she argued. "What was I supposed to say?"

Faith had walked up to them, stepping into the conversation. "You're right. It would've been rude to say no." She clasped her hands together, nodded and smiled to guests as they passed. If they'd been alone, the first lady probably would've been screaming by now.

"Melissa and I were trying to stay in the background," Zoe offered.

"Kadir favors blondes, and you're attractive. It's not a

214

surprise that he picked you out. He's left now, so I missed my chance for an invitation. I'll have to try a private invite."

"Did he say anything else to you?" Jason asked Zoe. He was all business now. She hated how he could turn his feelings off like that.

"He asked if I was available to give a tour around the city."

"I hope you said no," Faith said.

"I told him the White House would have someone who could recommend a tour of the city if he wished."

She nodded, seemingly pleased with that.

"Doesn't seem any harm was done," Jason said. "He probably wouldn't have had the time for a tour of the Red Tape Room anyway with the way he rushed off."

"You're probably right. At least we have a few interested targets, including the Algerian. Your presentation is tomorrow, Zoe."

Zoe had to catch her breath. This was going to happen. She glanced at Jason and was chilled by his deep frown. "I'll be ready," she said. Jason's expression shifted, and her heart felt heavy. She wasn't sure if he was worried or jealous. He didn't want her to do this any more than she did. Jason hid his emotions well. She had to find a way to convince him she could do this. "I'm sorry about what happened, ma'am. I hadn't expected to be asked to dance. I've never been to one of these cocktail events."

Faith sighed. "Delegates don't usually ask White House staff to dance. We might use it to our advantage. Did he ask you your name?"

"I told him I was Jennifer Brown." She didn't want to say he'd overheard Melissa call her Zoe. She'd screwed up enough for one night.

"The party's winding down," Faith said. "Go home and come back in the morning. Julia will go over what's expected of your presentation with the Algerian. Be on high alert now. We don't want any mistakes or accidents like with Alana."

215

"Understood," Zoe said. Tomorrow she had to face the reality of her first presentation. Tonight she had to convince Jason they could survive it.

Chapter 23

Zoe paced her office, reciting the step-by-step plan of her presentation with Muhunnad to Jason. She still had over an hour before the Algerian would show. "Okay, okay, I got it." She scrubbed her hands together. "I'll be glad when it's over."

"Hey." He blocked her path and lifted her chin. "Stop worrying. I know how you like to be in the middle of the action. But remember we're a team."

"I know," she snapped.

"Good." He kissed her, then smacked her on her butt. He turned serious again. "It's just a job. This won't change anything between us."

Staring up at him, she searched his eyes. She wanted to believe that.

He pulled something out of his pants pocket and held it up. A wide, black lace choker. "Since you can't wear your scarves."

She nodded and smiled, hooking the choker around her neck, afraid if she tried to speak she'd burst into tears.

There was a knock at her door. Jason opened it. Melissa stood there with a deep frown. Her eyes looked red, as if she'd been crying. "We're pretty sure there's a leak. Muhunnad suddenly changed his mind. You won't be doing your presentation tonight with him."

"One of the FLC?" Zoe asked. "Everyone seems so loyal. What would their motive be? And they must know the personal risk."

"It's a matter of time before we find out," Jason said. "Hopefully, we can stop them before any more damage is done."

She was relieved she didn't have to do her bondage scene yet, but she was disappointed, too. She hadn't slept most of the night, worrying about her first presentation, and wanted to be part of ending the wars. Each day she didn't hear from Damien made her more worried. "I wish it hadn't been canceled. Muhunnad would've been practice for Kadir."

Jason crossed his arms and gave her a grim look. "I guess the leak hasn't gotten to Kadir yet. The first lady met with him this morning, and he's agreed to an evening of entertainment in the Red Tape Room, provided he can have Jennifer Brown as his guest."

"Guess he enjoyed our dance together." She smiled. "How do we proceed?" She automatically went into operation mode.

"Julia and Faith are waiting for you in the Red Tape Room now," Melissa said. "But I have some bad news." Her voice quivered as she said that.

"What's wrong?" Zoe asked, her hand pressed to her chest. "Damien?"

"No, Alana passed away an hour ago. The burns were too severe. I'm sorry."

Swallowing back tears, she glared at Melissa. "Was she killed like Celia?"

"No, I don't think so." Melissa didn't sound as though she was sure, though.

"But I thought she was getting better." Zoe's voice cracked. Alana was loyal. Her only fault had been recklessness.

When they got to the Red Tape Room, Julia and Faith were there, arranging items on the leather bed.

"You told her?" Julia asked as she picked up a hanger that held a beautiful red corset with a short, black lace attached skirt.

"About the potential leak? Yes, she knows," Jason said.

"Good," Faith interjected. "Then you know we can't waste time. Other members of the FLC are trying to determine where the leak is coming from. Kadir is key to ending these wars and diminishing the power of the larger terrorist groups. Once they lose their connections and major funding from these leaders, their power will lessen. They'll always be a threat, but we're stopping them from becoming more powerful."

"I understand," Zoe said. "When is the presentation?"

"Two hours," Julia said. "You'll wear this. Melissa keeps

outfits and shoes here for last-minute presentations. No time for you to go home." Julia handed her the corset outfit along with stockings and a pair of spike heels. "You can use the ladies' room. No one will come down here. Secret Service is guarding the door to the basement. Tyler and the first lady will escort Kadir here. Be here with your mask on, waiting for him, in two hours."

"Two hours?" Zoe tried not to shout. "During the day? Isn't that risky?"

"It's a Saturday, so most of the staff is off," Faith explained. She picked up a pair of handcuffs. "He likes to use these, but they're not the real ones. You can easily get out of them."

"I can get out of the real ones if I have a pin or paperclip."

Faith raised her chin and frowned at her. "Under no circumstances will he learn of your background in the CIA. He thinks you're a lawyer. Keep it that way."

"Of course not," Zoe said, walking to the bed in professional mode. "Is this what Kadir likes?" She picked up a flogger, cane and a section of nylon rope. Then she noticed the butt plug, vibrator, dildo and lubricating gel. Crap, she hoped her session wouldn't go there.

"I asked about his preferences," the first lady said. "He's been given the rules about doing harm, cutting, fire play and needles."

"That's a relief."

Melissa touched her arm. "Don't worry, I'll be here and so will Jason and Tyler. The first lady will leave immediately after the session. She and the president have to fly to Oklahoma."

"We'll be back in a day or two," Faith explained. "Tornadoes have nearly destroyed a small town outside of Oklahoma City. We're going in to tour the area and show support for the victims."

"When will Kadir get to view the tape?" Zoe asked. The idea of having to wait for results of her mission didn't sit well.

"As soon as we get back. We won't be gone long, and it

takes a day or two to edit the video."

Zoe nodded and glanced at Jason. He had his usual stone-faced expression. Impossible to read. This was a job, a role. Even though there were sexual undertones, he'd understand. "I guess I should get dressed."

* * *

Zoe sat on the edge of the bed, head bowed, eyes downcast in a submissive pose. The pep talk Melissa and Julia had given her had done little to stop her hands from shaking. She squeezed them tighter into fists and pressed them into her thighs. The outfit Melissa had picked out was exquisite. Zoe had tried on several at the leather and lace sex shop in Georgetown, and they'd bought five outfits and three pairs of shoes and boots. The red corset outfit was part of Melissa's stash.

Jason's phone buzzed, and he checked it. "They're on their way."

Zoe's stomach did a flip, and she swallowed, consciously willing the wave of nausea to pass. Her heart was pounding so hard, she couldn't take in a full breath. Or maybe it was the restriction of the corset. She could do this.

Jason sent a couple of texts, probably acknowledging the message and then alerting the video crew. He stood by the door, his arms behind his back, wearing a simple Mardi Gras mask. There was no way to tell what he was thinking. "You okay, Zoe?"

She nodded. "I'm fine."

Melissa rubbed her hands. "You look a little nervous, but that'll work in our favor. Kadir will like the vulnerable look. Remember, he thinks you're a lawyer. Don't let him know otherwise."

She nodded. At the sound of the outside door opening, Zoe sat straight up.

"Relax," Melissa soothed. "Eyes down. Don't challenge him. You're a submissive, let him lead."

Julia, Tyler, Kadir and one of his bodyguards walked in.

The man was casually dressed in black slacks and a tan button-down shirt. "I don't suppose you'll let me be alone with her," Kadir said.

Chapter 24

Zoe's confidence drained when she heard Kadir's request to be alone with her. They wouldn't consider it, even as important as this target was.

"Now, Mr. President," Faith said with a polite smile. "We went over the rules. Mistress D will remain and assist or stop the encounter as she feels necessary."

Melissa introduced herself as Mistress D. "We protect the safety of our guests," Melissa said. "Your slave knows her limits and safe words. Your encounter is limited to the items on the bed. Two guards remain inside the room and two outside this door for your protection and hers. Your assistant may stay in the room or outside. Once the room is sealed, no one can enter or leave until Mistress D gives the okay. Do you understand?"

Zoe wondered who the guards were outside—Frank and Blake, or other FLC members? Kadir had his own bodyguard as well.

Melissa and Faith put on their masks. Kadir frowned. "To help our submissive feel less self-conscious," Faith explained. "And to add a little mystery and ambience."

He nodded, seeming to accept her explanation. "Yes, Mistress, I will respect your rules," Kadir said with a firm and arrogant tone. He turned his back on Melissa and Faith and strode to Zoe. Taking her hands, he pulled them apart. "Stand, my dear, I want to look at you."

She did as she was told, keeping her eyes down. Submissive, she must stay in a submissive role.

"No," he stated. "Any order or question from me, I expect a response from you. Yes, sir or no, sir will do. Do you understand?"

"Yes, sir."

"Better, slave Jennifer." He chuckled. Was he mocking her name? "You are very beautiful. I like what you've chosen to

wear, but I want you to take it off."

"Yes, sir." Her stomach grumbled, and a cold wave passed through her. Shaking fingers began to unhook the front of the corset. It was designed to be easy to put on and take off. Without thinking, she glanced at Jason, and he shook his head in warning. Too late.

A cane swatted her on the backs of her thighs, and her knees buckled. "Don't look at them," Kadir scolded. "I am the only man in your life. You will do my bidding without question, without hesitation. Do you understand?"

"Yes, sir." The words were forced through clenched teeth, but she couldn't help it. Her thighs still stung from the cane, and she had the urge to punch him in the nose. If she didn't get herself under control, she'd blow the operation. When she finished unhooking the corset, she opened it and let it drop to the floor. Cool air caressed her breasts and tightened her nipples.

His gaze studied her. The red thong barely covered her pubic area, and she didn't know if he wanted her to remove that, too.

"Beautiful," he said, staring at her breasts. His hand cupped her breast then slid down to her abdomen, his fingers sliding beneath the edge of her thong but going no farther. She held her breath, hoping he didn't make this too sexual because she didn't know how good she could fake it. "I know you're here to please me, but it will please me even more if I could get you horny." His hand moved to her ass.

"Yes, sir." Out of the corner of her eye, she saw Tyler take a step toward Jason. She couldn't imagine how he was feeling. Now she wished he didn't have to watch this.

"Your skin is soft." He took the items off the bed and placed them on a side table. "And this." He touched her choker.

"Don't slaves wear collars, sir?"

"Only when I give you one as a gift. Take it off and don't question me."

Eyes down, she slowly took it off and dropped it on the

floor. He lifted her chin and narrowed his eyes. "I see." His voice softened. "How did you get this injury?"

"Car accident, sir." He'd asked her that at the reception party. Had he forgotten or was he testing her?

He laughed. "I punish my slaves for lying." Reaching inside his pants pocket, he pulled out a black scarf. Her pulse kicked up a bit. What did he have in mind with that? He wouldn't dare strangle her with Jason and Tyler in the room. "I think you're distracted. I'm going to blindfold you."

"Yes, sir." She was relieved, although she didn't like giving up any one of her senses. As he removed her mask, Zoe felt naked knowing the video was recording her face now, but she also knew the AV guys would edit that part out. As Kadir tied the blindfold, she became aware of his scent. Spicy, expensive aftershave or cologne, mingled with sweat, filled her nostrils. She breathed through her mouth to shut out as much of him as she could. Rough fingers brushed her hair from her face and lifted her chin.

"Now, on the bed, facedown to start."

She did, then felt a crack across her thighs. "Ouch."

"What did you forget, slave?"

She had to think for a second. "Did I not say, 'Yes, sir'?"

He cracked her again. "No, you did not. Maybe next time you'll remember. You're not very submissive. I can tell by your tone and your body language."

"I'll try, sir." He was an experienced Dom. Melissa and Jason had warned her about him. Experienced Doms knew how to look for subtle changes in their submissives to understand their pleasure and their pain, to know when they were compliant or defiant, in subspace or in danger.

"She's new," Melissa offered in a whispered note.

"I don't care," he said. "She'll bend to my will or she'll be punished." Footsteps left the bedside, and Kadir's voice sounded from across the room. "She agreed to be my slave. Do not interrupt again unless you feel her life is in danger."

"Yes, sir," Melissa said.

Faith remained in the background, not saying a word.

The rustling by the bed told Zoe that he had returned. "I want to heat up your skin. Don't make any attempt to cover yourself or stop what I'm doing. Spread your arms and legs."

"Yes, sir." She did as ordered and waited for what would come next. He gripped her panties and ripped them off.

"You won't be needing these." She was naked now except for the thigh-high stockings and spike heels. The lashes of the flogger smacked across her ass without warning, and she yelped. He didn't question whether she liked it or not, but hit her again along her shoulders then down the backs of her thighs. The sting bore deep, and she tried to ride out the pain like she had when she was beaten in Turkey. After a time, the pain would become numbing, and her mind would drift. "I can see you're relaxing, slave. Good."

He struck harder, and she arched her back, her chest lifting off the bed, but she would not call the safe word. The video had to be good. "I bet you're getting wet now. If I stuck my fingers in your pussy, I bet you'd be wet. You want to be my slave, my whore. You want me to fuck you."

Who was in control and who was losing control? Zoe moaned and cried out, but in truth the pain didn't reach her anymore. She tried to believe Jason was commanding her. If he had been, this would have been a completely different scene. She'd gladly surrender to him.

Kadir's hand rubbed over her back and ass. "Yes, your skin has nicely warmed up. Turn over."

"Yes, sir." Her words slurred in her head.

He laughed. "Yes, you're my pain slut, a true submissive. I'm pleased." His voice was gruff. "Arms over your head and legs spread."

"Yes, sir. Ahh." The moment she had her arms and legs in place, he struck her across her breasts. Her arms came down, and he yelled at her.

225

"No. Do not move your arms."

She bit her lip to keep from spitting out a string of words that would have made her sound like a truck driver with road rage. It was a good thing her eyes were covered because he might have seen her defiance. She whimpered and moaned and hoped Jason realized she was faking most of it.

"Enough, now stand," he commanded. "And hands behind your back."

"Yes, sir." She wished she could see him. Standing naked in front of Jason, Tyler, Melissa and who knew how many video guys behind the walls made her feel vulnerable and awkward.

Handcuffs were snapped around her wrists. "They aren't too tight, are they?" He ran a finger around to make sure her skin wasn't pinched.

"No, sir. They're fine, thank you."

"I appreciate your politeness." He rubbed her back where the flogger had warmed her skin. "Is the pain too intense?"

"I'm okay, sir." One minute he was brutal, the next he showed concern. Was his brutality all a show to heighten the tension?

He grasped her arm and tugged her. "This way. I want you to stand here with your legs parted."

He stepped away for a minute, then returned. "Open your mouth."

She did, and he slid something large into her mouth until she started to gag. It took a moment before she realized it was the dildo. *What the fuck?*

"Hold this in your mouth," he ordered. "Do not drop it, no matter what, or you will be punished severely. Nod your head if you understand."

Zoe nodded.

"Sir, I need to interrupt," Melissa interjected.

"What is it?"

"She can't use her safe word."

He huffed as if impatient. "If she was my true slave, she

would not get a safe word. She won't need one. However, I will abide by your rules. If she needs to stop, she can raise the pinkie finger of her left hand like you mentioned in your rules."

"But she—" Jason started to argue.

"Is that acceptable to you, my slave?"

Zoe nodded. She didn't know if she could raise that finger high enough. That was the one that had been broken during her torture. But she didn't want to risk arguing the point.

"See?" He was annoyed, and Zoe didn't want Jason to interfere in case Kadir got frustrated and stopped the scene. They might have enough on tape, but she wanted to be sure. The cane smacked her thighs, and she cried out, almost losing the dildo. Now she got what he was doing. She couldn't scream without dropping the dildo, and if she did, he'd punish her. "Spread your legs wider."

She did, and the flogger swung between her legs, the tips of the thongs cracking on her raw clit.

"Mmmm," she mumbled. This time, the dildo slipped to the end, and she grabbed it with her teeth just before she lost it.

"Don't drop it." He laughed. "My punishments are severe."

Fine. Yeah, she wanted to kick him in the balls right now. She didn't want to be humiliated by this bastard anymore. The pain she could handle. She had a high tolerance for it. What if she dropped the damn dildo? What would he do?

At any time she could raise her pinkie, or try to, and stop the scene. The video guys had more than they needed to nail this guy. Kadir wouldn't question her stopping the scene. He knew she was a new submissive, and the FLC wouldn't question her, but she didn't want to stop. Not yet. She wasn't done with him.

She took a breath and tried to relax. She hung her head. Wasn't this attitude what had gotten her in trouble in Turkey?

"Good," he soothed. "I think you're finally surrendering to me. I can see it in your shoulders. You're finally relaxing. Don't drop the dildo yet. Not until I give you permission." He smacked her one more time between her legs, and she gripped the dildo.

Wait for it. The time isn't right. "Good girl."

He stopped flogging her, he stopped caning her, he wasn't even touching her. As she heard his footsteps circling her, a crack from the flogger made her jump. The tassels didn't connect. He was screwing with her. A breeze from the leather thongs stirred the air around her face. His cologne mingled with his sweat as he walked around her, smacking the flogger. Each time, she flinched, knowing by his laughter that he enjoyed tormenting her. The man was boring her, but she did her best to appear subservient.

"Kneel," he ordered.

She hesitated, uncertain of what he was asking.

"Do you not understand a simple order? Kneel." He pressed her shoulder down until she was kneeling. "Hands and knees, crawl to the sound of my whip."

Oh, for God's sake. From the other side of the room, she heard the crack, turned toward the sound and crawled. She would rather have felt the pain than endure this humiliation, especially knowing this was being recorded.

"Don't drop the cock," he warned, laughing. Another crack several feet away. "Hurry, slave, crawl to me."

She'd had about enough of this bastard.

"I bet you'd like my cock in your mouth instead of that dildo."

She stopped crawling. Sex was not supposed to be part of this. He cracked the whip again, and she crawled quickly in the direction of the sound.

"Stop. I didn't tell you to come to me yet. Don't anticipate my instructions."

She bowed her head, but inside she was seething.

"Our time is almost up. I would need many more sessions to train you." He sighed. She wasn't sure if he was pleased or not, and frankly she didn't care. "Stand up," he said. She complied. He smacked her once on the butt. "A minor punishment for your error."

When she knew he was standing in front of her, she opened her mouth and spit the dildo out.

"What the?" he exclaimed.

She'd had enough. Behind her, Melissa and Faith gasped. "I'm sorry, sir. My jaw cramped, and it slipped."

Apparently, he didn't believe her. Kadir picked her up and sat down in a chair, tossing her over his knee, and began spanking her hard. It was more painful than the flogger or cane. Then he laughed. "You are a pain slut. You did that on purpose because you wanted to feel more pain." He sounded pleased not angry.

"Yes, sir." Gritting her teeth, she withstood the pain as much as she could. Finally, she called, "Red."

He struck her one more time, then stopped. "Had enough?"

"Yes, sir." A moment longer, and she would punch the guy. The AV guys had better have gotten this down, because she wasn't going another round with him. He helped her to her feet and removed the blindfold. Melissa strode over and draped a robe over her shoulders.

Kadir hooked a finger under her chin. "Look at me." He studied her for several moments and frowned. "Did you enjoy our encounter?"

She didn't break eye contact and nodded. Inside she instructed her mind to go calm and complacent. Her eyes couldn't show how she loathed him. The skill to control what her eyes revealed was not easy to learn. "Yes, I did. Did you, sir?"

"Very much. A shame our time is over. Too bad you don't speak Arabic. I would offer you a position on my staff. I could use an assistant educated on international law."

Zoe glanced at Faith, who gave her a puzzled look. Zoe had forgotten to tell her she had told Kadir she didn't speak Arabic. "A thoughtful offer."

Melissa sent a quick text. "I let Julia know our meeting is almost concluded. Would you care for something to drink while you wait for her, Mr. President?"

"No, but Zoe will have some." He smiled, then kissed her cheek. "You're shaking, my dear. Is the robe not warm enough? Sit." He led her over to the bed and pulled a blanket off a side table and covered her shoulders. Melissa approached, and Kadir held up his hand. "She's my responsibility. If I need assistance, I will ask."

Melissa nodded and backed off. "I'm fine, sir," Zoe said.

"An intense scene can leave you off balance for a few hours. Will you be going home alone?"

"No," Jason said. "She won't be alone."

Kadir's mouth tightened, and Melissa glared at Jason. Tyler took a step closer to Jason. Probably a warning and a reminder that he shouldn't be saying anything.

Kadir picked up a bottle of antiseptic lotion. "There are a few areas that need attending. Permit me." He pulled the blanket and robe off her shoulders and rubbed some of the salve into her skin. He leaned close to her ear and whispered, "After we're done, I want you to get me the recording and delete all the copies, Zoe Summers."

There was dead silence for a long moment. Cautiously, she looked up at him, fighting her rising panic. *Oh my God.*

He whispered in her ear, "Yes, you heard me." He stood straight and spoke louder for the others to hear. "A sore area? I think you need a bit more." Then lower, "If you don't, I will kill every member in this room and ship your brother, Damien, back home in several pieces."

She jerked away and stared up at him, fury boiling inside her. *Damien. The bastard had him.* She'd kill him before he left this room.

His eyebrows rose at her response. "Easy. Don't do anything that will harm your friends or brother," Kadir warned.

Her mind raced for options. If she didn't think fast, she'd have to blow this mission. "How do I know you have him?" She stared up at him defiantly.

Anger flared in his eyes. Obviously, he didn't like to be

230

challenged. He quickly composed himself. "He's fond of playing a computer word game with you, and you haven't heard from him in a while."

Zoe felt the hatred turn to fear. An image of Damien in an Iranian prison made her ill. She didn't dare try anything with all the lives at stake. "Where and when?" she asked through gritted teeth.

There was a knock on the outer door. "Julia's here, Mr. President," Melissa said.

"I'll contact you," Kadir whispered. "Now smile if you want to see your brother alive again."

She forced a smile but felt like she'd throw up.

"She's doing much better. Right, my dear?" He looked at Zoe, and she nodded, covering herself with the robe. Terror turned her bones to ice. If she got the recording, she was a traitor. If she didn't, everyone in the FLC and Damien would die. She had no doubt of Kadir's power.

Melissa gave Tyler the signal to unseal the door. He unlocked the inside door to the Red Tape Room, then the outer door. The sound of tape ripping made Zoe cringe. The X of red tape being torn away meant it was over, but not completely. She didn't lose her cool and punch him out, although she wanted to.

To the others, the mission was successful and Kadir seemed pleased. Now she understood why Alana had enjoyed watching their faces when the sting occurred. The blackmail was icing when you could see their defeat. This time it wouldn't happen.

Tyler stood beside the door as Julia and Blake entered. A few other Secret Service men waited outside. Jason hadn't moved or said another word. The mask hid his features so Zoe couldn't make out his expression.

"Hello, Mr. President," Julia said. "I do hope you enjoyed your evening."

"I did, very much, thank you." He didn't take his gaze off Zoe as she tied the robe around her.

Faith stepped up to Kadir, her mask off. "Mr. President,

I'm pleased you enjoyed our little private affair. I do apologize for rushing off. The president is waiting to leave."

"Not at all. I enjoyed your hospitality. Thank you."

After Faith left, Julia approached Kadir. "I'll escort you now to the entrance, where your car is waiting. Tonight you and your staff will be guests at the Kennedy Center of Performing Arts for a concert by the Iceland Symphony Orchestra."

"That's very kind," he said, striding toward the door. "Shall we go?"

"The president will make arrangements to meet with you when they return," Julia said. "This way, Mr. President."

Kadir took Zoe's hand and held it close to his lips but didn't touch. Back to his polite, business manner? "Again, it was a pleasure, Ms. Jennifer."

Julia looked pleased by Kadir's demeanor, and Zoe tried not to show her worry.

"Enjoy the symphony," Zoe said.

Julia and Blake left with Kadir, meeting with the other Secret Service agents outside. Tyler closed the door. No one said anything for the longest time. Melissa and Zoe picked up the clothing that had been tossed aside.

"How long do we have to wait before we can leave?" Zoe asked.

"Julia may want to meet with us briefly," Melissa said. "How did it go?"

"Good. I'm a little sore, thirsty, and I want to take a shower, but it went well."

"I knew it would. I think we got good footage. We'll know for sure in a few hours, and it'll take some time to edit."

"Fuck!" Jason shouted. The others turned to him.

"Relax, buddy, it's over," Tyler said.

"Sorry. I couldn't stand watching him with his hands on you," Jason snapped.

Zoe sighed. "It's aftercare, a Dom's responsibility. No big deal. It's over."

232

Ripping off his mask, Jason paced around the room. "He spent a long time at it."

"It doesn't matter," Melissa said. "I'm sure we got good material."

"He'll try to contact her. He wants her as his assistant." Jason spat out the words as if they were sour in his mouth. "He wants her in his harem or as a mistress, or whatever he has going on. We have to watch her."

"You know that's not going to happen," Zoe said. "Especially with the UN, Secret Service and the media watching him, he's not going to try anything."

"Have you forgotten what happened to Alana?" he shouted.

"Of course not," Melissa said. "Calm down, Jason. Alana got reckless, and she wasn't trained like Zoe. Extra men will be watching Kadir's every move."

He leaned up against the wall and nodded. At first Zoe thought he finally was calming down but then, *Boom!* He punched the wall with his left hand, leaving a fist-size hole.

"What the fuck, guy?" Tyler grabbed his arm.

"Jason!" Zoe ran across the room, but he held up a hand, stopping her from coming any closer. He was shutting her out again, like he did after Turkey. When things got rough, he pulled away from her. "Brilliant." She crossed her arms and glared at him. She hoped his hand hurt like hell.

"Take it easy. We won't let that bastard bother Zoe. Let me look at your hand." Tyler turned Jason's hand over and gently moved a couple of fingers. Jason sucked in a breath and cringed. "I think you broke it, buddy. It's already swollen and black and blue."

"Terrific." Jason pulled his hand away.

"Do we have ice?" Zoe asked. "I'll take him to the hospital. Let me clean up in the bathroom first."

Melissa shook her head. "No, let Tyler take him. Julia wants to meet with us in her office. Then you should go home and rest."

"Melissa's right. I could be stuck at the hospital for hours. It's a broken hand, not life or death." He held his injured hand against his chest as he walked up to her. "I'm sorry."

"We'll have someone follow her home," Melissa assured him. "Kadir will be at the Kennedy Center this evening, and then he'll be at his hotel. He's being watched. We'll give you two a minute." She grabbed Tyler's arm and led him outside.

Zoe was glad Jason hadn't asked for her to be with him, otherwise she would have had to make an excuse. Standing in the middle of the room, she felt her stomach churn all over again. Once she stole the recording and they figured out what she'd done, she could be charged with treason. But what choice did she have?

Whatever chance she and Jason had had was completely destroyed now. This went beyond the failed-mission definition. She feared speaking with her throat tightening. This was not the time to get emotional.

He took her hand, then studied her. "What's wrong? Are you okay? Zoe, you're shaking." His eyes were wide, searching her face, demanding an answer.

"I'll be better after a shower and some rest." She looked at her hands shaking. "It's the tension releasing. That's all."

"Sit." Directing her to a chair, he pulled a blanket around her and handed her a bottle of water. "Drink."

"Thanks." She took a few sips and took a deep breath, trying to get her body to relax. She didn't have time for this. They could be editing the recording, making copies, sending them who knew where.

He looked away and clenched his teeth. "Why did you wait so long before calling your safe word?"

Now he was criticizing her performance? "I was told he had an hour. The tape had to be good."

He let out a breath. "You're right. At least it's over."

"Are you okay with what I did?" she asked, turning the

attention to him. When he didn't answer, she continued. "This was only an act, like actors on a movie set. Some have to play love scenes. It has no consequence on our relationship."

"I know." He relaxed a little. Studying his hand, he tried bending his fingers. He flinched. "Damn, I really fucked up my hand. I screwed up a lot of things."

"It's history. It was a tough job. Now go to the hospital and get your hand looked at."

Supporting his injured arm, he leaned toward her, his eyes gentle with concern. "You did great. I think I'm getting the idea you can protect yourself."

"Thanks." Her body shook, but not from her recent activity with Kadir. "I like that you have my back."

He nodded. "I do. I know this type of work wreaks havoc on relationships."

She gently took his injured hand to examine it. "We can talk more, but get your hand fixed."

"I'll come over after I'm done." He grinned then, taking her awkwardly into his arms.

She laughed. "Okay. I'll leave a light on in case I fall asleep. You have a key."

Melissa walked into the room. "Julia said we can meet tomorrow. Go home, Zoe. Get some rest. But shower first. You still look a little subspacy."

"Have Frank take you home, to be safe," Jason added.

Zoe sighed. "Okay. Tell Frank I'll be up in a few minutes." She grabbed her small duffle bag and headed toward the ladies' room.

Zoe stared at her wrinkled fingers gripping the loofa, still shivering. The pinkie of her left hand bent at an odd angle. It hadn't healed properly after her torturers had broken it in Turkey. She was fortunate to have all her fingers. The steam and hot water from the shower enveloped her and turned her skin a rosy pink. She picked up the lavender shower gel and squeezed a healthy portion into the loofa and started from her shoulders down again. Kadir's scent was long gone, but not the memory of his touch. How many times did she have to scrub to wash away memories?

Memories took the longest to heal. She'd gone through the presentation for nothing. The bastard would never sign the treaty, now.

How would Jason look at her when he discovered the deal she'd made with Kadir? When they all found out? Would this make her a target for the FLC assassin like Celia? She didn't want to think about that.

She now understood why she and Jason had failed, and why this would never work between them. What relationship could survive something like this?

The door to the ladies' room opened. "Zoe? It's me, Melissa. Are you almost ready?"

She forced each word to be steady. "Just finishing up. Scrubbed clean." She tried to laugh and hoped it sounded real.

"Good. Frank is waiting."

Zoe cringed. "I screwed up, didn't I?" She shut off the water and grabbed the towel, rubbing herself with it so vigorously she thought she scrubbed off another layer of skin.

"A little defiant, but I think Kadir liked the challenge. Don't worry about it. Kadir was pushing you, testing your limits, but he wasn't as hard as I thought he'd be. It went well, and you did great."

Zoe sighed. "Thank God. He seemed pleased with the encounter." She finished dressing, touched up her makeup and started drying her hair.

"Frank said Kadir left. They had three limos, and Frank has agents following."

"Frank does take his security job seriously." Zoe packed up her bag and followed Melissa out of the restroom. The sooner Kadir got in touch with her, the better. If his people didn't have Damien, she wouldn't be doing this. "I'll meet you upstairs. I have a few things to get in my office. Tell Frank I'll be right there."

"Okay, but make it quick."

After she saw Melissa leave, she ran to her office, grabbed the key for the Mason Room and a thumb drive. Swiftly, she moved into the Mason Room and listened. Silence filled the room but didn't give her any confidence. Determination and thoughts of the consequences for not doing as Kadir asked pushed her forward. Shoving back the drapes, she crept toward the AV room. Inside the passage, she opened the door and noticed one man sitting at a computer.

"Hi," she said with an upbeat tone. "How'd the recording come out? I was the star, if you hadn't noticed." She smiled shyly.

He frowned, glancing behind her and from side to side. "Oh, yeah. Okay. It looks good. It needs some editing."

"Great. Can I take a peek?" She moved behind him and to one side.

As soon as he called up the video, he glanced at her. "Are you sure you want to watch?"

"A little, just to get an idea." She glanced around. "Lots of equipment. How many copies do you make?"

"We won't make any until editing is complete." He began the video in the middle of a portion of flogging. If this ever got out, she'd be mortified. What was Kadir going to do with it?

The video continued for a few moments. "Seen enough?" he asked.

"I think so, thanks." She rapped him hard on the side of the head, knocking him off the chair. Stunned, he tried to get up. She found a rag and gagged him, then used an extension cord to bind him. Hogtie formation. Even if he could scream, he wouldn't be heard. She inserted the thumb drive and copied the file. Then she did one more thing for insurance before deleting the file. The guy was breathing okay and was coming around. She'd only dazed him. He stared up at her in disbelief.

As she walked upstairs, Zoe checked her phone.

"Checking on Jason already?" Melissa asked. "He'll be fine."

"I know he will. I was checking to see if I'd heard from Damien. His mission was supposed to be only a couple of days, and he always sends a text when he gets back."

Melissa hooked her arm over Zoe's shoulder and gave a squeeze. "Go home and sleep late. The meeting isn't until noon tomorrow."

Chapter 25

Zoe arrived at her house after eight, completely exhausted but revved on adrenaline, knowing at any minute Kadir would contact her. She gave Frank a weak and wan smile. "Go home, Frank. I'll be fine."

He held his cell to his ear. "Let me check in with Blake and the team."

Zoe wouldn't open the door. If she did, she'd have to invite him in, and Frank might decide to wait for Jason. She couldn't take that chance.

"Still at the Kennedy Center. Great. Don't let him out of your sight. I want to know when he leaves and when he's back at his hotel. And watch his men." He hung up and looked at Zoe. "I should wait until Jason gets here."

"No, really, I'm fine. I have an alarm and several guns in my house."

"But Alana, and what about the mole—"

Zoe lowered her voice, not that her neighbors could hear. "Alana was killed because she was reckless and she wasn't a former intelligence agent. Kadir hasn't even seen the recording yet."

He let out a breath. "All right. If you need anything, just call."

"Thanks, Frank." She pulled her cell phone out and sent Jason a text. "I just told Jason I made it home." She didn't tell Frank she'd told Jason she would change clothes, and then meet him at the hospital.

Frank nodded and waited until she unlocked the door. He jogged down the steps, got into his car and pulled away.

As she stepped inside, she did the puppy sniff. The first thing she smelled was roses. She dropped her purse and keys on the foyer table. Mrs. Snyder must've let the delivery guy in. Jason had probably sent them to ease her mind about her presentation. She smiled, and her heart soared, then her gut twisted.

How long would it be until the AV guy was found? She closed and locked the door.

She had no choice. He'd have to understand. All she wanted was something to eat and to curl up in bed. She checked her phone. No messages. She slipped it back in her jeans pocket next to the thumb drive.

As she entered the kitchen, she switched on a light and gasped. A huge bouquet stood in a crystal vase on her island. A note next to them was from Mrs. Snyder.

These came this evening. How nice. Dexter walked and fed.

She picked out the small envelope from the bouquet to read the note. Had Jason written something personal? She stopped.

Dexter.

Where was he? He usually raced to the door whenever she got home. She heard a whimper. Her dog. He hadn't greeted her. She sniffed again and smelled something else.

Drifting in the air was the pungent smell of cigarette smoke. Jason didn't smoke. And neither did Mrs. Snyder. She froze, and an icy chill slithered up her spine.

Walking into the living room, she turned on the light. Kadir sat in a chair, puffing on a cigarette. Dexter sat on his lap. Kadir's fist gripped Dexter around the throat. A 9mm rested on the end table, next to a teacup. After taking another drag on the cigarette, he snuffed it out in the cup and picked up the gun. She took in a long, slow breath and tried to calm her racing pulse. Her mind clicked through several options for action, for escape, and she knew she had none. Not with Damien's life at stake.

A surge of adrenaline made her heart pound in her ears, and a metallic taste coated her mouth. All her weapons were out of reach. One in the coffee table, one in the bedroom, another in the kitchen and one hidden behind the sink in the bathroom. How fast could she make it to the door? It was locked and chained. Even if he didn't shoot her, he could grab her before she got out.

"Aren't you going to miss the concert?" Zoe asked as calmly as she could. A shuffle behind her sent another rush through her. Kadir hadn't come alone. Glancing over her shoulder, she nodded to the man who had been with him earlier. "Good evening," she said. If Secret Service was watching Kadir, why hadn't they followed him to her house? Hadn't they seen him leave the Kennedy Center or his hotel? Thoughts of Alana's murder flashed in her mind. If Kadir didn't kill her, the assassin surely would now.

Kadir's bodyguard didn't acknowledge her in anyway.

"I'm not missing the concert." He grinned. "When you have as many enemies as I do, it's a good idea to have a double. Someone who can be seen in public when I want to go to other places discreetly."

"When my brother's released, and I talk to him, I'll give you what you want," she said.

"We'll get to that. I wanted to make a formal offer of employment," he said. "I mentioned I needed someone with your background in international law. I pay well. Fifteen thousand American dollars a month, and you'd live in a luxury apartment. But I expect a two-year commitment."

Was he serious? The man had to be out of his mind. Was this how he got his sex slaves? Offer them a legitimate job they couldn't refuse? "I like my current job, thank you." She was careful not to reveal too much contempt in her words, considering her situation. "I don't appreciate people walking into my house uninvited."

Kadir laughed. "You consider this an invasion of privacy then?" He raised his voice as he gestured with the gun.

"Yes, I do." She whistled. "Dexter, go lie down." She pointed to his bed. Her dog perked up and squirmed on Kadir's lap, but he was quick and wrapped his hand around Dexter's throat again. The dog whimpered. It took all her courage not to show fear.

"He's fine right here. And don't scream. I'd hate to have to kill your dog, your next-door neighbor, and anyone else who decided to come out to see the commotion."

She took a breath. "First you offer me a job. Now you're threatening me?" Her cell was in her back pocket, but she didn't dare reach for it now. Somehow, she needed to leave it where Jason would find it. One way or another, Kadir was walking out of here with the thumb drive and probably taking her with him to make her his sex slave. Boldly, she walked around the sofa and sat. As she did, she smoothed her hands over her jeans and slid the phone between the seat cushions, hoping he didn't notice.

Anger flared in his dark eyes. "Did I give you permission to sit?" he snarled. Knocking Dexter off his lap, Kadir shot to his feet and charged over to Zoe. Grabbing her by the hair, he dragged her off the couch. "Kneel." The gun was in his other hand.

She bowed her head in a submissive pose. "Yes, sir."

He sighed, calming down. Let the man with the gun think he had all the power, and he'd lower his guard. "It takes discipline to keep women in their proper place. As my mother obeyed my father."

She should've resisted responding, but she couldn't. "I have no problem with women respecting their husbands as long as the respect is returned. How many wives do you have?"

Kadir was silent, and she wondered if she'd pushed too hard. She was stalling. "I have one."

"How does she feel about your slaves? You must have dozens."

He smacked her on the side of her face, knocking her to the floor. The salty taste of blood filled her mouth. "A woman who speaks like this should be beaten."

"I may not understand your culture and religious beliefs. I can respect them, accept the differences, but abuse is abuse no matter how you try to label it or justify it."

He smiled evilly. Maybe he'd rather kill her than have her as his slave after what she tried to do to him. The only chance she had was to run for the kitchen door, knock over the vase of flowers on her way out and hope he'd miss when he started to shoot.

The plan set in her mind, she took a breath and leaped for the kitchen, swinging punches at the guard as she ran. The guard, skilled in martial arts, knocked her down and left her gasping for air. Kadir scolded him for being rough. He patted her down and took the thumb drive. When she was breathing normally again, she noticed she'd given the man a bloody nose. Little consolation.

Kadir picked up a small case he had on the floor, took out a netbook computer and uploaded the thumb drive. After a few minutes, she heard his voice and hers. His eyes widened. "Entertaining. I'll add this to my collection," he said. "A sophisticated system. I would expect that." He turned off the computer and slipped the thumb drive into his pocket.

"You have what you want. What about my brother?"

"I'm taking you to your brother," Kadir said, laughing.

"My brother isn't in Washington."

"He's in Iran," he said. "As you will be soon."

"You have what you want. I deleted the original copy. I'm not going to be your private slave." She had to keep thinking. Remember she was a lawyer, not CIA. If he found that out, they'd torture her for information and then kill her.

"My slaves are very loyal. They're educated, intelligent and beautiful. They please me in many ways. When they don't please me, I punish them. If they betray me…I'm sure you won't betray me."

"As soon as I get outside, people will see me, hear me."

Kadir picked up Dexter by the throat. The dog yelped. Reaching her arms out, she tried to get to him, but the guard held her back. "Let him go."

"After I kill your dog, I'll kill your neighbor and burn down these townhouses. And don't forget your brother. So, my little slave, will you come with me?"

"Fine."

"Excuse me? Is that how you answer your master?"

Her stomach roiled. "Yes, sir," she spat out between clenched teeth.

Kadir put Dexter down, and the dog curled up, shaking, in his bed.

"Better. Now, say, 'Thank you, Master, for not killing me.'" He held the gun to Zoe's head.

Hot and cold slithered up her skin. This was it. He was going to kill her. *Jason.* So much she wanted to tell him. She loved him and had never had the chance to tell him. And Damien. She couldn't help him either. Her throat constricted, and tears burned in her eyes.

"Say it," he ordered.

"Thank you, Master, for not killing me." She held her breath and waited for the click.

He put the gun down. "See, slave? I can be a forgiving Master."

The guard stood behind her and rested his hand on her shoulder. The sharp prick of a needle jabbed into her neck was unexpected. All her muscles went limp, and her vision blurred. Then everything went black.

* * *

It was well after midnight by the time Jason signed out of the hospital. The doctor had given him an envelope of pain meds to hold him over until he could get his prescription filled. A temporary cast supported his hand, but it throbbed and hurt like hell after all the probing and X-rays. The X-rays had shown two small fractures. He had an appointment to see an orthopedic doctor in the morning.

"You want me to drive you?" Tyler asked. "Didn't they give you something for the pain?"

Jason held up the small yellow envelope. "I haven't taken any yet. I will when I get to Zoe's." He took out his phone and checked his messages. "No frigging service in hospitals. We

might as well be in the middle of the jungle."

"It works in the lobby. I've checked in with Secret Service, and Kadir is at his hotel now."

On the way out the door, Jason's phone buzzed with messages. Zoe had sent a text a couple of hours ago. "Something's wrong."

"What is it?" Tyler asked.

"Zoe said she changed her mind and was coming to the hospital to wait for me. The text was over an hour ago."

Tyler stopped walking. "We'll take my car. It'll be faster."

Both his and Tyler's phone buzzed.

Before they reached the street where Frank had directed them, they saw a plume of smoke swirl up in a night sky illuminated by city lights. Emergency lights from several fire trucks and police cars flickered across the buildings and stopped traffic. The area was blocked off by police. Flames and black smoke billowed out of the windows of a small hybrid car. It couldn't be Zoe's.

"God, no, no, no." Jason jumped out of the car before Tyler stopped. He ran to the scene and was stopped by police. Jason identified himself and showed his ID. He ran to the ambulance. The gurney was there but no body. He stared back at the car. "Where is she?" he shouted at a police officer blocking his path.

The heat singed his skin, and the smoke reeked of oil and rubber. The firemen doused the flames, and a ball of black smoke billowed into the sky. Two policemen ordered a crowd of onlookers to get back. Frank came over and stood in front of Jason. "Hold on. We don't know yet if she was in there." Frank made a call on his cell while remaining a barricade to Jason. "I've sent security to her house."

Jason nodded, unable to take his gaze away from the car. *Please don't let her be in there.*

Once the smoke cleared, firemen pried the trunk open.

He held his breath as he waited for confirmation. The fireman slammed the trunk down. Jason let his breath out. Several firemen used pry bars to open the doors. If they didn't say something soon, he'd kick the crap out of them.

"No one's in the car," the fire chief announced. The man smiled. He had no idea what that meant. The news was brief comfort, though. If not here, then where? She was in danger.

Jason and Frank exchanged glances. "Where the hell is she?" Jason asked.

"We'll start at her house."

"Send someone to Kadir's hotel and his private jet," Jason added. "Do not allow that jet to take off."

"An all points bulletin has already gone out," Frank said. "We'll question Kadir and start looking for her. If he abducted her, they couldn't have gone far."

When they got to Zoe's house, Dexter bowed his head low and whimpered when Jason approached him. He picked him up. "She's not here either, but I bet someone was. Her dog is shaking. He never does this."

Frank's phone rang, and he answered it. "At the hotel? Has no idea? Yeah, right. Thanks." He gave Jason a worried look. "Kadir's at his hotel, getting ready to leave the country. His jet is still at the airport. The plane was searched. Zoe isn't there. She's vanished.

"Kadir was at the Kennedy Center all night with his aides," Frank went on. "We had him watched all night. He couldn't have left."

Tyler entered the townhouse. "We've questioned the neighbor. She said a man delivered flowers around six, and she let him in but watched him leave."

"Kadir must've hired someone to leave a window open or the back door unlocked," Frank said, making a face. "But how did he do it so fast?"

"Unless he planned it before he even got here," Jason said. "Did the neighbor see a delivery truck?"

Tyler nodded. "And later she saw a black sedan sitting out front. She thought it had to do with Zoe's work so ignored it."

Frank's phone buzzed, and he answered it. He swore after talking to the person. "Is he okay? Good. This changes things. I'll let you know." He rubbed his forehead then ended the call.

"What?" Jason asked.

"The AV guy for the Red Tape Room was knocked out. He said it was Zoe. The video has been erased."

"Fuck. Why the hell would she do this?" Jason placed his hands on his head. Another mission screwed, and Zoe might die this time. It was his fault for getting her into this.

"Any chance she made a copy for Kadir?" Frank asked.

"For what purpose?" Jason paced her living room with Dexter at his heels. He stopped.

"He found out about the recording and threatened her?" Tyler suggested. "He threatened to kill her like Alana was killed."

"Damien," Jason said. "Her brother's in Iran. Kadir must have him."

Frank started making a call. "I'll ask General Guzman to look into it. I'll have to let Rowland and Julia know. She probably compromised the mission and the FLC."

"She didn't," Jason argued. "Whoever the mole is did."

Frank got another call. When he was done, he explained to Jason. "Johnny Vargas is at the airport. Kadir is making a stink about being delayed. We can't hold him."

"We're wasting time." Jason had to keep his focus. "She can't be far. If Kadir doesn't have her hidden at the airport, he had someone else take her." Jason was reliving a nightmare. He had sworn this would never happen again if they got out of Langley. "Fuck!"

"Why would the bastard want the recording? I can understand him wanting it destroyed. And why take Zoe?" Tyler gripped his shoulder. "Why go through the scene at all if you know you're being recorded?"

Frank and Jason stared at each other, and reality clicked at the same time by the look in Frank's eyes. "Could Kadir have been planning this before the Red Tape Room?" Jason asked. "He met Zoe at the welcome reception, and he danced with her. The guy has his secret harem of slaves. What if he planned to take Zoe all along as his sex slave? When he learned about Red Tape, he decided he could use that against the US." Jason swore and gripped the back of the couch.

"Kadir wouldn't use the recording," Frank argued. "You all wear masks anyway, right?"

Tyler shook his head. "The unedited tape might have the participants without masks and clips of the first lady in the room. She brought him in and escorted him out. If Kadir has that copy, he has a high-resolution video of the first lady in a BDSM dungeon."

"When Kadir's slaves stop pleasing him, he sells them to white traders or kills them," Jason said, more to himself. How good of an actor could Zoe be and for how long?

"Easy, man. We'll find her."

Flashing blue and red lights from outside lit up the living room. There was a knock at the door. Tyler stayed with Jason while Frank went to the door. "We have company. We'll coordinate our efforts with local and state authorities, get her photo out there."

Frank checked his watch. "Just after midnight, so she's been missing at least four hours." He patted Jason on the back. "She was CIA. She's smart and trained."

Jason shot Frank a look. "I know. That's not why I'm worried. It's the moment they find out she's former CIA."

***

Zoe forced open her eyes, but she couldn't focus. Shadows swam in her view, and her stomach roiled. *Please don't be sick. Think logically.*

Her mind and thoughts kept drifting, and all she wanted to do was curl up and sleep. Her mind floated through the shad-

ows. Dreaming. She was dreaming she was in her bed, and Jason had his arm around her.

No. Wake up.

Forcing her eyes open again, she tried to stare at one point across the room until her vision cleared.

The room came into view. It was rectangular, no windows. A four-foot fluorescent light hung ten feet above her. The room was probably around fifteen or twenty feet long. A storage area or basement of some kind? The small mattress beneath her lay on the floor, and a blanket covered her. At least they wanted her somewhat comfortable.

Sitting up made her head spin, and she waited until the nausea passed. Her muscles felt sore and weak. From the drugs and partly from her encounter with Kadir? How long ago was that? She had no sense of time of day. Listening, she heard mechanical equipment and felt a vibration. Metal studs framed the room. Even the floor appeared metal. Maybe she was in the basement of a building, near a boiler room. When she tried to stand, the tug on her left arm caught her off balance, and she fell back on the mattress.

What the hell? Handcuffs clamped around her left wrist, attached by a length of chain to a thick eyebolt in the center of the room. She yanked on it but knew it wouldn't give. Testing the length, she walked from one end to the other, where there was a door with a sliding latch bolt. Probably locked. It didn't matter since she couldn't reach it.

Inside the room, she found boxes with bottled water, protein bars and apples. Under a tarp was a Porta John with toilet paper. Oh joy. They expected to keep her here awhile, several days by the supplies.

She rubbed her neck where Kadir's man had jabbed her with the needle. It was still sore, and she felt dizzy walking. Maybe from lack of food and water. No telling how long she had been out. The bottled water looked sealed, untampered with, and the protein bars looked okay, too, as far as she could tell. She tasted a small piece of a bar and drank some water. Her throat was so parched she could hardly swallow. Dehydration would kill her before anything else.

After she ate a couple of bars and drank more water, she felt better, but her head still swam a bit. The aftereffects of the drug they'd used on her might take days to wear off. Did Jason and the FLC have any idea she was missing? They must by now and know what she'd done. But did they have any idea where she was? If she was still in Washington, she wouldn't know. She couldn't hear truck or car traffic outside. Except for the boilers, she couldn't hear anything. And Damien…would a madman keep his word?

First thing she had to do was get out of the handcuffs. They hadn't taken her hoop earrings. She removed one, bent it straight and poked at the latch. After several tries, the lock released. Rubbing her wrist, she marched straight for the door and tried the metal latch. It wouldn't budge. It was held by riveted bolts. Unlikely she'd be able to pry them loose. The walls around the door had a fine covering of insulation. A cool breeze flowed through. She ripped at the spongy material and found a louver vent underneath. The vent appeared new compared to the dirty walls. Had they been expecting her company and didn't want her to suffocate? After taking the other handcuff off the chain, she used the edge as a screwdriver and took off the covering. A few feet in front was another metal wall. This had to be some kind of storage unit, a shed or a room in a warehouse.

She climbed out, figuring once she escaped she'd run until she found a public place. Outside, she breathed in fresh air that had an odd smell. With any luck, she'd find a gas station or a road where she could stop a trucker or get to a phone, *something*. She'd contact Jason and let him know she was okay. Had they realized she was missing yet?

It was dark, but a strange light shone from above. She stood outside her prison, looking up into a night sky. A brilliant moon and stars. She took a breath and relaxed a little. Thank

God, she was outside. Her prison had been a storage unit, and another one stood a few feet in front of her. In the dim light, she saw rows of them. She crept around the corner of her unit and froze. Zoe's lungs constricted as she tried to breathe. Blinking several times, she wondered if she was hallucinating, then wished she was.

A whimper came to her lips. As far as she could see, in every direction, she was surrounded by water. She was on a freighter ship in the middle of the ocean. The reality of her situation careened through her mind. A gust of wind swept over her, and her teeth chattered. She wasn't wearing a jacket, only the dress blouse and slacks she had on when she left the White House. Flashes of memories shot through her mind. Kadir with Dexter on his lap, her handing him the thumb drive, Kadir hitting her, pain in her neck, darkness and voices, then nothing. Her body shook violently now, from the cold and the anger at what she knew Kadir had planned for her. She might be going a little shocky, too, so she needed to find warmth. She rubbed her arms. The damp sea air coated her skin.

Standing along the railing of the ship, she had a better view of the stacks and rows of storage containers. Her prison was at the bottom of a tower of other containers with several towers side by side. There must be hundreds or over a thousand containers on board. The mechanical noise she'd heard was the freighter's engines. Since she couldn't see lights on the coastline, the ship had to be at least forty miles offshore. Even if she could get a cell phone, she wouldn't have service. But these ships did have Internet connections and a radio.

What kind of deal had Kadir made with the men in charge of the freighter? She had to assume they knew she was on board as private cargo. How much had he paid for her passage? Passage to where?

Survival mode kicked in as she considered her resources and options. *Assess the situation and make a plan. Determine her location and direction and communicate with her team, or anyone who could rescue her.*

As she crept along the deck toward the bridge at the stern, she tried to find something that told her what ship she was on. Lifeboats bore the words *Cape Sienna*. Spotlights shone onto a large blue smokestack with an orange S on the side. Far in the distance she saw lights on the water. An island? It was a cruise ship moving away at an angle and fast. Too far away to be of any help. The sky was partially clear, and by the stars, she estimated she was heading east. Even this much information wouldn't make it easy for them to find her.

Examining one of the lifeboats, she checked out the rigging and crane work. Then she looked over the port side. Even in the dark, she could see that a white wake churned along the hull of the ship. It was moving too fast to attempt to drop the lifeboat, even if she could operate the crane.

Footsteps on deck made her jump. She ducked behind a stairway, hiding in the shadows. A crewman walked up the deck, making his rounds, she assumed. She made her way toward the bow in the opposite direction, opened a door and went inside. Climbing stairs, she listened and peered around the doorway to the next level. The hallway was empty for the moment. She had no idea what time it was. Was the crew having dinner or asleep? She crept up the stairs to the top level, where the bridge was, and noticed two men in the control room, one at a wheel steering and another at a control panel. The radio was above the man steering the ship. The chances of her fighting off both men before she could get a call out and the rest of the crew stormed in weren't good. Sweat rolled down her neck, and she shivered as a gust of wind blew through the open windows.

She was on a ship full of men, and she had no weapons and very little nautical knowledge, nowhere to run. She was from Ohio, so she knew her way around forests and farms, not boats. Quietly, she backed up and returned down the metal steps. From one level, she heard voices. She traversed the passage and peeked into a crew dining area and lounge. Four men were sitting around a table playing cards and drinking something alcoholic by the looks of the amber liquid. Another man, stretched out on a sofa, was sound asleep. An old shark horror movie played in the background. A computer was set up on a desk in the corner, but she'd never get to it with those men in the way. A clock on the wall said one thirty. Good, the rest of the crew must be asleep. But how many?

Someone ran up another set of stairs. Zoe waited, unsure which way to go. Then another person ascended from the other side. Trapped. She was frozen in fear, her heart pounding so hard she swore they could hear it. They had to know she was here, or missing from her container prison. She had to move, fight, run, something, anything. She shifted along the bulkhead until she reached a door, opened it and slipped inside, closing the door behind her.

Listening, she waited. The two men talked, but she couldn't hear what they were saying. Then they continued down the hall.

"Hey, where did you come from?" a man's voice said from behind her.

A chill frizzled up her back. She turned around inside the small stateroom. A young guy with wavy, black hair and who looked barely twenty lay on a bunk bed, a laptop propped across his thighs.

"Sorry to barge in," she said. "I guess I got the wrong room. You get Internet on that?" Zoe pointed to his computer.

"Hey." He sat up and frowned. "You're not crew, and I didn't see you board. Stowaway?" He grinned, amused.

Zoe smiled and shrugged. Good, maybe all the crew didn't know she was Kadir's prisoner.

"I won't tell." He gave her a suggestive grin. "You can stay here." He patted the bed beside him.

Terrific. His price for silence.

"Thanks, appreciate that," she said sweetly. "May I?" She indicated the computer.

"What do you want with it?"

"I want to contact my friends, let them know I'm on my way. I have a backpack hidden in a storeroom." She frowned. "I shouldn't go out for it now. Someone might see me."

He rolled his eyes. "I'll get it for you later." He handed her his computer. "Make it quick, then get on over here."

"Thanks." She propped the computer on the tiny sink so he couldn't see the screen and started typing like a maniac.

"So why did you stow away? Running away from a boyfriend? Husband? Did he give you that black eye?" the guy asked with disdain.

Zoe glanced in the mirror over the sink. Her hair was mussed, and dark circles rimmed her eyes. Her right cheek was slightly swollen and black and blue. Hanging her head, she tried covering her cheek with her hair. "Boyfriend. He said he'd kill me next time. I had to get away."

He grimaced and brushed back her hair. "What a bastard. Does it hurt? Are you hungry?"

She touched it. "A little. And yes to hungry. That's sweet of you." *Gain an ally, good. Play along, but don't overdo it.* She hoped she didn't have to kill him. He was barely a kid and probably had no idea that this ship was carrying an abducted slave. What else could be in the containers? Typing in the Skype number, she held her breath, waiting for the connection. "I'll be quick."

She heard angry shouts from down the hall and running up or down metal steps.

The connection was taking forever to go through.

Hurry, hurry.

Chapter 26

Jason sat at Zoe's kitchen table, staring into a cup of cold coffee. Dexter lay at his feet. The dog hadn't left his side since she'd gone missing. A hand rested on his shoulder. "You've been up over thirty hours. Get some rest. The second I hear anything, I'll call you." Frank had been in touch will all the authorities, and there hadn't been anything concrete reported.

"What about Guzman?" Jason asked. "Did he get anything out of Kadir? I know the bastard knows where she is. What about her brother?"

"Diplomatic immunity prevents us from doing much. It's not been confirmed that Damien's team is being held, but he's missing. Usually, if terrorists have them, they like to send video with demands. They like the publicity. That hasn't happened," Frank said with a grim smile. "It could be a good sign or bad. Hard to say."

Jason rubbed his face. The weight of this disaster dragged him down where he barely had the will to breathe. "Any idea what happened?"

Frank made a face. "We've lost communication, and they missed their evac point. Could mean they had a change of plans."

He looked up at Frank and shook his head. "It's been over twenty-four hours. You know what that means with an abduction case."

"Jason, she's alive. Kadir wants her. She's White House staff but also CIA. General Guzman will authorize whatever military action necessary to get her back."

"A lot of good it will do if we don't know where she is." Jason got up and filled Dexter's water dish, then made another pot of coffee. "Want some coffee?"

Frank paced the room. He pointed to the bedroom. "Close your eyes for one hour. Tyler is going to take over here by then. I'll wake you if I hear anything."

Jason nodded, finally agreeing. His phone buzzed, a different tune. Not a phone call or text. Someone was trying to Skype him.

"Frank!" Jason waved to Frank as he answered the Skype. The screen opened up, and Zoe was there, her hair disheveled, eyes wide.

"Jason? You there?" she whispered.

"My God. Zoe, where are you? You okay?"

She glanced over her shoulder. He heard voices in the background. "They're coming. They know I got out."

"Where?" He gripped the phone so hard, he was afraid it might crack.

She took a breath. "Freight ship, *Cape Sienna*, heading east. We passed a cruise ship about an hour ago."

"What cruise line?"

"Don't know." She looked away from the screen. A male voice in the background asked her a question. "Talking to friends," she answered the guy.

"Who's there with you?"

"I'm Alex," the guy answered, chuckling. "Who are you?"

Jason ignored him. "Zoe, anything else you can tell us?"

"I don't know. Kadir uses doubles. He has Damien." She turned to the guy. "Alex, what port are we heading to?" The voices in the background were now yelling.

Jason clearly heard, "The bitch has got to be here somewhere." Then pounding on a door. He saw the face of a man, not Alex, and then the screen went blank.

Jason called up a Web site that showed the locations for all ships, trading vessels, private boats and fishing boats currently out to sea. Satellites used onboard GPS instruments to track the ships. He punched in a search for *Cape Sienna*.

"Where?" Frank yelled. He started punching in a phone number then stopped.

"Couple hours out in the Atlantic. Destination is Port of Valencia, Spain. They left out of Norfolk. Why aren't you calling

the Coast Guard or FBI?"

"What about the mission? The FLC? Won't we risk exposure?" Frank asked.

"Are you crazy? Screw the mission and the FLC. We're getting her back."

Frank rubbed his forehead and pressed his lips together. "What about the assassin? No one in the FLC knows who he is, but his primary job is to eliminate any threat of exposure."

Jason's body went rigid. His firearm was at his hip. Could he reach it in time if he needed it? Frank was armed, too. "Am I a threat?"

Frank shrugged. "It's something to consider. I don't know if the assassin would consider you or Zoe a threat, or me, if I helped."

Jason glared at Frank. "Zoe's a White House employee who has been abducted by a man known to have connections with terrorists and human trafficking. That's all we have to tell authorities. And she was CIA."

Nodding, Frank raised his phone and started calling.

* * *

"How did you get out?" a big man with dark hair and Middle Eastern accent asked Zoe.

Two other men stood in the hallway. They didn't have weapons. Perhaps the weapons were locked up and only the captain and supervisor had access. On the long trans-Atlantic voyages, lots of alcohol probably passed the time, so easy access to guns was not a good idea. The man turned to Alex. "Why didn't you report her?"

"Who is she? I thought she was a stowaway running from her boyfriend. Who hit her?"

Zoe took that opportunity to slam her foot onto the big man's instep, elbow his ribs, swing around and with the heel of her hand smash his nose. The sound of the crunch and his yells told her she had been on target. With the same momentum, she took out one guy's kneecap, and as he went down, she chopped the other guy's windpipe. With the three men gasping and screaming in pain, she ran. But where? How long would it take until Jason found her? Could she barricade herself inside somewhere? Would the name of the ship be enough?

Running up the stairs to a higher level, she looked for a pipe or something she could use for a weapon. Sooner or later, the captain would get the guns out. She'd be captured unless she could hole up somewhere. She tried several metal doors, and they were either locked or led to larger areas. No place to run, no place to hide.

Voices and footsteps were close behind. As she charged through one doorway, a man grabbed her. She fought, using martial arts and crazed-woman punches and fingernails. The guy released her. As she started to turn around, someone slammed her between the shoulder blades, knocking the wind out of her and shoving her down a flight of stairs. As she tumbled, her elbows, knees and head banged all the way down. At the bottom, she was too stunned and in pain to move. She wasn't sure if she'd broken anything.

Someone stepped on her arm. It hurt, bad. The barrel of an AR-15 pressed against her temple. "You done?" Another man—stocky, dark, bearded—glared down at her.

She nodded.

"Get up," he ordered. He got off her arm.

She rolled to her knees and tried to stand. Her head spun, but thankfully, she didn't think she had any—

"Ahhh," she cried out in pain and grabbed her left forearm. Already, the swelling had started, and discoloration had formed around her wrist.

"Serves you right if you broke it," he said. "Help her to the bridge. We may get company if her call got through."

"Alex, did she get a message through?" the stocky, bearded guy asked. Zoe suspected he was the captain by his authoritative tone and uniform.

Alex glanced at Zoe. He stuffed his hands in his jeans pockets. "I don't know. The Internet can be slow, and you all were yelling."

"What did she tell you?" the captain asked, his patience long gone.

"She was running away from a boyfriend and meeting friends. That's it."

The captain stared at him for a while to decide if he was telling the truth. "Changing course won't do any good. We can be tracked. We don't have enough fuel, and we have deliveries." He swore and rubbed his beard. "Expect company. I was given her transport papers if we ran into trouble. Kadir had a backup plan."

The medic on board gave Zoe something for the pain and immobilized her arm with a splint and bandage. She heard the captain comment that Kadir would be furious when he saw her condition. They gave her a blanket, pillow and some warm food. But they wouldn't let her out of their sight. It was obvious that keeping her alive was important. They didn't want to disappoint Kadir.

Zoe dozed off, from exhaustion and probably from the pain meds. When she woke, it was dawn. The sky had an orange hue, and the sea looked dark and rough. *Red in the morning, sailors take warning.* After they fed her some oatmeal and coffee, she was feeling better, but the pain in her arm returned.

"Captain, we have company," the man at the helm said, looking through binoculars. "And it's not the Coast Guard." There were five men on the bridge, and they all had automatic weapons. She estimated there were about fifteen men on board. They were probably strategically posted throughout the ship.

"It's too fast for the Coast Guard. Who the hell is it?" the captain asked.

"No, sir. It's a Navy vessel. They signaled for us to stop engines and hold position."

The captain gave a grunt. "The Navy has no right to hold

us up."

"Order from the Coast Guard, they said," the crewman amended. "I think they have more firepower on that ship than we have in automatic weapons."

"Fuck. Hold position," the captain said. He punched the chair he was standing behind. The Navy vessel approached and circled the freight ship like a giant, gray shark.

Zoe felt the butterflies waking up in her gut. They'd found her.

The distant sound of helicopter blades in the dawn stillness was a welcoming sound. She didn't make eye contact with the freighter's crew.

"Coast Guard vessel off port bow," the crewman with the binoculars announced. "And two helicopters."

"Take her below. Have the doc stay with her," the captain ordered.

"Captain," Zoe said, trying to reason with him. "Think of your cargo and your men. Turn me over and face a few fines. Claim you weren't aware I was trapped in one of those containers."

He narrowed his eyes. "You were my cargo, my most valuable merchandise, and now you're my hostage." He turned to Alex. "Get her off the bridge."

As Alex led her out, she overheard the other crewman ask the captain, "Who the hell is she? You said someone's spoiled daughter who ran away."

"Nevermind who she is," the captain said. "I want the crew positioned around the ship. No one is getting on."

Alex had a firm grip on her right arm as he pulled her through the narrow passageways toward the infirmary, where the doctor had checked her arm, rewrapped it and given her an ice pack. Alex's face was stern and confused. "You lied to me," he spat out.

"I didn't know who I could trust."

He glanced at her suspiciously. "You could've told me."

"That I was abducted? For the white-slave trade or worse?"

His jaw dropped, and he stopped walking. "Is that was this is? No lie?"

"It's more involved, but yes. It's true. The Coast Guard will board this vessel, and crew members who resist will face criminal charges and jail."

He groaned and shook his head. "Man, I don't want to do jail time. This is bad."

"Then help me. How can I get a weapon?"

He looked up and down the passageway before speaking. "I have a gun in my cabin. We're not supposed to, but I have one."

When they got to Alex's cabin, the *rat-tat-tat* of automatic rifles sounded above them on deck. Then footsteps raced down the passageway by Alex's room. More shots.

"Stay here," Zoe said as he handed her the small pistol.

"No kidding. I'm not going out there."

"I'll let them know you helped me."

She eased the door open a crack and peered out. The passage was empty for the moment. The silence made her more nervous. Blood pumped in her ears, and she could taste the adrenaline in her dry mouth. Stepping out into the hall, she ran for the stairway leading to the bridge. The only sound was two helicopters. A chill crept over her skin. Was everyone dead?

When she came out on deck, she saw ten crew members kneeling on the ground, hands on their heads, and two armed Coast Guard officers standing over them. On the bridge, the captain and his first officer had their hands secured behind their backs as two other Coast Guard officers talked to them. Was it over? Did they have everyone?

"Ms. Summers? I don't think you'll need that anymore." The voice was so familiar, she thought her heart would burst wide open. She spun around to see Jason standing next to two helicopter crewmen wearing headgear.

"Jason," she barely breathed his name as she ran into his

arms.

"I'll take that, ma'am. Just to be safe." One of the officers gently took the pistol out of her hand.

Jason held her back, kissed her quick, and tears dampened his cheeks. "Thank God." He squeezed her close and kissed her hair. "I thought I lost you."

"How did you get on board with all the armed men on deck?" she asked.

Jason and the Coast Guard guys laughed. One of the guys tilted his head. "Take a look behind you. We didn't need the help, but a little persuasion made the job easier."

Zoe looked over her shoulder and gasped. The Navy vessel, a huge warship, was so close she could see the men smiling and waving on deck. All the giant cannons were pointing directly at *Cape Sienna*. "Whoa."

"As soon as the Navy moved in and started moving those guns around, the crew put their weapons down. Even though the Navy had no intention of firing, the crew didn't have to be told twice."

"The Navy was bored and welcomed an excuse to play with their guns," the officer said.

Zoe rolled her eyes. "Hey, there's a guy in his cabin, a kid named Alex. He helped me. That's his gun. He had no idea about my abduction."

The officer nodded. "We're going to take you back, ma'am. You injured your arm?"

Jason lifted her left arm. "What happened?" He also touched her cheek and grimaced. "I can imagine. What does the other guy look like?"

"Pretty bad. He just lost his ship."

"Someone will take the ship into port where authorities will deal with it," the Coast Guard officer said.

Jason's arm came around her shoulder, and she leaned against him as he walked her to the waiting helicopter. "I screwed up another mission, didn't I?"

He shushed her. "We know what Kadir did. We also found your hidden file. Good job."

Zoe breathed some relief. "His copy won't be good after the third viewing."

"Virus? Good girl." Jason smiled and pulled her closer.

"But, Jason, he said he has Damien." The sick feeling was back.

"The authorities are working on that. And we know who the mole is. It's Charlotte Ellison. She has been opposed to the FLC during her husband's administration and was determined to shut it down."

"What are they going to do to her?" she asked.

Jason shrugged. "They'll watch her, closely now. She knows her life depends on keeping quiet."

Chapter 27

Zoe glared at the nurse hanging another IV bag and adjusting the drip. She'd been in Georgetown University Hospital in Washington, DC, for three days and pretty much out of it between a fever and the medications they had her on. "Another one? When am I getting out of here?" Zoe complained.

The middle-aged nurse gave her a calm smile. "You had a concussion, a fever and were dehydrated. The doctor wants to make sure you're well before we send you home." She raised an eyebrow at Jason. "She can have ice cream if you'd like to get her some from the cafeteria. The Rocky Road is excellent. No martinis." She gave Jason a wink.

"Funny." Zoe wasn't amused. Jason patted her arm.

"Want me to bring you something from home? A book, your laptop, Sudoku puzzles?"

She gave him the eye. "You're lucky they have the IV in my swinging arm." She groaned, then lowered her voice. "How did the meeting go with Julia? Are they going to use Kadir's video? Have they heard anything new from him? What about Damien?"

"Kadir has returned to Iran and refused further talks concerning the treaty. The FLC is considering an alternate plan."

"What kind of plan?"

He looked at her without speaking for a moment. Some questions were meant not to be answered. "No word, good or bad, about Damien. Try not to worry," he said.

She fought back tears. "What could've happened?"

"His team missed their checkout point, that's all. Change of plans is what I was told. General Guzman said it happens." He brushed her hair back behind her ear. "Are you ready for a vacation?"

"Not until I find out about Damien. Why?"

"You named the file Tahiti. When the AV guys edited it, they said it didn't look anything like Tahiti." He grinned.

"Ha ha. When I emailed the file to my Gmail account, I couldn't name it Sex Tape With Kadir. Gmail isn't very secure, but I didn't have much choice. Hide in plain sight."

Her phone started buzzing, and she reached her hand out. "It's probably my dad again. I should never have taught him how to text. Can you pass it over? Promise me when we both get our casts off and Damien is okay, you'll take me to Tahiti or the Caribbean, someplace with a warm beach."

"Sure." He handed her the phone.

She checked her phone. A play had been made on Words With Friends. The air caught in her throat. "Jason. It's Damien." She burst into tears. "He's okay. And he's still beating me." Frantically, she started texting him a message with her good hand.

"Still beating you? There's no way you'll catch me in this game," Damien said from the door to her room. He was grinning and wearing his desert camouflage gear.

Zoe squealed. "Damien!" She tried getting up, but he raced over and hugged her.

"Don't get up, sis." He stood back and looked at her. "You look like hell," he teased, but was serious, too. "Hi, Jason. How is she?"

"Much better. Broken arm, bump on the head."

"I heard some of the details. Kadir is one SOB. You'll be hearing on the news about some women we rescued who had been Kadir's slaves. That was our planned mission, an NEO, Noncombatant Evacuation Operation, of the women slaves. DOS and DOD received orders to deploy security forces and secure the evacuation. They hadn't realized there were so many. That's why it took so long."

"Who were these women?" Zoe asked.

"They were from various countries. A number of Americans, Canadians and British women thought they were being hired for consulting work and ended up as his private slaves."

"How many? And how did you get them out?" Zoe grasped Jason's hand.

"About seventy. All but fifteen agreed to leave. The World Health Organization and a few missionary services assisted in transporting and caring for the women. Every step of this mission was secret until we were sure the women were safe. We didn't want word to get back to Kadir's people."

"How is Kadir responding to this?" Jason asked.

Damien rolled his eyes. "He's insisting these women were contracted employees and consultants and were allowed to leave when their contracts were over. He plans to make another public statement about his trip to the US. He's not signing the peace treaty. From what I hear, his people are not happy with him." Would Kadir reveal the existence of the FLC to the world?

Zoe gave Jason a worried look. "But Kadir knew about Damien playing Words With Friends. I thought he'd captured you."

"Lost my phone or it was pickpocketed during the slave rescue, before you were abducted," Damien explained. "I'm sure it was picked apart. Fortunately, I don't keep anything that could be considered a security risk on it."

* * *

The American passenger strolled onto the commercial airline and took his seat in first class. He checked CNN news from his iPhone. The pretty young flight attendant approached his seat. She wore a hijab covering on her head that matched her uniform, highlighting dark, intense eyes and smooth, flawless skin. All the female flight attendants wore the same clothing on Iran Air. He wondered how she'd take the news. It hadn't hit CNN or local news, but he expected it would.

"May I get you a drink, sir? Coffee, tea? We should be taking off shortly," she said in English. Her passenger list probably told her who the Americans were. Not too many traveled to Iran since the new president had taken over.

He glanced out the window at the airport employees who were driving the luggage carts to be loaded. Several armed Iranian guards stood at various locations with rifles. "Coffee, black, thank you." He would have liked to have something stronger, but Iran Air didn't serve alcohol on its flights. Besides, he was still working until the plane was off the ground and he was out of Iran. Tehran was a nice city, based on what little he'd seen of it. Its people were kind, gracious and welcoming to an American posing as a computer software businessman.

A day ago, he had been at Sa'dabad Palace in Tehran, the president's residence and office, being introduced as the leader's temporary translator. Kadir's current translator was in the hospital with severe injuries after an awful car crash, and luckily, the assassin knew six languages. His connections had helped him to step in to get the job done. Too bad there hadn't been another way, but there was no quick and easy foreign policy fix. Serious reform took time, and overthrowing the regime through US intervention would have been a disaster. However, secretly creating a favorable environment to allow a more promising regime to step in could work. That's where he'd come in. A handshake, a tiny pinprick with a slow-acting drug that mimicked a heart attack and the job was done.

"Of course." She smiled and asked the next passenger the same before going to the galley. A moment later he had a cup of coffee on his tray. "Here you go, sir. Let me know if I can get you anything else." She also dropped off bags of cashews.

"Thank you." Outside his window, the sun was setting. The modern city of Tehran with its backdrop of snowcapped mountains was miles away. Two more armed police came out of the terminal and approached the baggage guys. His pulse kicked up a few beats, and he focused on his breathing to calm himself. He opened the bag of nuts and munched a few.

The flight wasn't full. It wouldn't be the first time the airline canceled a flight because of too few passengers. Not good. His flight would take him to Amsterdam, a six-hour flight, and then to London. If it ever got off the ground. He checked his watch.

"We should be leaving soon," the flight attendant said.

"There's a little delay, but it shouldn't be long."

He smiled and thanked her.

The flight attendants huddled around the kitchen looking over their phones and chatting anxiously. Was it his imagination, or did they seem pleased by the news? They were smiling, laughing, and hugging, so it did not look like they were disturbed by it.

"He's dead, he's dead," he heard one of them say in Farsi. He checked his phone, scanning Twitter, CNN and local news. Finally, a couple of Twitter posts and retweets. Iranian President Kadir was dead. Heart attack? CNN still hadn't announced it. Nothing on the local news, either. He sipped his coffee.

The flight attendants made announcements to fasten seat belts and turn off all electronic devices and prepare for takeoff. He checked CNN one more time, and there it was.

Iranian President Majeed Kadir has been pronounced dead of a heart attack. Reports indicate dozens of female hostages, many American, held by Kadir as his personal slaves were recently rescued.

There was no mention about the hostages or slaves on Tehran news. He turned off his phone and leaned back in his seat. The plane pulled away from the gate and started to taxi down the runway.

Moments later, the plane was in the air. The assassin scrolled through the selection of movies while he waited for his dinner.

Killing was the easy part when the target was evil.

Epilogue

"I think we might get some rain," Jason said, opening one eye and looking up at the sky.

Zoe took off her sunglasses and glanced over at him. With the approaching gray clouds, a few people lounging around the resort's pool began gathering their towels and belongings and leaving. "Don't care. It's too beautiful out here." The smells of the ocean and something barbecuing at the nearby tiki bar mingled with the warm breeze removed every last bit of tension from her body.

Waiting until both their casts were off had been well worth it. Who wanted to go to Tahiti with a cast and not be able to swim in the beautiful aqua water? Stretched out on a lounger by the pool, Zoe held her wrists side by side to compare.

"How are you doing?" Jason asked, one eye open. He looked so hot, naked except for his bathing suit. All bronze muscles with a sheen of suntan lotion on his skin. Only two days at the resort, and he was so tanned he looked like a lifeguard. She was trying in earnest to tan with her fair skin and mega sunblock, trying to avoid a burn.

"It doesn't hurt. But I do have a funny bump on the one that was broken."

"No, I mean, how are *you* doing? You've been through a lot." He sat up and took her hand. The butterflies in her stomach did a rumba.

"I'm good. Happy. Very happy." She leaned over and kissed him. "I can't remember the last time I felt this relaxed."

He nodded and looked past her, a line of worry creasing his brow. "I noticed you didn't bring any scarves on this trip."

"I don't need them."

He smiled and squeezed her hand. "What are we going to do when we get back? Leave the FLC? Go back to Langley? We can go anywhere, do anything we want. Do something less dangerous, more routine?" As he said it, she could tell he was saying this for her because of her ordeal.

"We would never be happy doing a routine job. We crave the adventure and danger. As long as we can take Dexter with us."

He grinned. "That's a given."

She knew they were ready to go home after two weeks on the island. "I'd like to continue with the FLC," Zoe said. "Their methods are unconventional, but bad things happen in the world when evil goes unchecked. Hitler, Osama bin Laden are a couple of examples. I'm going to ask Julia about deciphering the archives in my office. Many people have been a part of the FLC and influenced historical events. This knowledge should be translated and recorded, even if it's never made public."

"What do you think you can decipher?" he asked.

"Those who have been responsible for shaping the history of this country and possibly the world and are not in recorded history."

"Then we stay," he said. He didn't say anything about taking their relationship to the next level, but that was okay. They had time now. They'd been through a lot. Would she ever get tired of looking at him?

He checked his phone. "Interesting. Iran elected a new president, and there's celebrating in the streets. Sounds like this guy plans to sign the treaty."

"I hope so," Zoe said, grabbing the sunscreen and smoothing the lotion on her legs, arms and chest. "Good for the Iranian people. They've been through enough."

"It must be a good sign. Iran Air opened flights to London, Paris, New York, Chicago and Seattle."

"Really? Those airports have blocked them since Kadir took over. That is a good sign." She slipped the straps of her top off her shoulders and rubbed more lotion into her skin.

"You're getting me hot watching you." He bent over and gave her a slow and sexy kiss. "Later I'll rub lotion on you everywhere."

"Mmmm, nice. I brought a few items in my suitcase. I need more training for the Red Tape Room."

"What kind of objects?" He grinned.

"Flogger, restraining straps, vibrators, among other things."

He shook his head. "Didn't Customs go through your luggage?"

She nodded. "I asked the TSA agent if he needed a demo of any of those items. He blushed and stuffed them back in."

Jason laughed. "I'm getting hard. I need a drink."

"Good." She looked up at the sky. "I felt a drop, but the sun is still out. Catch a little more sun, then go in?"

He grinned. "I'm swimming over to the pool bar. Want anything?"

"Yes, a blue drink."

He laughed. "What's in a blue drink?"

She shrugged. "I don't know. It looks refreshing. Ask for an umbrella and extra pineapple, too."

She watched him swim to the bar, order the drinks and walk slowly back through the water. As raindrops fell, the wind picked up, and more guests scooped up towels and ran to their rooms or down to the beach to get under the covered tiki bar. She closed her eyes and enjoyed the feel of the warm rain. "Here's your drink. I asked for extra blue stuff and extra fruit," Jason said. "Going inside?"

"No. It's only rain." She opened her eyes, took the drink and sipped on the straw. "Yum. Thanks. And look, we have the pool to ourselves now."

Palm trees swayed, and ocean waves crashed onto the shore. She could have stayed here another two weeks. She closed her eyes. The image of her container prison on the freighter came to mind. She shoved it aside and replaced the thought with their gorgeous spa room overlooking the ocean. A big, Jacuzzi tub would be getting a workout later, as well as the bed.

"You like the drink?" he asked again.

"Yes, I said it was yummy."

"What about the extra fruit?"

She glanced at the wedge of pineapple and cherry with the paper umbrella. "What extra—"

The rain continued, but a speck of sunlight broke through the clouds, illuminating the top of the umbrella. Sitting on the pointed tip of the umbrella, a diamond ring sparkled brilliantly. A square-cut diamond was set with two smaller marquise diamonds on both sides along with a band of round diamonds. Zoe gasped, carefully plucked the ring off the umbrella and held it up. "Oh my God. It's beautiful. When…where did you get this?"

"Yesterday when I went into town, while you were having your massage. I snuck one of your rings to have it sized." He sat across from her and took her hand. "I love you, Zoe. I want you in my life always. Marry me."

The rain came down harder, and she started crying and laughing. "I thought you didn't even want to work with me." She laughed, and her heart swelled.

He smoothed wet strands of her hair over her ear. "That wasn't it. I didn't like being on a mission where I couldn't protect you. But I know you can protect yourself." His eyes were so full of love and anticipation as he waited on her answer.

She slipped the ring on her finger, then flung her arms around him and kissed him. "I love you, too." Her heart wanted to burst because she loved him so much. "Yes."

Standing up, she pulled Jason to his feet, too. The rain was now a downpour. "What are you doing?"

"Going for a swim. Bring your beer." She picked up her blue drink and walked down the pool steps into the warm water. "We have the pool to ourselves." Even the pool bar was closed.

"Right." Jason laughed.

"Think you'd like living in my Georgetown townhome? Or should we look for something else?"

"I like Georgetown. Dexter has a small backyard, and you have a nice neighbor who doesn't mind watching him while we're away." He took her drink and put it with his on the side of the pool, then scooped her up in his arms, swirling her around in the water. "So what do we do with the rest of the day?"

"Use your imagination, Merritt. Are you up for an adventure?"

Acknowledgements

Many thanks to the following people who are always there when I need them for support, brainstorming and insights, Karen Katchur, A.C. James, Cris Anson, Lynn LaFleur, Caridad Pineiro, Terri Prizzi, Desiree Holt, Joey W. Hill, Sabrina York, Diane Peters-Mayer, Vikki Jankowski, Irene and Stan Kulig, Joan Dawson, Joyce Lamb, Autumn Jordan, Kayelle Allen and others just too many to mention.

My deepest appreciation to Leo M. and Joanne C. Grudzinski for their help in researching this book. Michael is retired from the US Navy and works as a merchant mariner. Any errors in this story are all mine.

To my parents, Barbara and Donald Robinson, who have always supported and encouraged my dreams.

About Kathy Kulig

Kathy Kulig is a New York Times & USA Today Bestselling author of erotic romance whose works include paranormal, contemporary, BDSM, and suspense. She has published (or has contracted to publish) nearly 20 novels, novellas and short stories with various publishers and via self-publishing. Besides her career in writing, she has worked as a cytotechnologist, research scientist, medical technologist, dive master and stringer for a newspaper. In her spare time, she can be found mountain biking, traveling, lounging on the beach with a good book or having dinner out with her husband. Kathy resides in eastern Pennsylvania.

She raffles a FREE Amazon or Barnes and Noble Gift Certificate EVERY month to members of her Newsletter, so sign up here: http://eepurl.com/FC_nP

Also by Kathy Kulig

Dark Odyssey Series:
Spring Break
Summer Sins
Demons in Exile Series:
Desert of the Damned
Damned and Desired
Damned and Defiant
Single titles:
Burned Deep
Nightlord Lover
Risky Pleasures
Emerald Dungeon
Dragon Witch
Secret Soiree
Seducing the Stones
Wild Jade
"Tattoo Witch" in Something Wicked This Way
Comes, Vol. I (anthology)
"Spring Break" in Work and Play (anthology)
"Emerald Dungeon" in Dial B for Bondage
(anthology)

Where to find Kathy Kulig

Website: http://www.kathykulig.com
Facebook: http://www.facebook.com/kathykulig-author
Twitter: http://www.twitter.com/kathykulig
Blog: http://www.TheLustyView.com
Sign up for Kathy's mailing list:
http://eepurl.com/FC_nP

Author's Note

To my readers, you rock! Thank you for picking this book up! I write because I love to share my inspirations with you, the reader, and I'm sending you all hugs for taking the time out of you busy schedule to read my stories. I so appreciate your feedback in the form of reviews and emails. This helps me know what my readers like, and don't like.

Many of my stories deal with edgy topics like BDSM. Whether you decide to explore this lifestyle in your relationship, or not, please do so with care. Do your research if you're new. Be *safe, sane and consensual.* Use your head but follow your heart.

Happy reading!

Kathy

www.ingramcontent.com/pod-product-compliance
Lightning Source LLC
Chambersburg PA
CBHW060403180626
46817CB00007B/2501